A DIFFERENT KIND OF MIND

Naked, shoulder to shoulder in a circle that kept expanding and contracting...they were still doing their strange dance, eyes closed and hands joined...

As they approached, the tight circle uncoiled, came forward raggedly. At first glance there was nothing unusual about them, but Cal again sensed something profoundly different beneath the surface...the way they were still connected. It was subtle, unobtrusive—a hand there, an arm over the shoulder there. But from the first to last, they formed a continuous chain of flesh.

They continued to move closer.

July 8, 1985

Arlington

Avon Books are available at special quantity discounts for bulk purchases for sales promotions, premiums, fund raising or educational use. Special books, or book excerpts, can also be created to fit specific needs.

For details write or telephone the office of the Director of Special Markets, Avon Books, Dept. FP, 1790 Broadway, New York, New York 10019, 212-399-1357. *IN CANADA:* Director of Special Sales, Avon Books of Canada, Suite 210, 2061 McCowan Rd., Scarborough, Ontario M1S 3Y6, 416-293-9404.

THE TIME-SERVERS

RUSSELL M. GRIFFIN

AVON
PUBLISHERS OF BARD, CAMELOT, DISCUS AND FLARE BOOKS

for Ed and Annamae Vaznelis
with deep affection

THE TIMESERVERS is an original publication of Avon Books. This work has never before appeared in book form. This work is a novel. Any similarity to actual persons or events is purely coincidental.

AVON BOOKS
A division of
The Hearst Corporation
1790 Broadway
New York, New York 10019

Copyright © 1985 by Russell M. Griffin
Published by arrangement with the author
Library of Congress Catalog Card Number: 84-91192
ISBN: 0-380-89525-0

All rights reserved, which includes the right to reproduce this book or portions thereof in any form whatsoever except as provided by the U.S. Copyright Law. For information address Jet Literary Associates, Inc., 124 East 84th Street, Suite 4A, New York, New York 10028

First Avon Printing, February, 1985

AVON TRADEMARK REG. U.S. PAT. OFF. AND IN OTHER COUNTRIES, MARCA REGISTRADA, HECHO EN U.S.A.

Printed in the U.S.A.

WFH 10 9 8 7 6 5 4 3 2 1

CHAPTER ONE

THE FACT that somebody kidnapped the Ambassador wasn't shocking. It hardly took the Mission cybot to figure it was probably one of the Dey's brigand uncles from the north looking for investment capital. What was shocking was that for thirty-six hours, no one at the Legation even noticed the Ambassador was missing.

Not that he was a great ambassador. He was a career diplomat who'd never grasped that on Depaz you couldn't just be a spokesman for Home Office policy—not when it took six years for a query to reach Earth and another six for instructions to be beamed back. You had to be decisive; you had to formulate policy like the old ambassadors plenipotentiary of the sixteenth century.

Still, he *was* the ambassador. And it was only a week since the Deputy Chief of Mission had fallen into some sawgrass and bled to death. Losing them both that close together was damned awkward.

As soon as word got around, there was an emergency meeting of the chief officers of the Diplomatic and Consular sections. Calvin Troy came late because he'd been hung up with the code clerk feeding the Monthly Report into the high speed coder; the MR wouldn't reach the Home Office for six years, but you had to stick to scheduled feed times. Otherwise you got a bad End-User's Evaluation in your Home Office file, and that kind of thing always caught up with you. Which Cal, with a qualitative age of thirty and most of his career still ahead, knew only too well.

Cal found the chancery hall outside the C-level conference room so choked with chairs that he had to park his around the corner and walk back. The door was guarded by several sentribots and two human Marines. No question about it, he thought, big doings. Inside, the senior staff was huddled gloomily at one end of the long table, and the room was stuffy and close. Aircon broken down again, he thought.

"First Secretary Troy, how are you today," said the cybot-speaker over the door as he came through.

"Oh, buzz off," he said.

"Not even noticing the son of a bitch was missing," Grober, the Consul General, was saying with an elephantine shake of his head. "This could look very grim in our Annual Efficiencies."

A number of gray heads nodded back.

"Very grim," he added.

"Not if the Home Office never finds out," Hara said.

"Why wouldn't the Home Office find out?" Cal wanted to know, taking a static chair.

"Come, come, my boy." Hara smiled. "Be serious." She was a big woman, beefy and large-boned, with a broad Oriental face and almond eyes. Her straight gray hair was cropped short.

"I *am* serious."

"Because"—Hara sighed, trying to keep her temper—"the Home Office is six light years away, and all they know is what we tell them. And I trust we're not all dying to report ourselves, are we?" She glanced from face to face around the table, each in turn finding some excuse to look away.

Hara was on the rolls as Development Attaché. It seemed impossible for even a Depasian to believe an OWSR-2 rating was a Development Attaché, but the one time Cal had asked about it, Grober's face had gone hard and he'd changed the subject.

"You don't actually mean to misrepresent what's happened?" Cal said worriedly. "The regulations are perfectly clear about in-house misinformation."

Hara leaned back with raised eyebrows. She was

dressed as usual in a full, coarse native robe; it gave her a vaguely Old Testament look. "You mean, lie, my boy?" she asked.

Laughter rippled around the table, and Cal, still very much the new boy among the senior staff and not quite used to his promotion, flushed.

"I'm not suggesting anything you'd have to run down and confess to that MUDD religionbot you brought with you," Hara continued.

"I didn't bring it with me," Cal said. "The Home Office just happened to send us in the same shipment."

"I just mean, when we get the Ambassador back," Hara said, "we don't need to *emphasize* to him how long it took to get the old wheels rolling. We don't need to *stress* it in official documents."

There was a general nodding of heads. They were all as close to retirement as Hara and just as anxious to serve out their time without mishaps.

"Assuming we get him back in one piece," Cal said hotly, his self-respect stung.

"Of course we'll get him back. You've been Political Officer long enough to know kidnapping here's just a low-risk way to increase fluid assets."

"Or a national sport," Leon Baum observed from the end of the table with his unmistakable laugh, a burst of short glottal *heh-eh-ehs* way back in his throat like a pneumatic hammer. He had just received OWS/PD notification that six years ago he'd been promoted from Economic Section Chief to Counselor for Economic Affairs.

A servobot floated past, airmotor hiccuping, flat head clinking with glass tumblers and a water dispenser.

"If anything around here can be a sport," Hannibal Myers intoned gloomily from behind the blank discs of his spectacles. Myers was morbidly, pathologically despondent. He had been assigned as Fisheries Attaché, Depaz. Cybot error. He'd tried to explain that Depaz was a prairie planet whose largest body of water, the Marood, was a salt marsh a few meters across without so much as a single fish. The Home Office cybot had six years later explained it did not make mistakes. And so Myers's once bright future had been irrevocably blighted. Nowhere in his eight Annual Evaluation or Efficiency Reports was there any indication that he'd ever done a thing for the Depasian fishing industry. It was clear to the Home Office that he wasn't a team player.

The servobot's airmotor hiccuped and died, and the little machine veered and plowed into the wall, dropped straight down, fell onto its side, and rolled across the floor.

"Shall I buzz Maintenance?" Baum asked.

Grober shrugged. "When was the last time they actually fixed anything?"

"You're right," Baum said. "They never have the part they need."

"Still," Grober said uneasily, returning to the subject, "what if an OWS Inspector happens by to do a report? One's been due for five years at least."

"So has a Papal Nuncio and an entire Cultural Exchange troupe of actors," someone said. "But do they ever come?"

"Not according to O and D."

" 'There's a divinity that shapes our ends,' " Grober said, " 'Rough-hew them how we may.' "

"What?" Myers asked.

"Ancient playwright named Shakespeare. Private passion of mine," Grober said. "Pay it no mind."

Hara brushed it off with a shake of her head. "The only thing that bothers me is what a slick operation it was. Very un-Depasian. Really—who here ever heard of them grabbing an Ambassador out of his own compound? It must have taken planning, coordination, brains. . . . Who ever heard of a Depasian with brains?"

"Jesus, no," said Townsend. As Intelligence Section Chief, he was responsible for the Observation and Detection Unit. "Even they never blame their brains—it's always some other part of their bodies. 'A thousand pardons, master, my liver made me do it.' 'Forgive me, it was my bowels said I had to.' "

They all laughed, but Townsend looked worried. Cal figured he was afraid this might be somehow a non-Depasian operation, possibly an Albarian plot. And that made it an

Intelligence failure. Townsend's failure. An outside Inspector could easily assume the years of idleness on Depaz without any challenges for his training had blunted him, left him careless.

"You think an off-worlder did it?" Baum asked. "But we know everyone on the planet. And there hasn't been a freighter by in over a year."

"What other explanation's possible?" Grober asked. "There hasn't been a single attack on anyone from Embassy Row since the Dey agreed to adopt the diplomatic community en masse as second cousins."

"Are you saying it was done by someone from another legation?" Cal asked. "One immortal harm another? It . . . it isn't *done.*"

"On the contrary," Townsend said. "The Albarians have been known to do it."

"Well, they don't play by any of the rules," Cal said.

"Rules," Hara snorted. "Regulations."

Cal glanced at Hara. Like Townsend, she had the slack, gray skin and vacant eyes common to officers at the ends of their careers, when the rejuvenators could no longer stop the years from catching up—years of stupefaction from living on planets where the people, sometimes even the plants and rocks hated you, years lost in suspension during transfer from post to post that brought the eerie knowledge that everything you'd known and loved on your home planet was gone.

"When you've been around as long as I have"—Hara smiled grimly "you'll realize there's no rule, no law in the universe that isn't broken somewhere, sometime, not even the law of gravity. And not just by the Albarians, my young friend. Look at us—don't we defy time itself?"

"But there's a code of honor among—"

"I heard last time anybody saw the Ambassador was in the Code Room," the Air Attaché, Major Sedewski, interrupted. "Any leads there?"

"Yes and no," Grober said. "Indications are, he did receive a directive of some kind, but apparently the cybot dumped any record of it."

"Wouldn't that mean it was top security?" Cal asked,

turning to Hara because she was closest. "Isn't that standard operating procedure for Intelligence directives?"

"I wouldn't know," Hara said, looking down at her hands and nodding toward Townsend.

"Usually," Townsend said.

"Well," Grober said, anxious as always to smooth things over, "the immediate question is what we're going to do about the Ambassador." He looked around till he got to Cal, flushed sheepishly, then lowered his eyes. "Uh, what we were going over before you got here, Cal, was the chain of command."

"The way we see it," Townsend said, "the Deputy Chief of Mission hasn't been replaced yet, and the Executive Assistant's down with food poisoning."

"Gondolphi again?" Cal asked.

"The poor man's got the weakest stomach in the Service. You'd think he'd have learned by now to stay away from native cuisine."

"When did it happen?"

"Last night at a party," Myers said.

"Anyway," Sedewski went on, "with no DCM and the EA down, that leaves the rest of us. Grober here's in the Consular section, which eliminates him. Hara's out because she's only a reserve rating, I'm out because Baum's counselorship outranks my attaché status, and Baum's out because the economic section is routinely superseded by the political section."

"I guess so," Cal said.

"Glad you agree," said Baum.

"So?"

"So you're Acting Chief of Mission."

Cal's head snapped back as though he'd been struck.

"You *are* currently Senior Political Officer, aren't you?" Hara asked.

"Yeah," Cal admitted. "You know Bascomb's only been here a year."

"And you were even made Acting First Secretary after Welles died of fly bites, right?" Hara went on.

All his life Cal had dreamed of being head of a mission. But not like this, without being able to prepare, in the middle of a crisis . . . The whole meeting had been a setup so they could cover themselves by sticking him with operational responsibility. Even Grober, who'd been like a father since his arrival. And regulations were clear about the ACM's job. If the Ambassador didn't get returned, only one head would roll. . . .

He rubbed his sweaty palms on his thighs. "All right," he muttered. "I'll have somebody call Government House and get the Minister of State to arrange a meeting for me. And not with that go-between they call Gateway to the Dey. No point diddling around with middlemen. I'll say I want to meet with the Dey himself." He touched the intercom square by his right hand and told Bascomb to handle it.

"Shall I exaggerate a little and say the Counselor of Embassy or Political Affairs wants to see the Ineffable One?" Bascomb asked brightly.

Cal scanned the faces around him for any sign that they'd let him off the hook. Nothing. All right, he thought, then he'd use the power that the regulations gave him along with the responsibility. "Tell him the *Chargé d'affaires ad interim,* the Acting Chief of Mission, *demands* to see him."

"You've been promoted?" Bascomb asked.

"Something like that." Cal leaned back, already prickling with second thoughts. "You think that'll be all right?" he asked the others.

The faces looking back gave no indication.

"Well, I guess I'd better get a presentation ready. How forceful do you want me to be with them?"

"Hard to say," Grober said, sucking thoughtfully on his lower lip.

"Depends," Hannibal Jones sighed gloomily, "on how much you want him back."

Cal excused himself and headed for the door.

"Don't forget the reception tonight," Baum called after him.

"Reception?" Cal paused in the doorway. "How can we have a diplomatic reception when our Ambassador's been kidnapped?"

"Show of strength," Townsend said. "Everything normal. Don't want the other embassies to think we're running scared."

Cal looked from face to face. "We've got fifteen Marines with stun rifles and a bunch of metal sentribots, and we're going to tell Embassy Row we're not worried?"

"It's all in the face you put on things," Grober said. "The essence of diplomacy. Any strong preferences in hors d'oeuvres?"

In the hall, Cal threw himself into his chair and glided back toward his office. With the slightest burr, the turret head of a sentribot tracked him with its laser muzzle till he'd disappeared around the corner into the elevator to D-level.

Well, it was his own damned fault. At the end of his first tour, he'd had plenty of choices, but when the Service cybot showed an opening for a Political Officer, he'd grabbed it without even asking where the hell Depaz was. He'd been Protocol Officer his first assignment, and everybody knew Protocol Officers stayed Protocol Officers while Political Officers became Ambassadors. The fact Depaz turned out to have a nitrogen-oxygen atmosphere where legation personnel could wear civvies seemed like pure gravy.

He should have known there'd be a hitch when a mere OWSO-5 could get a political desk the second ten years out. He should have known it the minute he landed. Certainly the minute he saw the flies.

They had six wings, and they not only outnumbered the Dey and his barbarian nomads, but as Earth's crowning evolutionary achievement was man, so Depaz's was, apparently, the fly. Angry, voracious clouds of them buzzed everywhere you turned.

And aside from the flies, there wasn't a thing on that godforsaken, featureless prairie that wouldn't have bored even a camel inside twenty minutes.

Cal knew because the freighter that had brought him and MUDD had also brought a two-humped Bactrian as a gift for the Dey. When they'd opened the camel's pod, it had blinked, pursed its lips in puzzlement, and then closed its lids against the endless, dreary flatness of sun-blasted plain and refused to open them again.

It had been presented to the Dey in this somnambulant state because no one in the Legation knew how you got a camel to open its eyes and make the best of a bad bargain. It wasn't, after all, a professional diplomat.

It wasn't an immortal.

Only immortals understood what it was to crawl from planet to planet along the fringes of the galaxy, spending more time traveling in suspended animation between posts than on assignment. Only they knew what it was to serve the interests—or what they imagined were the interests—of an Earth whose very memory receded with every fifty or hundred years of fevered artificial sleep.

It was a special bond they shared with their brother diplomats from every system and which cut them off from their real brothers on their respective home planets. They formed a de facto club whose members might serve together on one planet and meet again a hundred years later on the Embassy Row of another. And it was that special exclusivity, that pride, which had attracted Cal to the Service. It made him feel more than human. It made him a citizen of the universe.

Back in his office, Cal tried to buzz Bascomb and got the Mission library.

"Sorry, sir," said the librarian. "The intercom's been screwy all day. We've called Maintenance, but—"

"Never mind," Cal said. He kicked away from his desk and swung down the hall to Bascomb's office.

"Sorry, sir," one of the OWSS clerks answered. "She's gone."

"Where?"

"Well, she couldn't get anybody to answer the phone at Government House, so she took a hoverbike over to see if she could rouse anybody."

"We spend eighty billions hauling in a communications system for the Dey as a goodwill gesture, another five billions installing it, and the son of a bitch doesn't even have somebody answering the phone?"

"They don't think like we do, sir."

"I know."

"They have this way of blaming everything on their lungs and gall bladders and—"

"I *know!*"

"And, anyway, I heard it broke down."

Cal sighed noisily. "I'll have to go over myself. Jesus—Bascomb should know driving over there in a bike will leave her so dusty not even the porter will talk to her. What's the matter with her? What kind of diplomacy is that?"

Cal kicked back into the hall to glide down the ramp to the foyer on B-level. Two Marine watch-standers snapped to attention as he floated past. "Come with me," he barked, suddenly conscious of being Acting Chief of Mission and rather liking it. "We're going to make a show of force."

Funny, he thought. Why did the Home Office go to the expense of sending Marines when sentribots were every bit as effective? No bot could replace a diplomat, of course, but they were certainly intelligent enough for simple security. . . . Intelligent enough to justify Congress passing the Cybernetics Laws to give them their basic bill of rights for consciousness protection.

But Cal knew the reason had nothing to do with efficiency. The Home Office sent the Marines for the same reason they chipped voices into half the furnishings, so the human diplomats wouldn't feel so cut off from Earth and home. So there would be a link with the rest of humanity light-years away. It was the kind of humane policy that made Cal proud to be part of the Off-World Service.

Maybe it was too bad that the Accords of those dim times after the Social Security Wars had outlawed clones. Cal would have preferred them to the medibots, sentribots, and cybots. But it was certainly not the place of a OWSO-5 to question the wisdom of his ancestors—or of anything Congress did, for that matter. Certainly not now, when there was an immediate task that needed doing.

He checked his belt to make sure he had salt tablets and a thermos in case the car broke down and he had to wait in some miserable sod hut till they got it fixed. And cyanide tablets in case he was stranded more than two days in the open. Then he left his powerchair bobbing and followed the Marines, ducking quickly through the door's billowing jets of perfumed insecticide and hurrying down the ramp to the official embassy limousine.

"Don't forget your face net and salt tablets, sirs," said the voice over the door.

The sky danced with black specks, and on either side the high-voltage grids crackled with incinerating flies. Beyond shimmered the water-collection towers atop the Albarian embassy, glinting with lenses and observation dishes trained on the Earth legation.

The old hovercar was known affectionately as Moby Dick because it was very big and very white. It had been shipped in parts and assembled by the last Air Attaché and the Marines to demonstrate the wonders of technology to the Dey and his court.

Unfortunately, the Dey and his court were largely indifferent to technology. They were perfectly happy with their ancestral steam tractors and family coal mines. They *liked* their village blacksmiths. There was even an awful rumor some Depasian had written a poem about one.

Even more unfortunately, no one had considered that Depasian roads were no more than grassless stretches through the prairie, widening occasionally to form the streets and squares of villages. Wherever the hovercar went, its progress was marked by shaking fists poking angrily out of the roiling dust wake.

The last Chief of Mission had beamed apologetically that perhaps something with balloon tires at Embassy Depaz would be better for biworld relations, but so far the Home Office hadn't found any other fossil fuel antiques—and the whole point, after all, had been to show the Depasians what benefits would accrue if they let Earth help them tap the vast oil reserves laid down before the ecological disaster that had nearly destroyed the planet.

Over a millennium or more ago, Depaz's third and lowest moon had exploded in the upper atmosphere and raked the surface with a shower of red-hot particles, which in turn had created a thick dust cloud for close to a hundred years—long enough, at any rate, to choke off all but the most tenacious and least desirable of the planet's flora and fauna—sawgrass, flies, and bandits.

The theory at least helped to explain the strange myth among the nomadic tribes about a huge yellow moon-face gobbling little white stones and anything else that moved. At least, that was the hypothesis put forward by an Earth archaeologist named Weston in the course of her study of pre-savanna hominids twelve years before, but she'd been declared persona non grata because she'd been injudicious enough to observe in her preliminary report that slavery and cannibalism were endemic among contemporary Depasian hominids.

As the Dey's Secretary-Cousin noted in a scorching letter of protest, cannibalism was common only in the *west* of Depaz, so the luckless scholar had been expelled post haste. Meaning she'd spent two and a half years under house arrest waiting for the next freighter to lumber by.

As Hara commented at the time, the real—albeit unstated—reason for Weston's deportation had been her being in the western steppes at all, though why the Dey wanted to close the west to off-worlders, not even their oldest hand, Hara, could imagine. And nobody at the time had paused to wonder how a copy of a report sent Highest Security via the high-speed coder had gotten back to the Dey.

Halfway between town and Government House, Cal's Marine driver had to swing off the road to make way for one of the Dey's relatives riding in traditional splendor on a two-wheeled *mels* drawn by a puffing, shuddering, clanging steam tractor. It was déclassé to ride in the motive power itself, of course—no one but a slave would have been caught dead *on* a tractor.

Another reason, Cal thought, that the hovercar hadn't won their hearts. In the rearview mirror he watched Moby Dick's brown wake roll outward and engulf the nobleman and his entourage. Given Depasian status symbols, the Home Office should have sent them one of the ancients' steam locomotives and a string of commuter cars.

Government House, maintained by the Dey to satisfy the incomprehensible need of off-world diplomats for a formal seat of government (the true seat of government being wherever the Dey happened to sit), dated from the pre-savanna millennia. Once the center of a vanished metropolis, it now stood forlornly in the middle of the empty prairie. It was built simply but elegantly of huge stone blocks, reminding Cal of a Renaissance imitation of a Doric temple or a Tennessee courthouse. Weston's notes indicated it had been approached by a fifty-foot stairway, but long ago the whole complex had sunk into the prairie. Now awash with sawgrass, the three and a half remaining steps were occupied largely by nesting animals.

Cal's driver slid to a stop at the foot of the steps just behind Bascomb's hoverbike and tapped the rear door open. Cal pulled his face net down just in time and waved the two Marines out first. They hurried up the steps, kicking several nondescript prairie creatures and dismal birdlings out of the way—among them, Cal noted, several mouselike *misha*, a carrion-gnawing *pulgarg* dragging a mange-eaten fur wing, and two of the Rhode Island Reds which, with the camel, had been part of the Mission's program to curry favor with the Dey by finding some Earth species that could overcome the biological imperative to keel over dead after less than twenty-four hours on Depaz. These had done better than most, certainly better than the forlorn-looking Albarian lizard-dog gasping in the middle of the doorway as the Marines clicked up the steps and positioned themselves on either side.

Cal kicked at it as he strode past. The dog was too depressed even to groan.

Inside, the porter was drowsing against the stone wall of the huge foyer. Bascomb suddenly appeared from somewhere, hurrying toward Cal and pursued by a cloud of black flies.

"You come over in Moby Dick?" she asked, puffing and swatting to keep them off her face net. Her face was visibly streaked with dust inside the netting, but for the first time, Cal noted something unexpectedly but distinctly attractive about her. He nodded.

"Just on my way back," Bascomb went on. "Found another of the Dey's cousins in there—claims to be Minister of State. Guess he's the one you want to see."

"You're sure?"

"Well, he asked me who I wanted to see, and I said the Minister of State, and he said it just happened that's who he was."

"And I suppose he's right in that office over there?" Cal asked, pointing toward a doorway of beaded curtain.

"How'd you know?"

"Because last time I was here—to present that Universal Endangered Species Agreement for their ratification, remember?—that was the office of the Minister of Foreign Affairs."

"Maybe they moved offices."

"Look around, Bascomb—it's the *only* office."

"What do you know?" Bascomb said cheerfully. "You're right."

"Never tell them who you want till you get them to commit themselves," Cal said. "Otherwise they claim to be whatever it is you're looking for."

"I'm sorry."

"Never mind—no point worrying after the damage's done," he said, annoyed with himself at having made her feel badly. "Wait here while I see if we can get anywhere."

Cal strode across the foyer to the door, knocked perfunctorily on the door frame, and pushed his way through the clattering beads.

He fully expected to see the very same Minister of Foreign Affairs he'd met last time. Sure enough, the man before him was indeed going through his predecessor's same metal box of file cards, but the man himself seemed different. He looked up as though surprised.

"Ah," he said, "may your nostrils be free of dust."

"And may the grass not cut your feet," Cal answered correctly. His Depasian was imperfect, but he was one of the few in the Legation who could even attempt to speak the language.

"Please tell me how I may be of service to you, most welcome visitor," said the Minister, "that the clamor of my bowels for me to aid you may be stilled." He removed a card from the file and used it to pick between his two front teeth, yellow as kernels of ripe corn. Like all the other cards Cal had ever seen from the file, it was blank.

"If this is about the last Agreement in Principle you brought my government, let me assure you that our Minister of Foreign Affairs is even now closeted with our Minister of the Interior to ask the advice of their organs how to discover any animal or plant that may be threatened. When they've been led to one, rest assured that we will all rush out and threaten it most fiercely."

A great black fly landed on the Minister of State's forehead and made its way unhurriedly down the bridge of his nose. His Excellency gave no sign he noticed. The fly eased itself under the tip of the nose, paused to preen all three sets of wings, took its bearings, and burrowed into the left nostril.

Cal's flesh crawled. And to think the first explorers to reach Depaz had suggested the Depasians might be of human descent because the physical parallels defied the laws of probability.

"This has nothing to do with the Endangered Species Agreement," Cal said. "I imagine Your Excellency knows perfectly well why I'm here."

"My mind is empty as the grass sea," protested the Minister of State innocently.

If this guy was going to play dumb, Cal thought, then he'd have to be blunt. The exquisite distillations of diplomatic language were wasted on Depasians, anyway; only another immortal could savor the subtleties.

And it was Cal's ass that was in a sling.

"Then I'll just have to see His Ineffable Limitlessness himself."

"The Dey?" The Minister leered, returning the used card to its proper place in the file. "Would not everyone like to see my illustrious cousin?"

"I wouldn't know."

"And would not every man wish to kiss the moons? First you must make an appointment with my cousin Gateway to the Dey, then—"

"See here, friend, my Ambassador's been abducted, and it's obviously the work of one of your illustrious Dey's illustrious uncles."

The Minister of State extracted a crusted relic of handkerchief from his sleeve and blew his nose. "I will convey this sad news to the Gateway to my Dey," he said, crumpling the handkerchief. The fly suddenly emerged from one of the folds, shook itself, climbed onto the Minister's thumb, and bumbled off. "He will be grief-stricken at your loss."

"I hope so. My Ambassador's person is protected by diplomatic immunity, and my government will hold the Dey personally responsible for his safe return."

The Minister of State's mouth opened slowly in an empty grin of apparent incomprehension.

What incredibly stupid people, Cal thought.

Or was it possible this one had just enough low cunning to see through Cal's bluster? Did he realize it would take years for Earth to get even a platoon's worth of military threat within striking distance of Depaz?

"Look, there may not be many of us here," Cal conceded, "but we don't go around on steam tractors and we don't carry potassium-nitrate firearms. We've got the real gear. So you'd better tell His Remarkableness to have whichever of his uncles did this get our man back here by sunrise"—he raised his finger in a rhetorical flourish—"or we'll do it ourselves, and the Dey will find himself an uncle or two short at the next family picnic."

A tired black fly looped over and settled on Cal's extended index finger. He shook his hand, but the fly clung tenaciously.

"I will convey this to my Dey," the Minister said mournfully. "My stomach tells me he will be prostrated with displeasure."

"Tell him we're *already* prostrated," Cal said, waving his hand more vigorously. "And we're getting more unhappy by the minute. We don't think kidnapping's a joke." He spun and strode toward the door, his hand flapping terribly.

"It has died, I think," the Minister of State called after him.

"What?"

"The fly. Old age, perhaps. It happens sometimes."

Cal stared at the motionless fly.

"Pluck it off," the voice from behind him continued. "Otherwise it will fester."

Cal emerged into the foyer flicking bits of dead fly from his finger. They had the most persistent feet; even dead, they didn't let go. He'd have to get the Agricultural Attaché to explain the mechanism someday. He found Bascomb staring at something on the floor.

"How'd it go?" Bascomb asked, looking up.

"I gave them till dawn. We'll just have to sit tight and see if it works." Cal glanced down at the area Bascomb had been studying. A perfectly circular dark spot. "What is it?"

"Looks like moisture."

"On the prairie?"

"Well, it seems to be shrinking. The only reason I could think of for that was evaporation."

Cal bent down and touched it. "I'll be damned. You're right—it's wet!"

"Maybe someone from the Albarian delegation? You know how they never go anywhere without a bucket of water."

"If anybody from Embassy Row'd been here today, we'd have known. We all keep tabs on each other."

"Well," Bascomb said, "whatever it was, it was recent. So, what do we do next?"

Cal looked over at the still-dozing porter, black with resting flies. "The reception tonight," he said. "What else?"

CHAPTER TWO

RESPONSIBILITY.

What a bitch.

And the aircon conked out in Moby Dick.

All the way back from Government House, Cal sweltered, sweat pouring off his forehead, soaking the back of his shirt.

"Why," he asked no one in particular, "does nothing around here ever work?"

"Dirt, most likely," the driver said. He swung past the fortresslike Albarian Legation on Embassy Row, then turned down the back way along the residence section of the Earth compound toward the chancery garage. Cal caught a glimpse of Grober's house.

Might not be a bad idea to stop by and talk with Grober privately. Cal was positive the idea of sticking him with operational responsibility this morning hadn't been Grober's. The old man had been his mentor since his arrival, and talking with him always seemed to help. In the twilight of his career, Grober had outgrown whatever ambitions he might have had—if so kindly a man ever really had any—and he was always happy to share whatever treasure of special knowledge or general wisdom a lifetime's experience had given him.

But there were questions that nagged. If he was really to be responsible for the Mission, even temporarily, he had to know exactly what to expect. Like Hara. Why had everyone seemed . . . well, afraid to cross her?

As soon as the Marine driver had parked Moby Dick, Cal

hopped on a tramseat and headed back up the incline to the Grobers' end of the compound.

The Depasian houseboy came to the door wiping his nose on his sleeve. He let Cal in and showed him to the little upstairs room overlooking the back garden. Well, not a garden precisely. Call it a pocket of Depaz's rarer weeds.

Grober hadn't gotten back from the Legation, and Mrs. Grober was bent over a table-shaped workbot, unpotting a brown and bedraggled something perhaps best not named and trying to prod it into life before transferring it to the outdoor beds.

"Cal," she said. "What a nice surprise."

"Surprised me, too. I came on a whim."

"Frank told me at lunch what happened, how they stuck you with responsibility. Are you here for advice and comfort?"

"Something like that."

"Well, Frank should be in any minute. Can I get you something in the meantime? A little tea?"

"No, I'll just sit and get my land legs back. Moby Dick always gives me a touch of motion sickness."

He seated himself in a chair by the far wall next to the glass case displaying Grober's insectoid collection, each specimen pinned to its own neatly handwritten label. Grober was perhaps the only off-worlder on Depaz who'd gotten any good out of the six-winged black flies. In fact, he had some really remarkable specimens. There were three on the second row, next to the white worm-flies, the largest close to two inches from disease-ridden mandibles to poisonous ovipositor. Cal shivered and turned back to Mrs. Grober.

"What do you know about Hara?" he asked.

"Fly larva," Mrs. Grober said.

"Pardon?"

"Oh, I'm sorry—I meant this plant." She gestured toward several rows of whitish lumps scarring the stem of the plant and radiating down into the potting soil.

"Worm-flies?"

"Maggots. No matter how carefully you cover a plant, there's always at least one clever fly that finds a way in."

She scraped the squirming white grubs off the stem and into a cup of insecticide with her knife. "Now what were you saying, dear?"

"I was asking what you knew about Hara."

"Everybody knows Hara." Mrs. Grober laughed.

"No, I mean her character, her background, that kind of thing."

"What an odd thought."

"Pardon?"

"No, it's just . . . of all the people to want to know that sort of thing about," Mrs. Grober said.

"How's that?"

"Just that I guess Hara must be a very private person. I don't think I really know much about her at all."

"But you and Mr. Grober have known her for a good ten years."

"Longer," said Grober, head appearing suddenly as he came up by way of the spiral stairs. He swung away and then back again on the last turn, puffing from the exertion, the red spots on his florid cheeks burning brighter than usual. "Eleven, I think. It was her suggestion I sign on for another year here till retirement rather than transfer for a one-year stint somewhere else. Paths of least resistance have always appealed to me. Sorry, by the way."

"About what?"

"Sticking you with being Acting Chief of Mission. Sometimes I mistake my friends for specimens in my collection." He did a quick pantomime of skewering Cal with a huge pin, then bent to give his wife a peck on the forehead. "'The hind that would be mated by the lion must die for love,' eh, my dear? *All's Well That Ends Errors,* Cal. Make a note."

"What do you think of her?"

"My beloved wife?"

"Hara."

"Sometimes I suspect we just have conflations of separate plays. Like *A Midwinter's Tempest.* Some marvelous isolated bits, but too many unrelated characters. What's a statue of his wife doing on an uninhabited island with a monster? That's the trouble with a classical education—

you spend all your time trying to make sense out of the ancients' hopelessly garbled texts."

"I was talking about Hara."

"So you were. Whatever for?"

"Well, I need to know more about, well, the entire staff. What I'm up against. This could involve deep security, the Albarian mission . . . And I really wonder who I can count on, who's weak, that kind of thing. And frankly, Hara gives me the creeps."

"Cal," said Grober, easing himself with some difficulty into a chair beside Cal at the table, "let an old-timer give you a bit of advice. It just doesn't pay to tell a senior officer like me that another senior officer gives you the creeps."

"You'd report me?"

"No, but someone my age is so forgetful, I'm apt to let it slip in front of her. And gossiping about an officer behind her back isn't going to help your Annual Efficiency Report when it's made out."

"I'm not gossiping."

"What, then?" Mrs. Grober asked, snapping out a leaf as brown and dry as one of the liver spots on her hand.

"Just fishing, I guess. Like her Reserve rating."

"OWSR-2? What about it?"

"It strikes me as odd."

"Odd? Can you be a little more specific?"

"All right, what if she's an intelligence plant?"

"I thought you weren't gossiping." Grober laughed.

"And I thought John Townsend was chief of the Intelligence Section," Mrs. Grober said.

"He's legitimate intelligence-gathering," Cal said. "I'm talking about the kind of person with top security clearance and carte blanche in covert operations—*real* intelligence. They say there's one planted in every embassy. Be honest. Do you think she's ours? You seemed to handle her with kid gloves this morning."

"Cal, for a young fellow, you ask a lot of dangerous questions."

"Dangerous?"

"He means, my dear," Mrs. Grober said, "that if Hara

were with Intelligence, it wouldn't be very smart to talk about her in the compound because she'd have installed listening devices."

"Even here?"

"Especially here," she continued. "There are all kinds of things a Consul General finds out about when he's processing visas and passports. All kinds of—"

Grober stood up suddenly as though deliberately interrupting her. "You have time for a little something to drink? Whiskey?"

"Isn't it a little early, Frank?" Mrs. Grober asked.

The background drone of the aircon stuttered; the lights flickered with a momentary power interruption.

Grober reached into the cabinet and took out a glass. "On Depaz, Mary, it's never a little early." He poured himself a finger of something rich and green.

"Funny color for whiskey," Cal mused.

"On Depaz," Grober said, "nothing is funny."

Grober threw back half his drink and made a face. "You'd think the Depasians could at least learn how to make decent booze, wouldn't you? Even the universe's most dismal racial failure must need a good drink every now and then."

"You could give it up, Frank," Mrs. Grober said.

"I could commit suicide, too, but I don't think I will."

"You are already, drinking that stuff all the time."

"My dear, I would be committing suicide faster if I didn't keep my senses anesthetized. How else can you cope with the depressing realities of life on Depaz?"

The lights flickered again and went out. Grober poured himself another drink and sat down in the gray window light.

"Believe it or not, the lower classes have a drink that's even worse. They call it *miship*."

"Rat bite?" Cal asked.

"Very good. Must have gotten a class one in your language qualifiers. Right, rat bite. Fermented from sawgrass seeds and *misha* intestine."

"Were you saying I *should* be careful before?" Cal asked.

Grober said nothing.

Cal cleared his throat to try again. "What's happened to the Ambassador could be seen as some kind of Intelligence screw-up. I got the distinct feeling this morning that Hara seemed more anxious than Townsend to hush it up. Do you think she was responsible for the screw-up?"

"How quickly we leap to conclusions," Grober said. "One minute you wonder if she's Intelligence, the next you wonder exactly which part of Intelligence was her responsibility. Will you be reorganizing the staff now? Look, you have to understand folks like Hara and me that are going short. We're old gears with our teeth worn down to the nub. Most of the time . . . well, face it. We slip. But not always. We've still got some bite left now and then—when it counts."

"You must admit, she didn't seem too worried about the Ambassador. Matter of fact, she's pretty cool about life and death in general—completely indifferent, like none of it matters."

"Cal, there comes a time when . . . well, you just get tired. Too tired even to feel. Look, I've been at this what, two hundred years? Something like that. Can you imagine how tired that is? I used to be like you. So did Hara, I expect. But the years are like bricks. They pile up on your back, one after the other. At first, it doesn't seem so bad. But then another and another and another. You start to bend over with it. After a while, the weight is all you're able to feel anymore. It's unbearable. Gravity, Cal, that's what you're up against."

"Gravity?"

"Pulling at your jowls, tugging out the bags under your eyes, dragging you down. Sit, lie down, rest, sleep, die. The grave's the ultimate black hole. Maximum gravity. Eventually everything gets sucked into it." Grober paused thoughtfully. "It's hard enough growing old back home, I guess. But out here somehow it's twice as hard, like the gravity's more intense. I think Hara and I have earned the right to be tired."

"Okay, forget it," Cal said. "Guess I was imagining things. I can't help worrying. Especially when I think back to the Academy and all those textbook cases of Intelligence screw-ups like Avvanos."

Grober shot his wife a quick, hard look.

"But I forgot," Cal said. "You were there, weren't you."

"Yes," Grober said. "We were there."

"So you'd know all about that," Cal said. "Funny, you never mentioned what your assignment was on Embassy Avvanos."

"We were young," Mrs. Grober said. "We—"

Grober cut her off with another look. There was an awkward silence.

"Well," Cal said, "guess I should be getting back. But thanks for the talk. It's a lucky thing for me you decided not to go back to Earth for that last year you've got coming up."

Grober laughed. "The idea of going home is just too strange. You get burned out this far away. There's no going back. My brain's fried." He turned to Mrs. Grober. "You want to go back?"

She shook her head. "I used to," she said. "But somehow it just doesn't seem worth such a long, long trip. Not just to die." She looked surprised, as though she hadn't meant to say what she did.

Cal shivered. "Well, I guess I'd better get back to the office," he said.

"What for?" Grober asked. "Why not just get ready for tonight's reception instead? Eat, drink, and be merry, for tomorrow . . . tomorrow we'll wake up, and we'll still be here. And try not to look so shocked, Cal. By the time it's your turn a couple hundred years down the road, it won't bother you, either."

"Maybe," Cal said, heading for the stairs. "See you later."

"And Cal?"

Cal turned. Grober said nothing, but he seemed to be forming words with his lips.

"What?" Cal asked.

"Good luck till the reception," Grober said. "Be careful."

* * *

Receptions and parties were a necessity of life. The horror of Depaz, aside from heat and flatness, was the absence of people worth talking to.

The Depasians were as interesting as turnips. That left only occasional off-worlders—freighter crews, explorers, pirates. And when any of these happened by, every Embassy's personnel fell over each other trying to get the visitors first. Dinner with anything that didn't let flies crawl up its nose while it talked to you was at least a change. And on Depaz, any change was ipso facto an improvement.

Such visitors were, however, rare. In the interim, the diplomats had to fall back on each other.

All the civilized worlds maintained missions on Depaz on the assumption that any planet so wretched was bound to turn out having some extraordinarily valuable something or other—just as soon as somebody figured out what it was. Meanwhile, every world kept a diplomatic foothold on the prairie so it wouldn't lose out when whatever it was was finally identified.

So to pass the time, the staffs of each Legation had receptions for the others on a rotation basis. Tonight was Earth's turn.

Entertaining, however, was not without hazards. The Albarian Information Officer and his compeers, for instance, were pleasant enough in their crocodilian way—for members of the Legation closest to being Earth's diplomatic rival—but they *would* keep plunging their heads into the nearest liquid, which was sometimes one of the buckets they had carried for the purpose and sometimes the punch bowl and sometimes, if your glass was big enough, your cocktail. You couldn't blame them, though; every minute out of water meant holding their breath, which is an awkward way to spend any evening.

Then there was Nargom, who perched on the backs of chairs and excreted regularly and copiously as a sea gull and couldn't be persuaded there was anything wrong with it. And all those that breathed methane and acetylene and propane and had to stand by the wall in clumsy pressure suits like mummies, faceplates swirling with exotic gases while smokers were kept well away to avoid the embarrassment of exploding a guest with a careless flick of an ash—not to mention the diplomatic repercussions. Or the mess.

But the most urbane old hand and sought-after dinner companion of Embassy Row was, oddly enough, the one posing the biggest problems. Not only did Drofsko—sole representative and entire Legation of the planet Si—have to remain in a transparent tube of noble gases to keep from oxidizing his liquid-silicon body into solid glass, but the tube, kept at low pressure and temperature, had to be wiped clear of frost several times per party to maintain visual contact. And even if you could have shoved a cocktail or canapé through his tube, he neither ate nor even breathed; he operated on pure photo-voltaic energy. He was a giant, undulating silicon solar battery.

Actually, Drofsko was neither "he" nor "she," but more correctly "they"—a colony of tiny creatures that Grober described as multilayered microprocessor semiconductors with silicon metabolisms, thousands of them, carrying out specialized functions for the entire entity, like the body cells of a human being except that each cell was individually intelligent. A genius, in fact.

Working in concert, Drofsko's component creatures were capable of processing information at five hundred megahertz—a million times faster than the firing rate for human neurons. As a result, even with the automatic timing devices that collected and converted his electrical pulses into synthesized human speech at rates humans could understand, the pauses between question and answer must have been for him more tedious than the twenty-minute lags in Earth-Jupiter link-ups back at the Home Office.

But Drofsko was nothing if not accommodating.

Indeed, he was more than flexible or even pliant. He had no form at all. Because his component creatures used electrostatic attraction and repulsion to move within the mass, he was a kind of liquid-crystal silicon puddle capable of flowing into any shape.

For humans, he usually hunched himself up like a gravy-covered chicken croquette.

"Really, my dears," he was saying at tonight's party. *"Such* a dreadful world, isn't it?" His iridescent skin shimmered with pleasant, oily rainbows, and spots in his tube glowed blue with helium ionized by his thought pulses. That meant a relatively low level of processing; when he was really working on something, the vapor in his tube glowed white with the combination of excited krypton and xenon. Tonight he was only discussing the unfortunate archaeologist, Weston.

"As you know, my dears, she had an advanced degree—a doctor of philosophy, I think it's called—so everyone at the Legation here called her 'doctor.' Well, the wretched Depasians—stop me if you've heard this. . . ."

Everyone had, in fact, heard it, but no one said so. There were only so many stories to go around, and Drofsko told things so well, though the Albarian Chargé kept his head in his bucket longer than seemed altogether necessary.

"Yes, well," Drofsky continued, "when her academic title was translated for them—the Depasian is *tpurkhgai,* isn't it, Cal?"

Cal was always startled when Drofsko addressed him; since he had no eyes, you couldn't anticipate him because you never knew where he was looking. But Cal got hold of himself and nodded, knowing Drofsko spoke better Depasian than the rest of Embassy Row combined and was just being polite by including him in the conversation. Not that Drofsko's consideration made it any less of a strain to talk to a tube of glop.

"Well, the wretched Depasians, having not the least inkling of the distinction between an academic doctor and a medical one—why, goodness, any nomad with a rattle is a licensed physician out here, and they couldn't in a thousand years *begin* to grasp the idea of a university. Anyway, they thought *Tpurkhgai* Weston cured warts, that sort of thing—can you imagine? So one day when she was out on one of her digs, one of those miserable brigand lordlings arrived and demanded *Tpurkhgai* Weston help his ailing wife.

"Poor Weston tried to explain she wasn't that sort of doctor, but day after day the bandit returned, threatening, cajoling—they *are* so persistent, aren't they?—until at last she gave up and asked what the symptoms were."

The battery failed in one of the canapébots and it coasted smack into the wall, leaving a smear of green dip down the length of it. Drofsko ignored the shattering sound of the bowl.

"Well, the bandit said, his wife smelled more terrible than a thousand diseased *pulgargs*. By now Weston was sorry she hadn't stood firm, but there was no going back, and she told the bandit to bring his wife in. Of course, it turned out the princess was the size of a small moon, and it took two of their steam tractors to drag her to Weston's camp.

"Weston had her undress and lie on a workbench, only to discover that this was one of those rare instances of a Depasian telling the truth—the princess, if anything, smelled worse than *two* thousand diseased *pulgargs*. Well, Weston tightened a C-clamp on her nose, put on her work gloves, and began pushing aside the princess's rolls of corpulence with a garden rake, when lo and behold, a dead *misha* dropped out from a trough of fat. It had been squashed *paper-thin*."

The company laughed politely.

"Weston was a great lover of theorizing, as some of you recall," Drofsko observed, his tube spotting with neon-orange pleasure at his listeners' response. "Her theory this time was that the *misha* must have been scampering over the hills and valleys of her royal highness's sleeping body one night when said highness sat up suddenly, crushing it to death in the folds of her royal amplitude. It had apparently remained thus hidden on the royal person for months."

Everyone laughed again, and Cal drifted away among the other conversational clusters.

"Akh," lisped the unitrans at the neck of the Albarian Information Officer. "A moszht wonderful party you are having."

"Thank you," Cal said. This was almost certainly one of the higher-ups in the Albarian intelligence community. "It could not, of course, hope to rival the sumptuousness of the entertainments I've had the pleasure of attending at your own Legation."

"Yeszh, I supposzh not." The Albarian grimaced, running out of breath. He nodded to his pot boy for the cauldron of water and plunged his head into it, held it under for a few moments, and finally reemerged, water sluicing along his expression lines and dripping from his snout. "But be telling uszh, good friend, how fareszh your Ambasszhador?"

"Fine, thank you," Cal said.

"But he iszh not here?"

Cal's eyes narrowed. Did this one in fact know something about what had happened? "Of course he is."

"Oh?" The Albarian smiled so that the score of pointed teeth along the sides of his jaw were visible. "But I do not szhee him anywhere."

"Oh, he's here somewhere," Cal said. "But he's tired today, and he may have excused himself early."

He had to be careful of jumping to conclusions on the slender springboard of a single coincidental inquiry. It was possible the Albarians really had been involved in the kidnapping, but this might just as easily be a typical spy's inquisitiveness, a fishing expedition for an advantageous scandal, a useful rift in the leadership of Earth's Legation, a potentially valuable illness.

"I am szho glad. I was frightened Hiszh Excellenszhy might be, how iszh it you szhay? Szhick." "

"Pardon?"

The Albarian gave the unitrans a sharp rap with his clawed finger. "Ill," it buzzed. He smiled toothily.

Just then there was a loud whirring, and another diminutive canapébot wobbled past. "Crypto-pâté, neopig-in-a-hlanket?" asked its flat voice loudly as it floated to a stop, slowly rotating its Lazy-Susan head to offer in turn each of its delicacies to Cal and the Depasian. "Fresh marood pseudoshrimp?"

"Ak baggle palgg?" buzzed the Albarian's unitrans in tandem. *"Fodle-yop? Quiggle-moro?"* The Albarian looked down at the unitrans with a profoundly puzzled expression. Drofsko, on the other side of the room, spotted orange

and seemed to shift his mass uneasily, almost uncomfortably.

"Is something wrong?" Cal asked the Albarian.

The Albarian shook his head.

"Quasi-cheese dip, then?"

"Argabarga warg?" crackled the unitrans.

The Albarian put his hand to his neck.

"Don't worry about it," Hara said, passing by on her way to the bar. "Frequency of the canapébot's probably off, so it's coming through the unitrans as electronic garble."

"Gosh, I'm sorry," Cal said to the Albarian. "We'll get it retuned at once." He grasped the canapébot firmly by its tray head and gave it a good shove. It bobbed away in a spray of crypto-pâté and pseudoshrimp.

"Frankly," Hara said, "sometimes it's a real temptation to give one of these things a lobotomy." She seemed to reach inside her robe.

"Jesus, no," Cal whispered, grabbing her arm. "You want to wind up standing trial under the Cybernetics Law?"

"The satisfaction might just be worth it," Hara said, drawing out a handkerchief and mopping her forehead. "Is it getting stuffy in here, or is it just me?" She moved on toward the bar.

Getting too jumpy, Cal cautioned himself. He needed to get hold, stop seeing spies everywhere. He cleared his throat to resume his exchange with the Albarian when he caught sight of Bascomb in animated conversation with Nargom.

"You must pardon me," Cal said with the slightest bow from the waist. "Pressing business." He followed Hara.

"You're certainly looking good this evening," he said to Bascomb as he came within earshot.

"Unh," said Nargom, preoccupied.

A houseboy hurried up with a portascoop and a trashbot to clean up the mess behind His Excellency.

"Is this guy bothering you?" Cal whispered.

Bascomb laughed, slipping her arm in his as they moved through the crowd. "You're certainly cheerful tonight. Did a medibot slip you something?"

"Nope, just paying attention for the first time," Cal said. "Sorry if I've been a little short or anything today."

"You've been just fine for somebody who just found himself promoted to Acting Chief of Mission in time to take the rap for one kidnapped Ambassador."

Grober passed by on his way to the punch bowl. "By the way, Cal," he said, leaning close, "my contacts report hearing some grumblings to the effect that His Limitlessness, the Ineffable Dey, did not take kindly to the tone you used with his Minister-Cousin this afternoon."

"The man was insufferable."

"No doubt, but as long as you're ACM, you've got to be careful."

Cal bit his lip. "I guess I was a little pushy. I thought that's what the situation called for."

"It does, but when the fate of our entire Legation depends on how well one self-indulgent despot likes us, we can't be *too* pushy, no matter what the provocation."

"Cal was just worried about the Ambassador," Bascomb said.

"No, I was wrong," Cal said. "I wasn't keeping things in perspective."

"Don't be too hard on yourself." Grober laughed, winking at Bascomb. "We always have the autoshuttle and our orbiting Evac ship, just in case."

"Mr. Troy!" came an urgent whisper. "Mr. Troy!"

Cal turned to find their Protocol Officer behind him, looking slightly disheveled and terribly upset.

"What is it, Hendrix?"

"Oh, something terrible, just terrible." Hendrix's chest heaved as he struggled for breath.

"Get hold of yourself, Hendrix. What's the matter?"

"You know that dog the Ambassador keeps?"

"That little yappy thing—Snitzy or something?"

"Trixie."

"Who could forget? What about it?"

"She's just been running *distracted* since the Ambassador's disappearance, and she . . . she got out."

"Out?"

"Of her kennel."

"You've come bursting in here to tell me that the Ambassador's little yap-dog got out of its cage?"

"Yes."

"Jesus!"

Hendrix's eyes were wide with terror. "But there's more."

"All right, then, let's have it!"

"You know . . . you know the Eprapi?"

"Those little greenish pygmies? What about them?"

"Not all of them. Just their Counselor for Administration."

"All right, what about *him?*"

"It."

"It, then."

"They don't have gender on Eprap, except grammatically."

"Will you get on with it?"

"Oh, my, yes, yes, of course. Well." Hendrix pursed his lips. "His Excellency the Counselor for Administration was on his way here . . . and . . ." Hendrix's lower lip began to tremble.

"Out with it, man!"

"The Ambassador's dog ate it." Hendrix burst into tears.

"Snitzy?"

"Trixie."

"You're sure?"

"One of the Marines found Snitzy chewing on his teensy little walking stick out by the side of the ramp a few minutes ago." He opened his palm to reveal the six-inch staff covered with teeth marks.

Cal squeezed the bridge of his nose. "Acting Chief of Mission less than a day and I've already lost two members of the diplomatic community in my own compound. Look, Hendrix, pull yourself together and get the Gunny to roust out all his off-duty Marines and any available securibots and search every square inch of the grounds. And don't let a word of this get out until we're sure you're right about what happened."

Cal watched sourly as Hendrix fled out the door.

"What you need is a drink," Grober said, suddenly at Cal's elbow. He steered Cal and Bascomb toward the bar, where a knot of people had gathered around Hara and Drofsko. They were still discussing Weston, and Cal paused to listen for a moment. He'd always had an amateur's interest in archaeology, and he hoped for a tidbit to take his mind off his troubles.

"I remember when Weston first came," Hara was saying, her gray face flushed with sawgrass whiskey. "Wanted to see the sunset, and I was delegated to take her. I *told* her the flies were worst at twilight, but no, she had to see for herself. Then she spots the Depasian women squatting off on the west side of town—you know how they head out that way to take a dump. And Weston says, 'What a stunning image, all those women meditating on the beauty of a sunset. You don't see that except in a primitive culture like this that's still in touch with its natural origins.' And I says, 'Lady, you can't get more natural, because they're just trying take a crap before the wolves come out. And if you decide to stroll over that way, I'd advise you to watch where you step.'"

There was a profound silence. Nargom excreted delicately over the edge of the sofa.

"Shit," Baum said, seeming to appear from nowhere. He gestured for Cal and Grober to join him up in the C-level balcony that circled the foyer above.

Grober left for the ramp first, then Cal and Bascomb. Cal noticed Drofsko's tube glowing with xenon-blue patches of interest. Funny, Cal thought. He couldn't remember when talking with humans had gotten Drofsko past neon-orange. Maybe he'd never seen humans embarrassed before, and he was intrigued by the concept.

Halfway up, Cal happened to notice the frosty base of Drofsko's tube. It rang a warning bell in his head. But why? What did it remind him of? He hurried down the hall and along the glassed-in outer balcony after Baum, squinting against the surges of harsh, purple-white light outside as fly after fly bumbled into the protective grids. Even through the glass he could hear the air crackling with their burning, brief, livid stars against the night sky.

What was it about the ecotube? He remembered once watching Drofsko arrive at Government House in a wheelbarrow arrangement drawn by three scrofulous Depasian hirelings who had wrestled him out, lugged him up the steps, and rocked him into place for his presentation like a new water heater. Drofsko could no doubt have moved his tube by antigrav or some even more miraculous device, but, as he explained to Cal, it was better diplomacy to employ as many natives as possible. He could see the ecotube standing there upright on the . . . Of course!

"I know this is going to sound crazy," Cal whispered to Bascomb as Grober and Baum halted just around the corner so they couldn't be seen from the reception area, "but did you happen to notice that the base of Drofsko's container is just about the same size as that circle of moisture you found at Government House?"

"I didn't notice," Bascomb said.

"Listen up," Baum said, glancing around to be sure they weren't observed. "We've heard from the kidnappers." He turned to Grober. "Your houseboy says a man in a mask came over the compound wall and told him to give us a message."

"A man in a mask?" Grober said, sucking his cheeks. "A likely story. Kid's probably involved right up to his yellow baby teeth."

"No doubt, but the point is they want someone to meet one of their boys out in the prairie north of town." Baum's face flickered in the glare of incinerating fly carcasses.

"Did the kid say how big a ransom they want for the Ambassador?"

"Didn't mention any specific money figure. Guess that's what they want the meeting for."

"Naturally," Grober said. "After kidnapping, haggling over price is the national pastime."

"Well, if I'm Acting Chief of Mission," Cal said, "I guess it's up to me to do the haggling."

"That's not the half of it," Grober said. "You're going to need an Irregular Disbursement Voucher. OWS/IDV 47405. I remember a few years back this one officer didn't oversee

THE TIMESERVERS

the IDV personally, and the accounting boys just crucified him."

"Thanks," Cal said glumly.

Grober squinted, preoccupied with the outdoor flash of a meaty white worm-fly. "Lost two pay grades."

"I said thanks."

Wisps of fresh ash floated past the window. "And half his accumulated sick leave."

A low moan from Cal.

"You all right, Cal?" Grober asked.

"Fine, fine."

Grober shrugged. "Anyway, make sure you take somebody with you."

"Are you volunteering?" Cal asked.

Grober shook his head. "Sorry. But I did have somebody in mind."

"I'll go," Bascomb said.

"Not you, dear," Grober said.

"Who, then?"

"Hara."

"You're kidding."

"Nope."

"After what you—I mean, you're saying she's the type for this kind of negotiating after all?" Cal asked.

"I'm not saying anything except she's the oldest of the Depaz hands," Grober said. "She's been here longer and knows more than anybody else, especially about the nomads."

"Okay, that makes good sense. Bascomb, would you go back in and ask Hara to meet me down in the garage? You don't have to tell her anything else, except maybe mention casually she might like to pack one of those guns from that weapons collection she's got."

"Yes, sir."

"And Bascomb?"

"Sir?"

"Don't breathe a word within fifty feet of Drofsko."

"Why, sir?"

"Just don't."

"Yes, sir." Bascomb hesitated a moment. "You'll be careful, won't you?"

"Sure. I'm always careful. Something wrong?"

Bascomb looked down with a shy smile. "Too bad there isn't time to stop by my apartment for a drink or something before you go."

Cal shook his head. "Maybe when I get back?"

"Of course," she said. "I'd love that."

"Mr. Troy!" came a voice from the other end of the hall. "Mr. Troy! You can relax! He's all right! We've found him!"

Cal closed his eyes and slumped against the wall with a sigh. "Before we'd even offered to pay a ransom?" he said, a smile spreading across his face. "Thank God."

"Ransom? We just found him under the side door."

"*Under* the door?"

"Where Trixie chased him," said Hendrix. "The Eprapi Counselor for Administration. But we're going to have to punish Trixie, anyway."

CHAPTER THREE

HARA DROVE low, slicing through the sawgrass. The vicious stalks drummed a thundering tattoo along the metal sides.

"We'll lose all the paint on our underside and shred the rubber bumper," Cal shouted over the din.

"But if we keep low like this," Hara shouted back, "whoever's waiting for us'll be outlined against the sky. We'll see him perfectly—and however many friends he's brought with him. It's an old nomad trick, my boy."

The fraternal-twin moons had just begun their climb into the purple sky, one swollen and orange, the other pale and waferish. They glinted off the still surface of the Marood, glimmering through the sawgrass off to Cal's right. Strange, he thought, how what in daylight seemed so much dead muck, huge doughnuts of salt crystal solidifying around the yellow sawgrass roots at the perimeter, could be transformed into such a thing of beauty, like a hidden mountain mere mirroring the million stars of the night sky.

"Twelfth milestone," Hara grunted. "That was the landmark the Grobers' houseboy gave, right?"

"Right," Cal said.

"Then where the hell wait a minute. There he is!"

Cal followed Hara's pointing finger to the horizon where, silhouetted against the pale medallion of the lesser moon, stood a solitary figure. The bandit was seated brazenly atop an *elik*, the small-headed cross between a horse and an antelope that the true nomads preferred to the steam tractors of the Dey's court. Beside him loomed something large and not quite recognizable but which Cal thought might be some kind of prairie animal he hadn't encountered before.

Hara hovered for a moment, then let the car crackle gently into the stiff grass. They pulled on their face nets and slipped gingerly among the serrated blades, moving slowly and very cautiously toward the Depasian, to avoid slashing their clothes or cutting themselves more than necessary.

"All right," Cal called in Depasian when he was certain they were within earshot. "Where's our Ambassador?"

"Does the prairie bloom in one instant, or blade by blade?" said the mounted figure in flawless English. "One matter at a time, please."

Cal hesitated. He'd never heard a Depasian speak English, let alone so well. But he sensed the man was waiting for them to draw closer. No Depasian could discuss business without being so close that his breath blistered your nose. That was because all Depasian cooking was based on a leeklike root that could peel paint and take the temper out of steel. It was consumed raw or chopped up with pieces of *misha*, earthworm segments, left to decompose in a bucket underground for a year or two, and fermented into a sludge with which the Depasians flavored everything. Quality was judged by how copiously the eyes teared after each mouthful. The kindest thing anyone in the Legation had ever said was Major Sedewski's observation that it tasted like burning dirt.

"I am here to offer," said the Depasian, "on payment of an infinitesimally modest sum, the return of this valuable creature beside me."

Cal squinted at the dark shape. "What the hell is it?"

"You do not recognize it?"

Cal squinted again. "The camel? But it's not even ours! We gave it to the Dey." He supposed they were testing him, and he wasn't at all sure how he was expected to respond. Should he show generosity by ransoming the thing for the Dey, or should he show shrewdness by ignoring it? Would regulations even allow him to ransom it?

"Every gift is the giver's life-long responsibility."

"I'm only authorized to discuss my Ambassador."

The Depasian shook his head. "And my god authorizes me to discuss only this mound-back here."

The statement was startling, but before Cal had time to question it, Hara interrupted. "What's he trying to say?" she asked impatiently.

"He says he's only here to make a deal for the camel. He—"

Hara raised her arm swiftly, and there was a muffled crack as the laser discharged. The camel dropped to its front knees, then toppled sideways, the fur around the spot on its skull where the laser hit still sputtering with flame.

"Tell him the issue's resolved," Hara said.

"Hara!" Cal whispered savagely. "What the hell did you do that for?" He tried to mask his dismay and anger from the bandit. Textbook behavior—no good letting your adversary know about any internal divisions or weaknesses.

"You've got to show these people when you mean business," Hara hissed back.

The back of Cal's neck was frozen with sweat. He'd have to make the best of what Hara had done. "That was just a warning," Cal said in Depasian.

"It was an act of depraved cruelty," answered the rider in English.

Cal hung his head, taken aback by the moral condescension. Actually, he had been beginning to feel good about shooting the camel. At least it was something *tangible*.

Wordlessly, the rider tugged his reins and turned his *elik*. Carefully, it picked its way among the sprawled camel's legs.

"I hope to God you haven't blown it," Cal said, annoyed with Hara for tempting him into morally indefensible thoughts. "It's my ass, you know." He watched the *elik* begin to canter westward.

"He was just stalling to up the ante," Hara said. "And I called his bluff. You've got to remember, their only moral code is not losing face in the eyes of their tribe. With us, they're conscienceless." She reached inside her jacket and pulled out a second, smaller pistol with a long barrel that glinted in the moons' light. "Now that they know we mean business, we should get some action."

"You're not going to shoot him?" Cal gasped. "He's our only link—"

Thup went the gun.

"Jesus Christ, you *did* shoot him!"

Hara gave him a sour look. "Does he *look* shot?"

The horse and rider were still moving away through the tall grass.

"Planted a beeper, that's all," Hara continued. "Airgun syringe." She reached deep inside her native robe and brought out a handset. "All right," she said after studying the screen a moment. "The dart's definitely moving away, so it caught on him or his horse. We'll just wait a while and then follow."

"But he's headed west."

"So?"

"The Dey's forbidden anybody going west of the Marood. Diplomatically—"

"Cal, if you want the Ambassador back, you're going to have to be prepared to play fast and loose with local laws sometimes."

Cal hooked his thumbs behind his belt. "All right, you know Depaz better than I do."

Hara gave a quick, satisfied smile. "Thank you," she said.

"But where did you find out about all this tracking gear?"

"You pick up a lot in the course of a career, especially when you're posted to a prairie where tracking could mean the difference between life and death. Sometimes I think it's too bad they don't give you a second lifetime to use it in."

They waited nearly an hour in the gathering cold beside the stiffening camel. It didn't seem quite fair, Cal thought, looking at it. After all those millions of miles, and in the suspension pod right next to Cal's . . . It was like losing a relative, a third cousin, say; it didn't make the eyes water, but it hung a weight of ineffable melancholy about the heart. Cal sighed at the exquisite existentialism of it all.

"Time we got our asses going," Hara said.

Again they followed low, the hovercraft's cab filled with the plaintive animal cheep of the beeper. On the console screen, Hara punched in the orbital photomap of the northern prairie to look for possible hideouts the messenger might be heading for. It showed only the scattered white patches of nomad tent encampments, and here and there occasional dark squares: the remains of Weston's archaeological excavations. Cal gritted his teeth, eyes flicking from the map to the direction finder to be sure they were still on the bandit's trail. Moby Dick shuddered with the strain of hovering at a trot, while outside rose higher the big and little moons.

"You notice anything odd about that guy?" Cal asked at last.

"The bandit? They're all the same—dumb as dirt."

"Yeah, usually. But this one . . . I don't know how to explain it—he just didn't seem dumb at all, you know?"

"Oh, they're cunning enough when it comes to trying to screw you out of a ransom," Hara said. "But when you've been here as long as I have—"

"It's more than cunning. There was something about him. If I hadn't known he was a nomad, I might have mistaken him for a human."

"Ridiculous." Hara laughed.

"And didn't you notice how he said 'god'?"

"What about it?"

"The Depasians have no gods. They practice a primitive animism. A few tribes worship these vague nature spirits—dryads, hamadryads, nymphs. And, of course, there's that myth of the gobbling moon-face."

"Their lunar eclipse thingy," Hara said. "I kind of prefer my own people's story about a dragon eating the moon."

"Weston thought it was a poetic description of the explosion of Depaz's third moon. But the point is, they have no gods in our sense."

"Forget it," Hara said, her face green in the glow of the windshield instrument display.

They rode on in silence except for the incessant beeping and the drumming of the grass. Toward midnight, Hara began looking at the instruments more and more often.

"We're overheating," she said finally. "It's from all this hovering without forward momentum to pace that *elik*. We're going to have to set down somewhere and let her cool off."

"Where?" Cal said. "We're sitting ducks out here."

Hara thought a moment. "Last time I was out on the prairie overnight, I holed up in one of Weston's old excavations. If we can find a big one, we can drop Moby Dick into it and be completely hidden unless they actually come up to the pit edge."

"You go out in the prairie often?" Cal asked.

Hara ignored the question, concentrating on the screen of the on-board cybot. "Well, well," she said. "There's one just a few minutes off our course."

Cal glanced at the screen. "What's the notation code there?"

"One of mine," Hara said. "That was the excavation Weston was working when the Dey's cossacks arrived to arrest her."

"I wonder if there's anything of interest there," Cal said.

"All I wonder is whether it's deep enough to hide Moby Dick," Hara said.

As it happened, the gaping black hole in the eternal flatness was a good two stories down. To one side still stood the abandoned cluster of pipes and scaffolding of Weston's sonic digger and a huge mound of molecularized dirt.

"Wonder what she was hoping to find here," Cal mused, glancing out at the earthen walls rising above them on either side as they settled into the excavation. They touched down on the pit floor with a gentle lurch.

"Same old saw about the Depasians being humanoid," Hara said. "Frankly, I knew Weston was nuts the minute I laid eyes on her."

"Yeah, I guess it would be pretty depressing to think the Depasians were descended from us."

"Depressing? I'd slit my wrists."

Cal eased his seat back to stretch out. "But we can't be completely sure."

"How's that?"

"Well, there's a century or two missing from the history."

"You mean the Social Security War?" Hara asked.

"The magnetic flux storms after the holocaust erased all their cybot records."

"It's what you get for storing everything on magnetic tapes and discs." Hara closed her eyes sleepily.

"Yeah, but what if an expedition left Earth just before the war—"

"They didn't have space flight then," Hara objected.

"On the contrary," Cal said. "Most historians believe the twentieth and twenty-first centuries *did* have space flight."

"Forget it."

"But think about it," Cal said. "An expedition whose records were entirely lost in the storms, an expedition nobody knows about anymore. It landed here, had no Earth to phone home to, the members interbred . . . It would explain a lot."

"The degenerating effects of mating within a restricted gene pool?"

"It would explain why they're so—"

"God, do you have to be so metaphysical all the time?" Hara asked. "If you don't stop, you're going to decide that the Depasians' most revolting customs are terrestrial. Next you'll tell me the Gobbling Yellow Moon Face is an idea from Earth."

"You have to keep an open mind," Cal said.

"When you're my age," Hara said, "you get the right to close your mind on some issues. My boy, you're worse than Weston." Hara settled back again. "The Social Security War. I wonder why they called it that."

"Something else history's forgotten."

"Worst case of amnesia in thousands of years."

Cal turned to face Hara. "Tell me, how did you happen to know Weston? She's gone a good twelve years."

"I took an extension on my ten-year tour."

"Like Grober?"

"I was three years to retirement when my time was up. I couldn't see dragging through fifty years in suspension just to wake up and spend three years as a short-timer ten light years away."

"That's why you advised Grober to do the same? What'll you do when you finally finish here?" Cal asked. "Go back home to Earth?"

Hara looked pained. "After three hundred years? Wouldn't recognize the place, my boy. No, I think maybe one of the places I toured—Albar, for instance."

"But Albar's the enemy."

"That's professionally. On a personal level, Albar would suit me fine."

"But we claim their government—"

"Cal, stop playing rule-book warrior with me. What's important isn't government, it's climate. Albar's kind of swampy, sure, but it's only a few light-years away, and it's mainly agricultural, so it wouldn't have changed all that much. It's familiarity you want when you get older. You get so you hate change."

Cal shook his head. "It's funny," he said aloud.

"What's funny this time?"

"You and Grober. I have yet to meet anyone about to retire from the Service who wanted to go back to Earth. It's like you get allergic to it after you've been away for too long."

"That so?" Hara said. "Tell me, my boy—are you dying to get back to Earth at your age?"

"Why, uh, no, I guess not," Cal said, "but after all, I've got my career to worry about right now. I couldn't think of going back right now. It would mean giving up being an immortal."

"Ah," Hara said. "I see." She turned her head away to face the side window. "Well, after my long drive on top of an evening's worth of whiskey, I think I've had enough talk for one night. What do you say we rest up for whatever's in store?"

"Sure," Cal said.

He closed his eyes and lay back. For a few moments his

head whirled with faces and crises:—this morning's meeting, the Ambassador, Snitzy(or was it Trixie?), Grober, the maggots on Mary Grober's plant—until at last he felt himself drifting, drifting, warm and happy, long ago, long ago. . . .

Gradually rolling hills began to emerge from the darkness around him, falling away on every side, their flanks blemished by the scudding shadows of fair-weather clouds high above. He felt a warm hand closed around his, but every time he tried to look up, he saw only a dim shape towering over him in the blinding sunlight.

He looked back to the valley again, down toward a dark green blotch in the center of it. What was it?

Trees. That's what it was. A grove of trees. So long since he'd seen trees . . .

It was one of those municipal parks marking the site of some ancient, ruined city, a few foundation stones left exposed by archaeologists, signs explaining where the sewage treatment plant was, which blocks marked the generating plant.

He knew it was his father holding his hand. He looked up again, longing to see his face, squinting against the white corona of light, but the face was an empty shadow. Then all at once lumps began to emerge from the silhouette, excrescences, goiters swelling into the shapes of subsidiary heads, scores of them, hundreds of them writhing Medusalike all over his body.

Cal wrenched his hand free, terrified, took two faltering steps backward, turned, and ran. Down the hill he pounded, each footfall shivering up his shinbones as he fled, the mutation that had been his father lumbering after him, gravity pulling both of them down into the valley. Struggling through the undergrowth, vines and thorns tearing at him, then up again, a black cave mouth yawning ahead.

There was something horrible, something unnamable there. Yet his fear of the father-thing forced him to stumble inside.

It lay sluglike in the inky shadows at the back of the cave, huge, pulsating. Completely shapeless. Yet he felt himself drawn inexorably toward it. He grabbed out at the granite of the cave wall, but his fingertips scraped uselessly across the rough stone, leaving long, thin smears of blood as his legs dragged him closer and closer to the thing. An orifice, that's what it was, living, shimmering, raw muscle tissue undulating in peristaltic waves, swallowing, swallowing . . .

He awoke with a start. The first fierce sunlight glared over the grassy edge of the pit. Hara was still asleep in the shadows of the cab, and the direction finder still beeped with the movement of the receding blip.

His heart pounded in his ears, and he closed his eyes to try to calm himself, barely able to catch his breath. What had he been dreaming? Was it some long-buried childhood nightmare? What had the thing at the back of the cave been?

Get out and walk, that's what he'd do. Walk off his fright.

Trying very hard not to awaken Hara, he rolled to one side and stood up. The flies were usually paralyzed by the early-morning cold, so he could get out and stretch his legs without smothering himself in a face net. He opened the hovercar door.

"Don't forget your face net and salt tablets," murmured a hidden speaker.

Cal eased himself down the skirt to the ground.

What a dumb thing, getting spooked by a dream. What he had to do, he told himself, was concentrate on the real world around him.

The excavation was like a huge cellar hole. Cal knew nothing about archaeology, and he wondered how someone like Weston went about deciding to dig in this particular place rather than anywhere else on the endless prairie. Slowly, he walked the length of the pit, kicking at an occasional clod of dirt, keeping to the cool, flyless shadows to avoid the brilliant band of sunlight along the far wall and a widening strip of floor.

At the far end, the excavation had collapsed and covered Weston's herbicided soil with fresh earth. New shoots poked up through the debris. Cal pushed the clumps aside with his toe, wondering what might have made the wall give way despite the nearly solid mass of interlocking sawgrass roots in the soil of the rim. Sod bricks, after all, were the *ne plus ultra* of Depasian architecture.

He felt something slip and give way under his foot. Idly, he kicked the grass aside, then bent down to push some dirt away.

Wouldn't it be something if an amateur like him with no training in archaeology made a major discovery? What might that do for the extravocational specialties and avocational subheadings of his Annual Evaluation?

With disappointment he uncovered a corner of polyethylene sheeting. A piece of tenting from Weston's camp, probably. He tugged at it, scraping away dirt, sawgrass roots, and the glistening midsection of a worm plump enough to make a Depasian's mouth water.

No—something smaller, a packet of some kind. Maybe an artifact Weston had unearthed and wrapped before she'd been arrested? Suddenly, it pulled free, a polyethylene bag opaque with dirt-filled scratches. But there was some kind of identifying number stenciled in one corner and there was a lumpy but very light object inside the bag.

Cal broke the seal and folded the bag back to reveal a thin scrap of something blackish made of a hard, light substance. It was still caked with dried earth, but on one side Cal could see clearly where Weston had scraped some of the dirt away to reveal lettering of some kind. What struck Cal was that the lettering on this Depasian artifact looked very much like thousand-year-old alphabets he recalled from museum exhibitions of twentieth-century life and fire-blackened art.

Mind racing, he hurried back to Moby Dick and hopped up onto the running board. Back inside, he touched the square for the light over his seat and studied the artifact more closely. Of course, he had no idea what the shapes of the letters meant or even how to pronounce them, but their outlines were quite clear.

But maybe the cybot would know! He flicked the in-dash switch and pulled out the lightpen. Carefully, he began to trace the lightpen over the outline of each letter in turn, as a corresponding shape drew itself on the screen.

A triangle on legs, *A*. Then an upright with a horizontal crosspiece, *T*. Another two-legged triangle. Then an upright with a half circle supported on a canted leg, *R*. And finally an unadorned upright, *I*.

Cal studied the flickering shapes he had transferred to the screen.

ATARI.

CHAPTER FOUR

WHEN HARA AWOKE, she found Cal hunched over the cybot console.

"What are you doing?" she demanded sharply.

Cal looked up, startled. "Patching through to the Mission cybot. You ever see anything like this?" He pointed to the shakily drawn symbols on the screen.

"Looks like old Earth writing," Hara said.

"The cybot says so, too," Cal said. "Twentieth century. Even told me how to pronounce the symbols—*ah-ta-ree.*" He held out the lump he'd found, dark and encrusted, like an oyster grubbed from the muck. "But the number on the bag doesn't match anything on the itemized list Weston left in the cybot."

"Why should it?" Hara asked, taking the fragment and holding it under the light from the windshield to study it.

"Because I found it right out there in Weston's dig."

"Oh?"

"Not only that, but there is an allusion in Weston's notes to 'a fragment of unidentified device, probably manufactured, apparently terrestrial in origin, possibly late twentieth or early twenty-first century.' Do you realize what that means?"

"No," Hara said, scratching sleepily and yawning.

"This must be an artifact from Earth. Except that it's been buried here on Depaz for eons."

Hara looked up from the artifact. "Nonsense. You found it in one of Weston's plastic bags, right? Probably something she brought with her, maybe something she saved from some dig she went on back on Earth when she was a student or something."

"You mean like a keepsake or a good-luck charm? Then why didn't she take it with her when she left?"

"You forget, she didn't leave voluntarily—she was arrested by the Dey's cossacks on this very spot. And she left in a hurry."

"But if she'd dug it up back on Earth, wouldn't she have cleaned it up back there?"

"That's probably dirt that got on it after she dropped it in the scuffle."

"*Through* the polyethylene wrapping?" Cal asked.

Hara stooped to look glumly up through the windshield at the sky. "We'd better get moving if you're still hoping to find the Ambassador," she said. Without comment, she slipped the artifact quietly into the pouch at her belt.

The beep stopped moving an hour later. Hara slowed to a stationary hover when they were within two miles and had the cybot lay out a photomap of the area. It showed the dark patch of another of Weston's excavations just off the white thread of a trade route and near a white checkerboard of nomad tents. A regular camping site on the western trade route.

"What do you think?" Cal asked.

"My bet is they're keeping the Ambassador somewhere in that dig—same trick we used last night."

"Makes sense."

Hara pulled out her pistol.

"We're not going to attack them, are we?" Cal asked.

"Depends," Hara said. "First we'll just scout around, see exactly how many of them there are."

"I don't want another camel slaughter like last night," Cal said. "Not till I'm sure there's no other way. If I'm Acting Chief of Mission, and I have to take responsibility for what happens, then I want to talk with them first without any violence—even if we find the Albarians there. If they really have the Ambassador, he could get hurt in the cross fire. Anyway, we're supposed to be diplomats. The least we can do is try diplomacy."

"You bucking for a promotion?" Hara said. She opened the small locker under the dash and removed a second pistol. "You'd better take this, just in case the other side don't turn out to be big talkers." Then she slapped the throttle back and cut the engines. The whine died into a clattering of sawgrass scraping the hull as Moby Dick settled onto the surface.

In addition to the guns, they took from the supply locker between the seats two sets of teles, a communicator to range themselves and keep in touch with the hovercar cybot, a day's worth of food tablets, and salt pills. Then they fastened their face nets and plunged out through the puffs of insecticide, easing themselves down gingerly among the deadly grass blades.

"Don't forget your face nets and salt tablets," said the hovercar.

It was hard enough going for the first three miles, picking their way slowly to spare their shoe leather and clothing, but after that, Hara insisted they drop to a crouch, and a mile later she stopped again.

"From here on, we crawl."

Cal looked into the tangle of vicious grass blades. "You're kidding."

"Nope. You want the grass to get you, or a Depasian bandit?"

They crawled. Almost at once a grass blade sliced through Cal's sleeve into the flesh of his forearm, almost to the bone. Another gashed his forehead. Blood pooled in his sleeve, saturated the cloth, dripped down his face. The juncture of his right earlobe and jaw stung where his sweat trickled into another deep cut. His hands were wet with blood inside his ribboned gloves, and every inch they moved forward was like putting his palms on a burning griddle. There was an acid in the sap of the grass. It ate away at cloth and flesh.

Gradually, through the dry hissing of the prairie wind in the grass, Cal thought he could make out tatters of voices. Perhaps singing, perhaps talking, he couldn't be sure.

"Do you hear that?" Cal whispered.

Hara nodded, studying the handcom.

"You think it's coming from down inside the excavation?" Cal asked.

"Cybot doesn't show anything moving above ground for twenty miles in any direction."

With excruciating slowness, Cal and Hara eased themselves the last few feet to the rim of the pit. Cal reached out, hands trembling, and bent back several ironlike blades of grass.

Below was the excavation, perhaps thirty feet down. Along the far earthen wall ran a string of interconnected translucent domes, like soap bubbles or wave spume. Cal had never seen anything like them anywhere on Depaz—except, perhaps, on Embassy Row. Depasians could never have conceived of such things, let alone built them. No question—the Albarians had to be at the bottom of this.

On the near side of the domes, Cal could see a cluster of nomads in the mid-morning sun, naked, shoulder to shoulder in a circle that kept expanding and contracting. Off to one side was a bundle of rags next to a post. He slipped his teles from their charger-pouch and hooked them over his ears.

The bundle of rags was the Ambassador! Occasionally, he shook his head violently, like a madman. Perhaps he'd been injured. Or drugged. Or tortured. But at least he was still alive.

Cal swung his teles across the rest of the camp. No sign of the Albarians, but it was like them to lurk out of sight in the shadows. He turned back to the Depasians. Far from appearing dangerous, they were still doing their strange dance, eyes closed and hands joined. Some appeared naked. Gradually, they pressed inward toward each other, condensing into a close, pulsing knot. For an instant he recalled the heads erupting from his father's body in his dream.

"You think it could be some kind of religious ritual?" Cal whispered.

"More likely some weird sex thing," Hara grunted.

"Well, my dears, what a pleasant surprise."

The buzzing voice was so close that Cal rolled into Hara in fright.

"But then," the buzzing continued, "we knew one of you

would come sooner or later. We hoped it would be you, Cal."

A great sphere, like a transparent beach ball, loomed over them.

"Drofsko?" Cal asked.

Inside the sphere, Drofsko shimmered pleasantly, carefully hunching himself up in the center to keep the ball stationary.

"But how did you get in that—"

"Container? Really, my dear, a much more mobile home than that ecotube of mine." Drofsko shifted his weight, and the ball rolled away along the edge of the cliff, Drofsko constantly flowing upward to keep it moving. The air inside was spotted with neon-orange. "And no mechanical devices for sensors to detect."

"But they'll *see* you!" Cal hissed, trying to wave Drofsko back into the sawgrass.

"What of it?" Drofsko said. "They're perfectly friendly."

"Forget it," Hara said, standing up. "I should have guessed before."

"Guessed what?"

"He's behind the whole thing, don't you see?" Hara answered.

"I thought it was the Albarians."

"Not unless they've gone partners with our friend here," Hara said. "They never had a thing to do with it, did they, Drofsko? No, my boy, this is some kind of move on this character's part to outflank us in local politics. I just haven't figured out what it is yet."

"Outflank you in Depasian politics?" Drofsko said, stopping momentarily. "Whatever for?"

"What do you mean 'whatever for'?" Hara said. "Isn't that what we're here for, to outmaneuver each other? Just because your Intelligence officer happens to be part of you rather than a separate operative—"

"Nonsense! If I wanted to steal a march on you in local affairs, getting involved out here would hardly be the way to do it. If the Dey knew about my work here, he'd be furious. The last thing he wants is any improvement in his nomad cousins' lives. Why do you think he closed this area to diplomatic personnel? I'm constantly running grave risks of discovery."

Suddenly, Cal saw the pieces fall together. "Were you at Government House yesterday?"

"Perhaps."

"I should have known it! Why didn't I see through you at the reception last night?"

"Really, my dear," Drofsko purred. "What besides this sphere is there to see through?"

"But how could you get to Government House without being spotted by our O and D?"

Drofsko moved forward again. "How often must I tell you, Cal, to hire native help. They know *all* the back ways. Now come along."

They reached an earthen causeway that led down into the pit. Drofsko shifted his weight backward to brake his descent, and began to let himself roll down. Shoulders bowed in defeat, Cal followed behind Hara.

What an idiot he'd been, he thought. He hadn't just failed to get the Ambassador back, he'd gotten himself captured to boot.

At the bottom, Drofsko rolled toward the pile of rags. But as they approached, the tight circle of Depasians uncoiled, came forward raggedly. At first glance there was nothing unusual about them, but Cal again sensed something profoundly different beneath the surface. They didn't hang their heads or avert their eyes.

And there was something else—the way they still were connected. It was subtle, unobtrusive—a hand there, an arm over the shoulder there. But from first to last, they formed a continuous chain of flesh. If the first had been handed a live wire, the last would have twitched.

They continued to move closer.

"Cal?" croaked a voice. "Is that you?"

Cal turned toward the Ambassador. His hands had been tied to the stake behind him, and he kept whipping his head violently from side to side, gurgling and moaning. His hair hung in lank clumps, and his face was swollen with angry red welts.

"What have you done to him?" Cal demanded. His impulse was to go to the Ambassador, but he was afraid of making any sudden movements.

"Nothing," Drofsko said. "It's the flies."

"You left him exposed?"

"Only since morning."

"It's barbaric," Cal said. "Aren't we all immortals? You could at least have put him in one of those domes you've got over there."

"They're not *ours,* my dear. They belong to the Depasians. They're the ones who built them."

"Impossible."

Drofsko was silent a moment. "As you will, then. But the Depasians did try to keep him inside. It's just that he was too noisy for them to bear. They're a quiet people, you know. They're accustomed to the silence of the prairie. And for an ambassador, your man is as loud as any I've ever encountered."

At that moment the Depasians halted some twenty meters from the stake where the Ambassador was tied. Hara eyed them watchfully. They didn't so much as whisper among themselves but stared directly at Drofsko. As though in answer, Drofsko's sphere spotted with blue.

Telepathy, Cal thought.

"The shapeless one informs us that you have come for the Ambassador," one of them said in English.

"Yes," Cal said, startled to find a second Depasian fluent in an Earth language. He scanned the group for the one who'd spoken, but none stood out. That was another thing—there wasn't any obvious leader. At last he found one he thought might be the rider he'd met the night before. With the sense of relief of meeting an old friend in a crowd, Cal addressed him. "This is a serious violation of diplomatic conventions," Cal said. "We demand his immediate return without conditions or ransom."

"There was never any mention of ransom," said a voice that was not the rider's. It seemed speakers were selected spontaneously and randomly, as though all were equal and any one might serve as well as any other. As though, Cal thought, the members of the group were merely mouthpieces for some external intelligence that formed the thoughts, chose the phrases, manipulated them.

Drofsko.

But why would Drofsko bother? Had he finally found the incredibly valuable whatever-it-was that all the Embassies had been hoping for?

"That is exactly the misunderstanding we were afraid of," said one of the voices.

"What?" Cal said, startled.

"That you'd think I was controlling them, or that the abduction had some complicated, intergalactic purpose," Drofsko said. "My friends here merely wished to discuss a small matter with your Ambassador."

"What small matter?" Cal asked.

"A directive he received from your Home Office two days ago. I tried to explain to my friends it was hopeless—he's not the sort who understands that when there's a six-year lag between a Home Office decision and its implementation here, one needs to feel free to exercise a certain amount of interpretive latitude, a certain amount of discretion in foreign policy."

"He's a loyal OWS officer," Cal said. He turned to the Ambassador. "Are you all right, sir?" he whispered.

"As he admitted to me himself," Drofsko continued, "for him policy is policy, a directive a sacred trust. So my friends decided they had no choice but to detain him until they could bargain with someone more . . . well, flexible."

The Depasians nodded in unison. There was something machinelike about them that made Cal's flesh crawl.

"Such as who?" he asked.

"You," Drofsko said.

The Ambassador moaned again. Cal struggled with the urge to risk loosening his bonds.

"You may release him," a voice from the crowd said as if in answer.

Cal's head snapped to scan the faces. He hadn't been surprised that Drofsko could read his mind, but this was as though the Depasians could, too. Was one Drofsko's protégé?

The Ambassador moaned again. Cal hesitated, then knelt by him.

"Get them *away*," the Ambassador was muttering, whipping his head at the flies. Then he looked up. "Cal!" he croaked. "Hara! Thank God! You got the directive, too?"

"What directive?" Cal said, reaching behind to get at the dry and crusted cords.

A mad smile spread across the Ambassador's face. "That's right, don't let on," he whispered hoarsely. "Not with *that* thing around. Got to watch even what you *think*."

Cal busied himself with the knots. "You mean Drofsko reading minds?"

"Ridiculous," Drofsko said from behind.

"It admits it picks up all kinds of energy waves—light, infrared, radio," the Ambassador said. "It just never let on that it can pick up the electrical pulses of brain waves, too."

"Your brain waves are too slow, all low-speed garble," Drofsko sniffed.

The Ambassador's eyes were unnaturally wide, the irises too open, the lenses unfocused. "But what about the high-speed coder?"

"Excuse me, sir?"

"The high-speed coder, you monster!" the Ambassador shrieked, bending forward to see Drofsko. "That's not garble, is it?" He sank back, exhausted. "Who do you think got the Dey to seal off the west in the first place—leaving it nice and safe and empty, one big private laboratory? Who do you think intercepted the prelim of Weston's report and slipped the Dey a copy so she'd be kicked out of this area? And how do you think they knew all about the coded directive to me?"

"Utterly uncivilized," Drofsko said.

"What *were* those orders, sir?" Cal whispered, releasing the last knot.

"Termination, of course," the Ambassador said, barely moving his lips, head down as he rubbed his wrists.

The cluster of nomads shifted uneasily, and Drofsko's sphere rippled with a rainbow of colors.

"Go ahead," the Ambassador hissed into Cal's ear. "However clever he's made them, he hasn't given them weapons like ours. *Kill* them! Kill every last motherfucking one of them!"

"Sir?"

"These are Home Office orders!"

Cal stared at him dumbly.

"What are you waiting for, mister? Just look at them—can't you see how he's changed them? Clumped together like a bunch of amoebas, all part of this perverted megabeing here . . ."

Cal leaned closer, so they wouldn't be overheard. "You mean Drofsko?" Cal asked, glancing back at the creatures behind him, hands clasped, shoulders pressed against one another.

"No, don't you see? He's remaking them in his own image—he's playing God."

"Really, my dears," Drofsko said, rolling nearer. "You've got it backward."

"I get it," Hara said. "The classic pocket-revolution gambit. He gets these chumps under his power, then has them overthrow the Dey's government we've spent twenty years building ties with, brings in his own stooges here, and pretends it's the people's will."

"Honestly," Drofsko said. "You were better off talking about the sunset scene on the west side of Kabugar."

"Don't worry," Hara said. "I only count eighteen of them, and no weapons that I can see."

"Of course not. If anything, I've been working to decrease their natural capacity for violence."

"Don't hand me that," Hara said.

"But I do. It's so difficult to make you people understand when you insist on imposing your own values on others' motivations." Drofsko's sphere wobbled slightly with what might have been indignation. "Just because *you* bribe the Dey with chickens and camels, you assume everyone else—"

"Then what were you doing?" Cal asked. "Why all the

stories pretending you had nothing but contempt for these people, when all the time you were actually working with them?"

"Like the *misha*," Drofsko said. "Protective coloration. But why are you displeased?"

Cal stared at the clasped hands and pressed bodies, suddenly as obscene to him as the bands of flesh linking one Siamese twin to another. Involuntarily, he took a step away from the Ambassador, as though being close might transmute him into what they'd become: less than whole, simply dependent parts. "How can I be pleased after what's been done to my planet's chief representative?"

"And they were so counting on you to understand," Drofsko said sadly. "But why do you think the lot of these nomads is now worse than it was? Might it not possibly be better?"

"At the cost of their individual identities? Never."

"We fail to understand your objection. But we know only too well that the prairie has a way of dulling and deadening things, Cal," Drofsko said. "The way a snake hypnotizes its prey before it swallows it. We would have thought someone who tried to waken the prey might be said to be doing it a service."

"They're the prey, all right," Cal said. "But you're the snake. You went to a lot of trouble buttering up the Dey so he'd seal off the area, getting rid of Weston before she could change the way we thought about these people. It wasn't just for this little group of nomads, was it? How many more of these . . . nests are there?" He still didn't want to believe an immortal would plot against his fellows. An immortal, after all, was above the petty rivalries on individual planets. An immortal . . .

Cal felt a strange warmth flooding through him. No, he thought. It was so much easier for them now. So much more sensible. The prairie melted into a meadow flecked with gold. Daisies, were they? Dandelions? A field from his childhood, he thought, blades of shadow slicing swiftly across the green as occasional clouds raced through the blue sky above. A puppy, was it, a reddish brown dog bounding through the field toward him, black nose glistening, good, loyal . . . ?

"You've got to fight it," Hara managed through clenched teeth.

Cal blinked, and Hara's contorted face emerged through the wisps of memory. Then he felt it—like a band around the base of his skull and the back of his neck, drawing him face-first toward the others. His scalp blossomed with prickles. Drofsko was forcing him; it was all he could do to hang on.

Suddenly, Hara seemed to wrench herself free, like a hunter struggling out of the underbrush. She staggered back and dropped to one knee, raising her pistol with both hands. She fired.

One of the Depasians in the middle of the line toppled forward, and a knot of three or four caromed off to the side, disconnected, stumbling aimlessly, then recovered and lunged forward to catch up as the rest charged.

For an insane instant Cal found himself surprised they could act in smaller groups. He stood transfixed, watching them pound toward him in slow motion.

"Come on, man," the Ambassador shouted. "Shoot or give me your gun!"

But even then he thought how pleasant the warmth had felt, how reassuring. Then he thought of the artifact he'd found in Weston's excavation. "We can't just shoot them, sir! They might be human!"

"Not these!" the Ambassador shouted. "Not anymore!"

"Anymore?" Cal said.

"Just shoot!"

"Drofsko!" Cal shouted. "Drofsko, why don't you stop them?"

"How? I have no power over them."

"What are you lying for? Make them stop before I have to shoot."

"I can no more stop them than you can stop Hara."

Several more were already torn away by the surges from Hara's gun, but the rest had nearly reached them. Cal fumbled in his waistband, found the pistol, yanked it out, held it like an alien thing, raised it, and sighted through it. He could see Hara's bent back. He paused an instant, weighed the possibility, then raised the barrel slightly and fired.

A Depasian stopped suddenly, head exploding in a reddish-white puff of vaporized bone and brain, and dropped like a sack. Cal felt a surge of sour sickness in the pit of his stomach. In front of Hara were already crumpled a pile of grotesque and rigid bodies, and the air rang with the insect whine of the pistol's recharging capacitors. The remaining Depasians had stopped. They stepped back.

"Don't shoot, Hara!" Cal called. "Give them a chance!"

Drofsko waited, poised within his sphere.

"Do you see?" Cal screamed. "Do you see? They're no match for our guns! Call this off before any more of them get hurt!"

"Kill him too, boy!" the Ambassador shouted. "Don't let him get away! He's the one responsible!"

Cal struggled for breath. "If you've got no power to stop them, then how were you almost able to make me join them?"

"I didn't do that," Drofsko said. "They did."

"Nonsense," Cal said. "No Depasian's capable of such a thing."

"Well, my dear, you know best."

The Depasians lurched forward. Cal glanced at Drofsko; his sphere seemed to be suddenly gray and opaque. Then something moved to the right—two Depasians sneaking up behind. He dropped to his knee Hara-like, and fired. Then movement to his left. He swung back just in time to see Drofsko's great ball rolling forward, shimmering huge, inexorable. . . .

For an instant Cal saw the creature from his dream, waiting at the back of the cave, swallowing, swallowing everything.

He was not even conscious of firing.

The molten ring where his beam struck Drofsko's sphere puckered inward with the rush of oxygen-rich air into the semivacuum of the bubble. But Drofsko made no effort to protect himself. He remained motionless, a silent emblem of reproach, as the oily rainbows of his surface dulled and grayed with the oxidation of his silicon component creatures. He became inside his sphere a solid slab of glass, dead and white as a fish eye. Two or three flies found their way inside the hole, buzzed about in search of carrion, and settled disappointedly on the smooth, hard puddle.

"Cal, you idiot!"

It was Hara's voice. Cal shook himself, saw Hara struggling to rise from the pile of dead Depasians about her.

"What the hell's the matter with you?" she was shouting. "Where's the Ambassador?"

"I didn't mean to," Cal said, his eyes drifting back to Drofsko's motionless sphere. "I never meant to. He came at me—"

"*Cal!* The Ambassador's gone!"

Stupefied, like an exhausted swimmer, Cal shook his head. "Gone?"

"There must have been a bunch of them behind us," Hara was muttering. "Snuck up while you were having your little crisis of conscience." She paused to peer into Drofsko's motionless sphere. "Well, at least we don't have to worry about this son of a bitch anymore."

Cal turned and stared at the stake where the Ambassador had been tied, his bonds intertwining and separating like snakes in the breaths of prairie wind. There was a dark maroon stain in the dirt where the Ambassador had lain. Blood.

"Come on, Cal," Hara said. "Help me find the son of a bitch. They can't be far."

Numbly, Cal followed Hara toward the strange domes along the wall of the excavation. The structures seemed to have been built of some incredibly hard foam material that hardly sagged even under the heat of Hara's laser. The rooms inside were neat and largely empty. In the third, Cal and Hara found one of the Ambassador's shoes.

"Weird, isn't it?" Hara said. "For a basically filthy people, it's amazing to see them keep anything this neat."

But neither the domes nor the excavation yielded anything, and when they went back toward the nomad encampment, they had no better luck. The women came fearfully to the flaps of their tents to shake their heads.

No, they had not seen the off-worlder. They had not seen anything. And the cybot in Moby Dick gave no indication of movement on the prairie for miles in any direction.

"We're going to have to face it," Hara said. "The Ambassador's gone."

"We can't go back to the Mission empty-handed," Cal protested.

"We can't stay here."

"Leave the Ambassador?" The burden of responsibility suddenly weighed heavier than ever. Gravity again. Somehow Cal had never quite considered that they might not get the Ambassador back one way or the other in the end.

"We don't know where he is, my boy. We've done everything we can."

"I guess you're right."

"Who knows, there might even be some secret exit. We'll bring in a sonar probe and scan the place. I'll get the bastards."

They didn't bury the dead. As Hara said on the way back in Moby Dick, what happened to the corpses was the flies' business. She'd bring Drofsko's remains back to the Legation when she did the sonar scan. She didn't think there'd be any problem coming up with a story to satisfy Drofsko's home planet.

"We haven't even established a consulate on Si," Hara chuckled, "so it's a moot point whether old Drofsko was telling the truth that it was the Depasians that read our minds, not him. Still, maybe it'd be smarter to make sure whoever makes the presentation to the intermediary embassy doesn't know the truth. This mind stuff's hell on Intelligence. And I think you and I ought to keep the details to ourselves."

Cal tried not to look at Hara's eyes slitted against the sun as she steered. He sat leaning well away from her. "We lost the Ambassador," he said at last. "And I killed an immortal."

"Drofsko? Strikes me as a perfectly reasonable action," Hara said. "In a way, it's lucky. You came close to disobeying the Ambassador's direct order to fire. That's disregard of Home Office directives. Wouldn't look good in your

Annual Evaluation. 'Course, I don't have to tell you about regulations."

"You don't understand," Cal said. "It was just a gut reaction. I never meant to shoot. Or maybe . . . maybe I did do it on purpose. Maybe I was afraid how close he came to making me part of them. Is that what happened to you, Hara?"

"I don't knock myself out trying to find cosmic reasons for what I do. It was a tight spot, and things were starting to go against us. We've got a big investment in the Dey, and according to the Ambassador, there was a directive outlining a threat Drofsko posed to that investment. Anyway, our main concern is still finding him. We're going to have to do a lot of explaining, coming this close to having him and then—"

"What if there are other pockets of these . . . mutants all over the west?" Cal said. "Drofsko didn't exactly admit it, but—"

"That's where our investment in the Dey pays off. We'll just tell him and let him take care of it."

"But what was Drofsko trying to do?" Cal wondered. "Why was he meddling with another species?"

"Be like me—don't worry about it. Dead is dead. All I worry about is retirement next year. It's a simple equation—follow directives, and collect your pension at the end of the road." Hara turned toward Cal, her face greenish as the daylight around them failed. "And, Cal?"

"Yes."

Her lips were pressed tightly together, her mouth a cruel blue scar. "Neither one of us says a word about any of this without checking with the other first, understood?"

"Why?"

"Common sense, my boy. For one thing, think what jerks we'd look like if it got out that we'd had the Ambassador in our hands and let him get away, eh?"

"Yeah," Cal said, "I guess you're right."

Hara glanced over at him again. It was almost as though Cal could look through the hanging folds of flesh to see the death's-head within.

"Not that *I'm* worried," Hara said, smiling. She seemed

to relax her grip on the wheel. "But *you've* still got a career ahead of you."

Cal sank back in his seat, feeling dirty with sweat and fly traces. It would be six years before the Home Office even knew how its directive had been acted on, another six for promotions or demotions to be beamed back. By then Cal would be sleeping away the years to the next assignment in the hold of some freighter, drifting across time as well as space, away from his fellows in the Legation, Grober and Hara living through into their retirements. When he arrived, his demotion, his punishment, retribution would be waiting for him at his new post.

But by then, maybe he'd understand things like this better. All he knew now was that there wasn't anything in the regulations that covered it.

CHAPTER FIVE

THE FIRST THING Cal noticed outside the cocoon of pain that licked like flame along the line of each and every sawgrass cut was that the view from his bed was wrong. He ought to have been able to see the tops of the Albarian collection-communication towers through the tinted glass of his window. Instead, the cool and glass-muted blue-gray square of prairie sky was radiantly empty.

The window was in the wrong wall, come to think of it.

Cal jacked himself up on his elbow and looked around.

What do you know? Wrong room.

Then the pain flooded through him and he dropped back flat on his bed. Help, help, he thought. I've been kidnapped.

"Well, how are we this morning?" a voice behind him asked cheerfully. The pain in Cal's neck and head was too intense for him to roll over and see who it was. He felt suddenly helpless, weak, maddeningly soft.

"Who the hell are you?" he asked.

"That's not a very nice question," said the voice. "Especially when the time to ask it is long past." Footsteps came toward him across the room and circled around the bed.

"Bascomb!" he said. "How did you get here?"

"I live here."

"Ah," Cal said quietly. The significance of it sank in. *"Oh."*

"I *thought* you'd remember," she said, smiling. She sat on the edge of the bed.

"Agh," Cal said.

"Sorry." She hopped up and moved to a chair, from which she flashed him a sympathetic smile. "All those cuts and bruises must have gotten kind of stiff overnight."

Cal managed to get himself back up onto one elbow, sorting through the few shreds of memories he could grab hold of. Yes, she'd met him after he and Hara had parked Moby Dick, they'd had supper, grass wine, some relaxants . . .

"This is against regulations," he blurted.

"What?"

"Us. It's a violation. Two officers from the same section getting involved. Its terrible for discipline. And as ACM, I'm supposed to be setting an example."

"All right, all right—I was raised by the book. But I couldn't help myself."

Cal blushed.

"There's something, I don't know, kind of sweet about how you're so confused all the time."

Cal stopped blushing. "Raised by which book?"

"The Service rule book. I told you last night—I was an OWS brat."

"Oh, right," Cal said. "Of course."

"It's all right," she said. "You don't have to pretend you remember—I know how exhausted you were. I was only teasing."

"Folks in the OWS, eh?"

"I guess my dad would seem like a homebody to you. Farthest post was the consulate on Ganymede. But he taught me to love the Service."

"But not obey regulations?"

"Within reason."

"Where is he now?"

"Retired."

"On Earth?"

She shrugged. "Well, you know how it is, six years before any word from home . . . I guess he must have gone back by now." She looked puzzled. "Funny, not knowing."

"Sure," Cal said. He started to lie back. *"Ouch!"* He eased himself back more slowly.

"Are you sure you're all right?"

"Except for the excruciating pain."

"No, I mean . . ." She smiled sadly. "You kind of had me worried last night."

"How's that?"

"The way you kept mumbling in your sleep, groaning. Once you even screamed."

Cal felt the skin behind his ears tighten with fear. Through his mind flashed Drofsko, the running Depasians, the *crack-crack* of the lasers, the thin blue line of Hara's lips as she swore him to secrecy. "I didn't say anything, did I?"

"Just that you didn't find the Ambassador. You didn't say anything else."

"That's good."

"Did you want to?"

"Of course not," he said. "An OWS brat ought to know you don't discuss security matters at home."

"I wasn't trying to pry," she said. "It's just, well, I remember sometimes I'd see my father talking to my mother off to one side, privately. No serious breaches of confidentiality, I'm sure. My dad was a professional—he'd never have compromised security. But even he had to get things off his chest once in a while just to stay sane. Part of his job was being go-between with some of the shadier characters the Consulate used but couldn't acknowledge official ties with—smugglers, counterfeiters, some downright pirates. 'I've seen things that would curl your hair, kitten,' he said to me once. That was one of his expressions, 'things that would curl your hair.' Things that would eat away if he kept them bottled up."

"I'm not your father."

She laughed. "And I'm not my mother."

He looked away from her to the window. Yes, it would help to talk to somebody about yesterday, somebody who could help him make sense out of Drofsko's death, or even somebody who could just listen sympathetically.

There was a buzz. Bascomb reached over and touched the intercom square.

"Cal?" asked the voice.

"Hara?" Cal was shocked. "How the hell did you know—?"

"Never mind," Hara said. "I just wanted to get hold of you and ask if we couldn't get together sometime today for a little chat."

"I don't know if—"

"I think it would be a really good idea."

Cal glanced over at Bascomb, but there was nothing in her face to suggest she found anything out of the ordinary in the conversation. "Are you just asking or telling?"

"What is it with you, my boy?" Hara laughed. "Asking, of course. You're Acting Chief of Mission. But Grober reminded me that we have to sit down with Townsend and have him debrief us. You know me, I'm all thumbs when it comes to security, but Townsend's a trained specialist, and if we go over what happened with him, he might notice a clue or something we overlooked."

Grober! Why hadn't Cal thought of him before? "All right," Cal said. "I'll be at the chancery in an hour or so."

"Good. See you there."

Bascomb palmed the mute square for the intercom. "Shall I make you some breakfast?"

"No," Cal said. "I've got to go."

"But you told Hara an hour—"

"I was just thinking about what you were saying about your father. There's something I need to do before I see Hara." Yes, he thought, Grober would make it all right.

Grober looked up and smiled when he saw Cal enter. "Good morning, good morning," he beamed. "And how are we today?"

Cal slumped in the unpowered chair by the door for visa applicants. So far, no Depasian had ever come to the Consular Section on B-level and applied for a visa to Earth, and it was not clear whether current policy would allow granting a visa if one did, but the chair, like the Consular Section itself, was maintained as a kind of monument to the sanctity of regulations.

"You're pretty cheerful this morning," Cal said.

"Yes, I suppose I am. Why shouldn't I be? But I'm surprised you're so gloomy."

"Gloomy? Why shouldn't I be?"

" 'How silver-sweet sound lovers' tongues by night,/ Like softest music to attending ears.' " Grober leaned back, smiling hugely.

"What?"

"Romeo and Rosalind."

Cal found himself getting annoyed. "What are you talking about?"

"Love."

"Well, I'm talking about losing our goddamned Ambassador."

Grober's smile faded. "Yes," he said. "I was sorry to hear you didn't find him."

"Didn't find—did Hara tell you that?"

"Not in so many words, no," Grober said, chewing thoughtfully on the inside of his cheek. "To use diplomatic language, I guess you could say that there were strong implications in that direction. But don't worry, Cal, it's not the end of the world. We'll get him back, I'm sure of it. I've been here a good long time, and I've never known these people to kill when they could collect a ransom instead. I'd never have let them stick you with being ACM otherwise."

"Exactly how it happened—"

Grober held up his hand. "Never mind. I don't want to know."

Cal bit his lip angrily. "Thanks for the help."

"Look, Cal, if there's one thing I've learned in the Service, it's to do my job and keep my nose out of other people's business. If I had only one thing to bequeath you, it would be this: Never find out more than you have to."

"Great."

"Come back when you're about to retire and tell me how wrong I was."

"Who do you talk to to keep yourself from going crazy, then?" Cal asked angrily.

"You need a shoulder to cry on?" asked a voice from the door. Baum had poked his head in. "Heh-heh-heh. Why don't you try that dumb religionbot down in the basement? It's got a facet and a program for every form of worship devised by man."

"The Multi-Modal Unitized Devotional Device?"

"Who could have guessed that one of the thousand names for God was MUDD?" Baum cackled, and disappeared.

"Begone, varlet!" Grober called after him. "Pay no attention, Cal—the man thinks everything's a joke, and you have serious things on your mind. The last thing you need is flippant suggestions."

"Was it flippant? You and Mrs. Grober go to mass there every week."

"Yes, well, good Catholics have to do *something,* even on Depaz."

But Grober was right, Cal thought. It wasn't fair to trot out all his doubts and fears and burden his colleagues with them. But the MUDD machine down on A-level—wasn't that exactly what it was designed for? Cal stood up.

"Another engagement?" Grober asked.

"Something like that." He paused at the door. "But tell me, what was all that about love when I came in?"

"Something a little bird told me."

"And what did it tell you?"

Grober chuckled. "That you and a certain junior political officer were deep in consultation after your return from the prairie."

"Just who was the little bird—Hara again?"

Grober thought a moment. "Quite honestly, I don't think it was. Come, come, Cal, Embassy Depaz is hardly a large place. Secrets are never secret very long."

"On the contrary—it's funny the kinds of secrets that *do* get kept around here," Cal said. "Are you going to tell me it's against regulations and I should stop seeing her?"

"By no means." Grober smiled. " 'Let me not to the marriage of true minds admit impediments.' "

Cal stepped out into the hall only to discover Hannibal Myers slumped against the opposite wall, weeping softly to himself. His lips and chin were streaked like a mad dog's with some kind of whitish foam.

"Hannibal, what's the matter?"

"Nothing," he said, sobbing. The tears cut clean channels through the white foam.

"What do you mean nothing? OWS officers don't cry, man. Tell me what's happened."

"I was about to rinse my mouth out with the usual thimbleful of water after brushing my teeth, when I looked down into it and . . . and thought—*water.* I just lost control." His body was racked by a huge sob. "Please, please, please tell me my transfer came through this morning."

Cal laid his hand gently on the other man's shoulder. "I'm sorry."

"No word?"

"Not yet."

"Oh, God, it's *so* depressing."

Cal slipped into a powerchair and swung down the hall, feeling strangely self-conscious. He bypassed the elevator and parked in a secluded alcove to take the emergency foot stairway down to the A-level basement. No point advertising where he was headed. What he did was his business.

At the foot of the stairs, he checked to make sure there were no Marines or even sentribots about. Then he clocked quickly along the corridor. The machine had been designed to Home Office specs for Missions whose remoteness or size prohibited chaplains, and it had arrived on the same ship that had brought Cal, but somehow he'd never actually been down here to see it. He'd never been particularly religious, even as a boy, and he wasn't quite sure what to expect. He stopped at the end of the hall. On the door before him had been stenciled MUDD. He took a breath, feeling reluctant and a little afraid, then stepped forward. The door slicked open automatically.

The dimly lit room was cloaked in a white-noise hush piped in from outside. In the shadows at the far end of the room stood a huge, seven-foot polyhedron, and on the wall to Cal's right, a bank of lighted squares. On each was some kind of label. He leaned over to read them. BAPTIST. BUDDHIST. COPTIC CHRISTIAN. PRESBYTERIAN. TAOIST. ZOROASTRIAN.

There—the red square: ROMAN CATHOLIC. That was it. He'd never been a Catholic, of course, but if it worked for the Grobers, it was probably the one he wanted. He reached out and touched the square.

Solemnly, the great polyhedron began to revolve. Past Cal slid the first facet, decorated with glistening blue tile with some kind of navigational instrument mounted in the center. The Islamic face, of course, with a direction finder for locating Mecca among the stars. Next came something covered with rice paper—the Shintoist face, probably. Then one writhing with plastistone figures. Shiva and Krishna, the Hindu facet. Even with all their arms, they looked downright homey after all the tentacles and feelers and sucker-pods Cal had seen. Funny how grateful you got for anything that smacked of home.

He shifted his weight anxiously. What business did he have asking somebody else's religion for help? What if it refused to listen to him? What if it rose up like a medieval priest driving the infidels and heretics from the village?

But at that moment the plastistone trefoil Gothic arch swung into view, the hydraulic arm for elevating the Host bouncing slightly above the narrow altar as it eased to a stop. A processional hymn suddenly blared from the soundwands.

"Excuse me," Cal said. "I want to confess."

"Infinite Thy vast domain," thundered the digital chorus. "Everlasting is Thy reign."

"I want to confess!"

"Holy—" sang the chorus and snapped off. A small, metal lattice rose noiselessly from a slot to obscure the altar.

"Confessional access number, my son?" the machine asked solicitously.

"Guess I don't have one," Cal said.

There was a disapproving silence.

"I'm not Catholic. Matter of fact, I'm not anything."

"I see," said the machine glumly.

"But something's been bothering me, and I needed to kind of talk it out. In the strictest confidence, understand."

"Everything said to me is processed and stored in a failsafe, zero-access mode," the machine soothed. "The secret of the confessional is inviolable."

"The thing is," Cal went on, turning his face away, "I killed somebody." He paused. "I *think*. Or some*thing*. That's the problem with off-world diplomacy—you never know quite what you're dealing with. Fact is, this person that I—who *died*, I mean—he . . . Actually, not *he*, exactly, because he . . . *it* . . . well, *they*, really."

"Take your time, my son."

"No, I think *they* is technically correct. A colony of, well, liquid-silicon semiconductors. But they functioned as a single entity. As if each of our body cells—I mean, *my* body cells"—he smiled apologetically at the machine—"were individually intelligent. Do you see what I mean?"

"Absolutely," the machine said. "I have never heard so cogent a confession."

"Oh. Yeah, I guess it would make sense to you." Cal scratched his head. "Anyway, where it gets sticky is that this colony was . . . another planet's Ambassador." Cal sighed helplessly. "But it was an accident. See, being liquid silicon, he . . . they had to live in a sealed krypton-argon atmosphere, and when my gun, uh . . . went off, so to speak, his capsule got punctured, and oxygen got in and, uh, crystallized him into a puddle of, well, um, to be perfectly candid, glass."

"An accident, you said?" the machine asked. "Were you cleaning your weapon, something like that?"

"Yes."

There was a pause.

"Uh, sort of," Cal added miserably. "I was shooting at him."

"Not an accident, then," the machine said, as though making a note.

"No. But I didn't *mean* to. It's just everyone else was shooting when his Depasians rushed us—or at least Hara was—and he rolled at me, and I . . . Well, damn it, as near as I can make out, he was meddling in the local social dynamics. He was trying to make the natives like him, submerge their individual identities into his collective super-consciousness. And they're *humanoid*."

Cal paused to take a deep breath.

"Not *human*, necessarily. I want to stress that. But *close*—in a distant way. That makes it unnatural, doesn't it?"

"Insufficient moral data field," said MUDD.

Cal thought about the bit of plastic Hara had slipped in

her pocket. He wished he still had it. "But if they *were* human . . ." he said. "I know it's unbelievable, crazy. But just suppose, for the sake of argument, they were a pod of one or two clone-types sent out by some pre-Federation country on a mining ship before the Social Security Wars, the way they used to do when cloning was legal. When the clones were cut off by the war, they interbred. That would explain why the Depasians were so godawful, you know?"

"All Creation is the Almighty's handiwork," murmured MUDD.

"Yeah, but I'm talking a gene pool of two types. Think of the recessive traits in just one generation. I don't think you want to hang that kind of degeneracy on God."

"Processing," said MUDD. Background digital hums and whines began to bleed softly through the analog soundwands.

"But it would make what he did even more reprehensible, more unforgivable. Damn it, I *shouldn't* feel guilty. It was like shooting a big bowl of jam. Silicon jam, I admit. Intelligent silicon jam. Pleasant, friendly jam, in a lot of ways. I *liked* Drofsko at parties. Really. But we couldn't let him get away with something like that."

Cal sighed, and his shoulders slumped. "I never learned much about religion. Somehow I can't even remember whether my family went to church. But have you got a category like, say, preemptive homicide? Well, not *hom*icide, but—"

The pager on Cal's belt beeped, registered that he was in a secure area, and opened a noncoded channel.

"Cal? Baum here. Finder says you're in the MUDD room."

"What about it?"

"Took me at my word, eh? Heh-heh-heh—each to his own. I gave up on it when I found out it was orthodox. Let me tell you, waiting for that thing to give me an electronic *parve* would have been worth my life. Think about it, Cal—there's nothing on Depaz that *isn't* unclean!"

"You wanted me for something?"

"Well, a couple of things have come up, and since today

was my turn to be Officer of the Day, I thought I'd better check in with you."

"Well?"

"First, an unidentified starship of apparent Earth origin has been picked up on our scopes, presumed to be a tramp freighter, smugglers, or pirates."

"How far away?"

"Just entering transfer orbit."

"Transfer orbit? At the autoshuttle station? Impossible! We should have known about any ship out there years ago and been tracking it, shouldn't we? What's the matter with everyone? How could it have snuck up on us without at least one person knowing about it?" Cal asked.

"Well, actually," Baum said, "somebody did. Seems Townsend's Observation and Detection Unit sent down a memo a few years back, but it got misdirected and a few days ago someone in Procurement punched in for hardcopy of a stack of validated G-eighty-slash-five purchase orders for some local Kabugar merchants from three years ago and out came the memo. Another mechanical problem, but at least they forwarded it."

"A few days ago? What took till now?"

"Had to be routed through channels."

"Great. So how come for three years no one at O and D ever wondered why nobody answered their memo?"

"It's their business to send out memos, not expect answers from OWS officers. They're Off-World Service Staff down there with, OWSS nines and tens. They're supposed to report and await orders like good soldiers, period. Standard Operating Procedure. The last thing they want is a reputation for bothering people."

"I know, I know—don't quote the rulebook at me. But why didn't some O-and-D-er so much as happen to mention it to anyone in the Diplomatic Section over lunch or something?"

"OWSO's and OWSS's don't have lunch together. It isn't done. And even if they did, they couldn't discuss anything over lunch. *Everything* in O and D is classified. You know that."

"Yeah, I wasn't thinking. Regulations. What now?"

"Wait for it to land."

"The autoshuttle?"

"The ship itself. It's already headed in."

"How could a starship land, Baum?"

"Don't ask me. I'm an economist. All I know is what O and D tells me—that the ship's not much bigger than the average shuttle, and its trajectory indicates that it's headed for the landing area. I hate to say this, but as ACM, you ought to go meet it. It could turn out to be the OWS Inspector making a surprise visit."

"Great. That's all I need."

"At least the readings are consistent with a Federated Earth ship, and Major Sedewski didn't see any indication of armament before he passed out."

"Passed out?"

"You forgot the major's drinking problem?"

"Oh, yeah. But I thought he was in some kind of rehab program."

"He is, he is, and the medibots report he's making terrific progress."

"Great."

"But we still don't get any response from the crew. Either they're still in suspension—and the landing's going to be one memorable wienie roast—or it's some kind of cybot drone with battery failure. The big mystery's how the ship picked the landing field out of an entire planet where the variation in elevation is on the order of three hundredths of a percent. I mean, this place is flat as glass."

"If it's not the Inspector, then maybe it's that other ship we're tracking," Cal said.

"Actually, that was the other thing I was going to mention. O and D just updated us on the status of the starship *St. Ulfilas of the Goths*. It's within two weeks of arriving in orbit."

"Saint Who?" Cal said.

"If you want answers to questions about saints," Baum said, "don't ask Jews."

"Ahem," thundered the voice of MUDD from behind Cal. "St. Ulfilas, a missionary to the German barbarians about three thousand years ago."

"I see," Cal said, shaken by the unexpected interruption. "Then this is . . . ?"

"Right," Baum said. "That Papal Nuncio we've been expecting for five years. He's about to be here."

Cal slapped his forehead in despair. One of the complications of representing Federated Earth was that the Vatican had never surrendered its diplomatic independence. Even diplomats from binary systems who gloried in endless replication had trouble understanding why anyplace as insignificant as Earth had two diplomatic corps.

"All right, at least I've still got two weeks to think about that one. I'll swing by the office for a quick check and then head out to the field to see what the stars have sent us."

"One last thing, though."

"What's that?"

"Hara asked me to remind you that you're supposed to meet with her as soon as possible."

"Right," Cal said. "Check."

When Cal reached his office, he found Bascomb already there. He felt awkward in front of her, embarrassed. He wanted to pretend nothing had happened between them. What he'd allowed to happen had been a stupid aberration. As ACM, he couldn't allow it to happen again.

"You still all right?" she asked.

"Fine," in his best formal manner.

She looked hurt. Then she raised her eyebrows. "Oh, I get it," she whispered, leaning forward. "You don't want to let on when we're at the office, right?"

He licked his lips. "Uh, yeah. Right."

"Right you are," she said. "Regulations."

"Regulations, right."

"So," she said, leaning back, "shall I call down to the garage and have them get Moby Dick ready?"

"Oh, right, right. And get me all the Marines we can spare, and any mobile sentribots, and have them meet me at the front." Cal had to get out of the office. Why had he been so weak-willed last night? "And call Hara and tell her I'll have to talk with her later. I've got pressing business right now."

"You're leaving already?" she said. "You know it'll take a while for them to give Moby Dick even a quick once-over. It always needs repairs when it's been out in the grass."

She looked hurt again. Why did she always have to look hurt?

He gave her a *c'est-la-guerre* shrug. "Duty calls, Bascomb, duty calls." He paused in the hall to hear the door slick shut before he dropped into his powerchair.

If Bascomb called, she never got through. Cal found one of their Depasian mechanics face down on the griddle-hot tarmac of the garage interior, covered with four-winged flies and completely gone on *miship*.

Cal shrugged it off. It was the sort of thing that happened all the time, like never having the aircon or the lights working for a full twenty-four hours. Garage dome echoing with the flies' buzzing, Cal stepped over him and stalked through the impossible heat to Moby Dick. The hovercar was still warm from his and Hara's odyssey, battered and nearly stripped of paint, stalks of sawgrass sticking out of every nook and cranny like a scarecrow's stuffing and hanging like arrows from the shredded remains of the rubber bumper. One had been driven into the sheet-steel door.

Maybe he should have waited for that once-over of Bascomb's. He certainly wasn't anxious to be stranded by a breakdown in the middle of nowhere. At least one OWS-10 stranded out in the open without protection from the flies some years back had committed suicide.

But he didn't want to wait.

In another moment he was inside at the controls. With a roar, he floated backward under the opening doors and into the sunlight's glare.

"Don't forget your salt tablets!" thundered the cybot voice triggered by the door.

He swung around front and waited while as many Marines as Bascomb had found piled into the rear of the car or, faces muffled in face nets and bodies protected by leather jump suits, swung themselves up onto hoverbikes. Their little motors chattered to life. Behind them wobbled the mobile sentribots, turret heads swiveling warily from side to side.

Grimly, Cal swung onto the dusty road that led past the architectural extravagances of Embassy Row. There were a little over two dozen of them, but only one caught his attention, a one-roomed tower. It had been Drofsko's. Now it stood empty, one of his Depasian servants squatting disconsolately at the door and staring dully out at the horizon, awaiting the return of his master.

Yet the man's eyes, Cal thought, glittered under the shadow of his hood as they followed the little cavalcade from Earth's Embassy Depaz.

Was he one of *them?*

Cal tried to keep his mind occupied, but there was nothing in the empty flatness to snag his thoughts before they skipped on, skimmed over the horizon, and burrowed into the obscene, squirming pile of Depasians he and Hara had found, that writhing mass of indistinguishable bodies slick and glistening with excrement and dew. And Drofsko, his liquid-silicon component creatures piled up into a pillar to hold his sphere steady, his atmosphere spotted with white flashes of ionization.

Had Drofsko meant to crush him or only to plead with him to stop? Had he fired out of mistaken fear? Or was it something about that black piece of plastic he'd found and Hara had kept? Had he perhaps shot out of some bizarre sense of kinship with those Depasians, horror at how they'd been subjugated by Drofsko's superior will?

Or had he been but Hara's mirror image? Had he simply fired to protect Federated Earth's share of influence on Depaz? An act of political expediency?

But he couldn't quite recapture the instant. It kept rolling away from him, dispersing like smoke. Something about Drofsko pitching toward him and then—nothing till the startling whine of his laser's recharging capacitors, the molten ring in Drofsko's sphere puckering inward with the rush of oxygen, the two flies settling on the glassy fish-eye slab of his dulling skin.

Would the pain ever stop? Would he spend the rest of his life agonized by it? Why couldn't he be like Hara?

"Sir?"

She was hardened to everything. She—

"Sir?"

Cal blinked and looked over. The young Marine was sitting hunched forward on his seat.

"Yes?" Cal said.

"The landing strip, sir."

"What about it, corporal?"

"We passed it about two kilometers back."

"Check. I was planning to come in from the west side."

"Right, sir. I knew you had a reason."

Trailing a column of dust and the tails of hoverbikes and gleaming sentribots, Cal swung around and headed back toward the burned and blackened circle in the center of the prairie.

"You did see there were people there, sir?"

"People?"

"Depasians. Maybe some others."

"Funny," Cal thought aloud, "wonder what's brought them out here."

They were within sight of the field again. The Marine had been right—there were clusters of people around the field. And one or two strange land vehicles, along with several figures in various forms of pressure suits.

"Well, that explains part of it," Cal said. "Personnel from the other legations. They must have picked the craft up through their own O and D units."

"Yes, sir," the corporal said. "But what about the others?"

"Looks like Depasians."

Beneath the usual nimbus of black flies, a ragged cluster of them hung on the far side, jabbering among themselves and giddy with this rare possibility of a distraction from their dusty days and unrelenting banditry. They kept themselves a respectful distance from what appeared to be an official Depasian welcoming committee—another of the Dey's cousins in a ceremonial robe, tracing a pattern in the field's carpet of dead flies. Behind him simmered his tractor of state, hissing and clanking as his slave blew off excess steam and hoped the boiler didn't let go. Drawn up behind was a paramilitary group on *eliks*. They were carrying either musical instruments or blowguns.

"You're right," Cal said, tapping the dashboard dispenser for a salt tablet and swallowing it in a gulp. "How the hell did they hear about this? You guys got your face nets up?" There was a chorus of affirmatives as Cal pulled his own face net up over his head and broke the doorseal.

"Don't forget your face nets and—"

The fierce heat rushed up to meet him as he dropped to the ground and began to crunch his way across the fire-blackened stubble toward the Minister-Cousin. Behind him crunched the Marines.

Halfway across, the Albarian Protocol Officer and two native bucket-bearers stepped forward.

"Thjkh shshsvvvfs psluhtoss packhrabmsh?" the Albarian hissed into the unitrans slung around his neck. "Who iszh it?" crackled the artificial voice of the unitrans at his neck, neutral and emotionless.

Cal shrugged. "We've got no more idea than you do."

"Plshfar Earth nabangzh," the Albarian protested.

"A Federated Earth ship, you say?" Cal asked, ignoring the unitrans. "How do you know? Were you tracking it on instruments?"

"A Depaszhian informed uszh," said the Albarian condescendingly, motioning a bearer to step up so he could plunge his head into the bucket.

Cal stepped back to avoid the spray. "A *Depasian?*"

"A szhtreet beggar."

"Didn't you find it suspicious that a beggar should know such a thing?" Cal said. "We may be rivals, but as fellow immortals it's in our mutual interest to keep each other informed of changes anywhere in the ecological or, ah, sociological structure of Depaz that might threaten the well-being of the diplomatic community."

"Aszh long aszh you will give up whoever comeszh on thiszh szhip for at leaszht one dinner with uszh."

"No, no, you don't understand," Cal said. "There are genuinely strange, possibly even threatening develop—"

"It haszh been *death* without anyone new for dinner," the Albarian said, cracking a saurian smile.

"Never mind," Cal said.

"You know the accordszh?" the Albarian persisted worriedly. "The rulszh?"

"Yes, yes," Cal said. "The agreement—I know. If the ship's under our jurisdiction, we promise to let you have the occupants for a dinner and reception."

Annoyed, Cal stalked on toward the Minister-Cousin. Couldn't even enemies think about anything but their dinner plans? "May the dust not clog your nostrils," he said as he drew near the Depasian official. He couldn't be sure whether or not this was the one he'd seen at Government House.

"May the grass not sever your feet," said the Minister-Cousin with a glance at the Armed Marines and watchful sentribots.

Cal made several assays at a conversation, but the Minister-Cousin remained impassive. For an eternity they cooked in silence, and the flies crawled unheeded over the Depasian's immobile face.

And yet they really did seem human, Cal found himself thinking despite himself. Smaller, brown skin, leathery from centuries of exposure, upper lip enlarged like a cartoon leprechaun's in some obscure natural adaptation, eyes heavily lidded against the prairie dust. If common sense didn't argue otherwise, he could almost . . .

A bright flash in the eastern sky, then a gleaming spot swelling into the silver of the autoshuttle.

"Remember!" Cal heard the flat voice of the unitrans saying. "If they're even remotely acszheptable, you must share them with the rest of uszh."

"I told you, yes!" Cal shouted back as the ship's blessed shadow swept over them and the craft began to descend into the dust of its retros. Stoically, Cal watched the dust cloud roll toward him, then slapped on his respirator and flicked on his belt light as the world around him melted into a brown gloom. He believed the report that there was no evidence of hostile intent, but he couldn't help a little stab of sourness at the pit of his stomach.

Patiently, they waited in the dust for something to emerge, but there was nothing, only the dying engine sounds and, from the nomads behind, earsplitting, unearthly noises. So, the riders weren't carrying blowguns after all. They were a mounted band. In fact, they seemed to be playing "Hail to the Chief."

In several more minutes, the cloud dispersed to reveal the silver ship now sitting on its landing struts.

"Look out!" shouted the corporal. "She's falling over!"

With an electric-motor whine, the ship began to tip sideways. Depasians screamed and scurried away.

"No, no, it's not," Cal shouted back. He could see now it was rotating on its cradlelike struts.

When the ship reached horizontal, the motor sound stopped. There was a nervous pause. The nomads had stopped running at the edges of the field; they waited there, jabbering ever more excitedly; the Marines fidgeted nervously with their lasers. The sentribots watched impassively.

Then suddenly, the entire side of the ship cracked open, and a light filled the widening seam. The Marines tensed. The ship's side was in fact a huge door hinged at the bottom. It swung out and down to touch the ground.

"Shall I blast it, sir?" asked the NCOIC, a young corporal. He held his gun up with his thumb on the safety release.

"Of course not!" Cal said.

"A warning shot, at least?"

"For God's sake, no. What's the matter with you, mister?"

"Just doing my job, sir," the young man said disappointedly.

With a *ker-lunk*, the door lay flat open to form a kind of platform, revealing the remaining three sides of the room within. To the left and right were doors, and in the center was a larger curtained area of some sort. Around the periphery of the hatchway burned a variety of colored floodlights.

The curtains of the exit bulged, went flat, bulged, rippled, bubbled again. There was somebody behind them.

"Now, sir?" whispered the corporal. He had already released the safety on his own.

"No, you ninny."

The curtain disgorged something. A figure stepped out into the room and came forward on the platform.

Cal sighed with relief and joy. A human! A living man!

He was wearing a strange suit with puffed sleeves and hips and tight leggings, and he carried a rod topped by a crudely painted chicken's head. His cheeks had been roughed with stylized circles, and his eyes exaggerated by blue-black lines around them. His shoes were pointed and curled.

The man struck a pose, one index finger pointing into the sky, the other touching his chin, his legs crossed and toes pointed like a dancer's.

Cal realized it was up to him to serve as toastmaster and chief greeter. The Depasians could never imagine any concept as complicated as a customs procedure. He stepped forward and cleared his throat.

"As *Chargé d'affaires ad interim* of Embassy Depaz, and Acting Chief of Missions of Federated Earth, I extend to you greetings as one I take to be a fellow human from that same great planet in a spiral arm of—"

"Thank you."

"Am I right then? You *are* human?"

"Nearly as human as you, my master," said the man with a low bow.

"Then allow me to do you the honor of introducing to you the most honorable representative and august Minister-Cousin of . . . ?" Cal glanced hopefully at the Minister-Cousin, then asked him in Depasian what he was.

"Of the Exchequer," said the Minister-Cousin.

"Of course," Cal continued gratefully, "of the Exchequer for His Imperial Limitlessness, Living Incarnation of the Gobbling Moon and Hope of All, the Ineffable Ancient of Deys."

"I am indeed most deeply honored," said the man with another low bow.

"May the dust not clog your nostrils," intoned the Minister-Cousin.

"Nor yours, my friend."

"He has not given the correct response," the Minister-Cousin said.

"It is no disrespect," Cal said. "He is not aware of what the correct response is."

"Not know the correct response?" gasped the Minister-Cousin.

"It is not one of our customs," Cal said. "In our world—"

"Is not what is true and right, true and right absolutely and in all places at all times?" the Minister-Cousin demanded angrily. "How could the correct response be any different in any other part of the universe?"

"Allow me to answer for him," Cal said, smiling grimly, "and express the hope that the grass may not sever your feet."

"May you live longer than the *elik* but more cleanly," said the Minister-Cousin petulantly.

"Don't forget about dinnerszh," buzzed the unitrans unemotionally. The Albarian had moved up almost directly behind Cal. There was another splash of water.

"Am I right in assuming that you are alone?" asked Cal, turning back to the visitor.

There was a sudden movement in the curtains behind the man, and suddenly others in equally strange costumes began to file out to take their places on either side of their spokesman. Cal lost count after twenty.

"A treaszhure!" gushed the Albarian in his own voice. "A divinely szhent szhalvaszhion!"

"Jesus," Cal muttered to no one in particular. "This is going to have the Consular Section up all night processing passports. Poor Grober." He searched out the man who'd appeared first. "And may we know what business it is that brings you to the planet of Depaz?"

"Business?" said the man, turning to his companions. Laughter rippled through their ranks. "Why, no business, my masters. Unless mirth and merriment be business."

Cal frowned. "And your name so we can get the Consular Section processing your forms as soon as possible?"

"You may call me," he said, "First Player."

"Yes, but what's your *name?*"

"That *is* my name."

"I see. I'll inform the Consular Section."

" 'When shall we three meet again?' " asked a voice from behind, " 'in thunder, lightning, or in rain?' "

"Shall I shoot now, sir?" whispered the corporal from behind.

"No," Cal said. "Now I understand!"

"What is it, sir?"

"That cultural exchange ship we've been expecting," Cal said. "That's what these people are!"

"Pardon, sir?"

"Actors," Cal said. "A troupe of actors out here in the middle of nowhere!"

CHAPTER SIX

" 'THE PLAY'S THE THING' " said the First Player in a rich, mellifluous baritone.

"Yes, yes, absolutely," Cal said, smiling wanly and feeling vaguely uncomfortable. There was something about the way the man's eyes bored into you, opening a way for an emptiness behind them that made Cal want to look away.

" 'Speak the speech, I pray you, as I pronounced it to you,' " the Player said, " 'trippingly on the tongue; but if you mouth it, as many of our players do, I had as lief the town-crier spoke my lines.' " He thrust his grinning face close to Cal's.

The teeth were perfect. That was one thing about actors. They always had perfect teeth. Capped. "Very good, very good," Cal said, trying to be a good sport. "Do you want to come in now and have the Consular Section start debarkation processing, or would your people like a chance to freshen up first?" He swatted at the cloud of flies collecting just in front of his face.

" 'Nor do not saw the air too much with your hand thus, but use all gently, for in the very torrent—' "

"It's kind of a long, involved process, so the sooner we get started, the better. I'm afraid we don't have enough room in the hovercar for all of your company at once—"

"—'tempest and, as I may say, the whirlwind of your passion, you must acquire and beget a temperance that may give it smoothness.' "

"But we could do it in several trips—kind of a shuttle

back and forth. And in the meantime, we could probably get some staff together for a little luncheon. We could tell you how things have been going here, and, ah, you could tell us what experiences you've—"

There was a growl from behind. Cal didn't have to look; he knew it was the Albarian.

"And, of course," he hastened to add, "you'll want to make arrangements of your own for a variety of other engagements. I don't know if you've met Albarian diplomats on other planets you've visited, but we happen to have the honor of the presence of the Chief of Protocol for the Albarian Mission here with us today, and he's expressed a *very* strong interest in having me extend an invitation to you and your people for dinner tonight."

"Dinner?" The First Player looked surprised.

"Don't tell me you've made other plans," Cal said with a sinking heart. The Albarian growled again, sending shivers up Cal's spine. He could almost feel the creature's breath on his neck, ravenous for dinner talk. In fact, Cal would have had no compunctions about disappointing the Albarian were it not that next time the shoe might be on the other foot, and it would be the Albarian who had the interesting dinner companion available. "What other plans could you have made on Depaz already?"

"Ah, well, but you see, it's not like that at all," said the First Player.

"What is it like, then? You don't want to eat?"

The First Player hesitated as though caught in a lie. "Well, ah, yes and no. It's just, ah, that we must get ready for the performance."

"I see," Cal said.

" 'O for a Muse of fire, that would ascend the brightest heaven of invention,' " said the Player. " 'A kingdom for a stage, princes to act, and monarchs to behold the swelling scene!' "

"No, no, I understand you want to put on a play," Cal said. "It's just that I'm afraid you've come to the wrong place."

"This *is* Depaz, is it not?"

"Yes," Cal said. "I wish I could say it weren't."

"Well, that's a relief because we were supposed to perform for the indigenous population of Depaz. Our orders are quite specific on that point. For a moment I was afraid our navibot had made a mistake."

"It has if you think you'll be able to get the indigenous population to sit through a play."

"But this is an historic occasion," the First Player said. "We're here to stage the first production of Shakespeare on Depaz in the entire history of this fair planet."

Cal's eyes wandered off to the wide and featureless barrens beyond. Just above the horizon, a cluster of distant thunderheads brooded like somber black ghosts. "Shakespeare? Somehow I don't think that's going to make much of an impression here."

"The Immortal Bard not make an impression?" the Player asked.

"On a planet where the most highly developed art form is pillage?"

"If 'music has charms to soothe the savage breast,' has not the greatest poet in the history of our planet that same power a hundredfold? Give these people just a taste of great art, and they will grapple Shakespeare to their bosoms with hoops of steel."

"You don't know the half of it," Cal said. "If Shakespeare were still alive and they thought they could get a ransom for him, they'd have him grappled before he knew what hit him."

The First Player shook his head. "It's hard to believe," he said.

"I'm afraid we live in two different worlds." Cal laughed. "Figuratively speaking, I mean."

"Oh, no," the First Player said, brightening. "Not at all."

"Art and government aren't separate worlds?"

"Not in this case. We're just like you. We were sent by your Home Office."

"What?"

"Yes—we're from Federated Earth's Cultural Exchange Program to bring living theater to the stars. We're thespian diplomats for the Immortal Bard."

Cal gave a soft low whistle.

"And the HO expects you to use your good offices to get the local head of state to attend, whoever he is," the First Player added. "Can you tender whatever invitation is required?"

"You don't mean the Dey?"

"He is the principal of this particular state, is he not?"

"Well, yes, he is, but—"

"Then the Home Office wants him invited."

"I think you're asking for trouble," Cal said. He leaned forward. "A play must run a couple of hours, and I'm not sure His Ineffability has ever kept his mind on anything that long."

"But think of the benefits," said the First Player. "Is there any higher good than to share with the rest of the universe our sweet swan of Avon, the greatest single treasure of our heritage?"

"I guess not," Cal said. "But the Dey is, well, he's not the sort of, uh, man who, uh . . ." He glanced around. It was difficult to say much with both the Minister-Cousin and the Albarian so close. There was little chance of the Depasian understanding anything he said, but the Albarian might translate for him, and that garbled version would almost certainly get back to His Ineffability. As he knew from trying to negotiate with those sneaky Tithonians when he was posted on Rhea, his first assignment, there was nothing worse than being cut off at the knees by faulty translation. Except for being cut off at the knees by misunderstandings owing to deliberate mistranslation. Diplomacy was full of pitfalls.

"Tut, tut, friend, have him here at eight."

"Wait, I don't think you understand. We're going to have to talk this over at the Mission before we can grant a clearance, agree what would be, um, helpful in cementing our relations here and increasing understanding."

"We have our orders."

"I appreciate that," Cal said, "but I don't think the Home Office realizes the risks involved on a planet with such a potentially unstable domestic situation." He thought of Drofsko's altered nomads. What if there were more of them? "I don't think the Home Office really understands the dangers of coaxing the Dey out into a crowd. If we sponsored the performance, we'd be responsible for the Dey's safety. If anything happened, it could jeopardize the reputation and credibility we've spent years trying to build up here for Federated Earth's mission to Depaz."

"I have our OWS Information Agency papers on the ship," the First Player said, a little stiffly. "You seem to forget that the Home Office must have carefully considered all this before it decided to send us out. I should be most reluctant to have to report that their wishes were ignored by the Acting Chief of Mission on Depaz. Shall I cite the regulations governing the Cultural Exchange Program?"

"Right," Cal said glumly. "I'll just check in with my people and then call on the Gateway to the Dey and see if we can arrange a mutually agreeable time. By the way, you and your people will probably need face nets if you're going to be outside at all."

"Face nets?"

"For the flies," Cal said, swatting at the thundercloud of insects regrouping around his head.

"Flies?" said the First Player. "I hadn't noticed."

"Hadn't noticed?"

But the First Player had already turned and ducked back inside his ship.

Back at the chancery, Cal called a meeting of the senior staff and section heads.

"Here we are with our hands full, trying to find a missing Ambassador," he said, "and we've got to play nursemaid to a bunch of temperamental thespians."

"I don't know," Hara said slowly. "It might prove very beneficial."

"I don't see how."

"You did say Shakespeare, didn't you?" Grober asked. "God, what I wouldn't give to see a production of *Lear of Denmark*. Why, I'd even process the forms for a whole regiment down in the Consular Section to see that. I think I'm just beginning to get old enough to understand him as a character."

Hara closed her eyes and pinched the bridge of her nose. "Did they happen to say which one they were planning to put on?" she asked.

"Maybe it's *Twenty Thousand Leagues Under the Sea*," Hannibal Myers offered, his face cracking in a rare, hopeful smile.

Grober looked disgusted. "That's not Shakespeare."

"Oh," Myers said, all the lines in his face beginning to droop.

"It'll be all right," Cal said.

"*A Midwinter's Tempest* has a fair amount about the sea," Grober said kindly. "Maybe they'll do that."

Cal surveyed the faces around the table. "Frankly, I wonder whether we want any performance at all."

"Not have a performance?" Grober asked. "The Home Office has these guys travel six light-years to bring us Shakespeare, and we're going to say sorry, none today, thanks?"

"But can we can trust them?"

"How do you mean?" Major Sedewski asked.

"Well, what do we know about them?"

"We all know that traditionally the Home Office has sent out different kinds of cultural outreach programs over the years," Farouq, the Cultural Affairs Officer, said.

"But how do you know these guys are part of that program?"

"I wouldn't. I don't have the faintest idea what a cultural outreach program looks like. I've been waiting eight years for one to reach out this way, and I'm not even sure I'd recognize one now if it bit me."

"Did any of them say or do anything to make you suspicious?" Townsend asked Cal.

"Nothing I can put my finger on," Cal said. "But there's something about them that's not quite right."

"Some things you can't put your finger on aren't very helpful," Hara said.

"Yeah, yeah," Cal said. "Well, what about the fact that their ship is much too small to hold all those actors?"

"Maybe they're not planning to stay," Baum said. "Left their luggage at home."

"No, I mean, there must be twenty of them at least. How could they possibly have squeezed the suspension chambers, the cryogenic pumps, life-support systems, and everything else you'd need for twenty into a ship the size of the autoshuttle?"

"I prefer to think they're catching us on the fly," Baum said. He laughed through his nose.

"Fly," Cal said thoughtfully. "That's another thing."

"What?"

"Something about flies," Cal said. "I just can't remember what it was."

"Heh-heh-heh," Baum laughed. "What else is there to think about around here?"

"No, it's . . . I know! The flies didn't bother the First Player at all. In fact, he let them crawl all over his face. It didn't register at the time, but—"

"And here we thought nobody could sink to the level of the Depasians," Baum chortled.

"What if they *are* Depasians?" Townsend mused.

"That's right," Sedewski said. "No one but a Depasian would put up with letting flies crawl all over its face."

"How could they be Depasians?" Cal asked. "They don't have the technology for starflight."

"Who said anything about starflight or deep space? What if the reason we didn't spot them before is that they were never out there in the first place?" Townsend said. "Then some plant in the Mission, say a local FSSE working as a mail clerk, forged the memo? Then they just fly in from a few hundred miles away like they'd—"

"But they don't have any kind of flight technology," Major Sedewski objected. "They're still using steam tractors."

"Right," Townsend said, eyes narrowing with craft. "But we still can't rule it out altogether."

"I thought the story was that O and D spotted them years ago," Cal said.

"Maybe somebody should go check them out," Hara said. "I'm free this afternoon."

"But you're Attaché for Development," Cal said.

"Well, think of it as a kind of development," Hara said.

"What about the performance?" Grober said. There was a note of desperation in his voice, the kind of desperation only someone who'd been on Depaz more than ten years without theater, without a ripple in the flat sameness, could understand. "You're not going to stall them indefinitely, are you? They might get discouraged and leave."

"There's also the fact that the Minister-Cousin by now has told the Dey all about it," Baum said.

"You're right," Cal said. "Okay, Hara, go ahead and check it out. Meantime, I'll go see the Gateway to the Dey and find out if the Dey's liver or whatever organ's in charge of aesthetics really wants to know anything at all about a rival in greatness."

"I just hope to God they're not Depasians," Grober said. "For one thing, they'd be as wretched at acting Shakespeare as they are at everything else. And for another, if the Albarians ever found out we'd misled them into inviting Depasians to a dinner, they'd probably declare war on Federated Earth."

Cal took the hoverbike. Somehow he felt like he needed the fresh air. He bobbled along Embassy Row at a modest rate, enjoying the rush of prairie wind through his face net and glorying in the living tremor of motor vibration from the handlebars up through his palms, to his shoulders, and into his chest.

The Albarian embassy was quiet, the collection towers standing like silent sentinels, metal ears cocked. Further on, Drofsko's squat tower was still empty; even the Depasian handyman seemed to have left it. The spidery spires and aeries of Nargom's people twinkled with an occasional light.

Then the flatness of the stretch of prairie between the isolated embassies and Kabugar itself, the roadway a slice of naked topsoil between towering walls of sawgrass. Occasionally, Cal passed a weedman walking beside his *elik*-drawn cart; clots of hooded women walking three or four together, their children plodding behind them, heads down; once, the tractor-drawn *mels* of a young nobleman, who looked away and pretended not to see the inferior off-worlder. All were inundated alike by the dustcloud of the hoverbike. And finally out of the flatness ahead rose the swollen excrescence of Kabugar.

Closer to the city, there were more pedestrians to be drowned in dust, and freshets of sewage could be seen sparkling among the sawgrass roots on either side of the road. And beggars, beggars everywhere. Beggars with exotic deformities, beggars with rare diseases, beggars with running sores, beggars with missing parts. Cal fixed his stare on the Elik Gate before him to avoid eye contact with any of them as they pushed and shoved one another, trying to get closest to him. Open hands clawed at him, reached hopefully out, palm up. Strange birdlike cries rent the air.

But by then Cal had tipped under the lintel of the Elik Gate and banked to the left, down a winding canyon of sod huts and lean-to's called Way of the Flies, and around onto the principal thoroughfare of the city, the Street of Robbers.

Here the buildings were built of sod brick, sometimes two or even three stories, with small windows out of which occasionally poked a dark and furtive head to see what the buzzing was below, only to jerk back inside like ferrets with the realization it was an off-worlder's hoverbike. Children, beggars, peddlers, *pulgargs,* and *eliks* alike scurried to get out of Cal's way as he roared on toward the last entryway on the Street of Robbers and eased to a stop.

It was perhaps the most important doorway on Depaz, though despite the presence of two Depasian guards in cossack dress on either side of it, it was modest even by sod-brick standards.

But it was the conduit through which all contacts with the Dey had to flow. It was the home of the Gateway to the Dey.

The precise relationship of the Gateway had never been established to the satisfaction of any off-worlders. He was apparently closer than a cousin. Many theorized he might be a half, or even a full, brother. But whatever it was, the Gateway had absolute and final authority about who and what did or did not get to the Dey. Ordinary mortals, of course, could not expect to approach the dazzling magnificence of the Dey directly. This made the Gateway perhaps the most sought-after man on Depaz.

If not the most popular.

Today, the Gateway received Cal from his customary recumbent attitude. He was slender but somehow fleshy, with a round, puffy face in which glimmered two rich brown eyes surrounded by long, luxuriant lashes. About him bustled several cherubic serving boys, one presently engaged in adjusting the stiff, squared-off sleeves of the Gateway's heavy robe of gold thread and matching pointed cap. Another held a bowl at his elbow, into which the Gateway occasionally dipped his thumb and finger to pluck out and pop a single tender seedling or raisin-size fruit between his full, sensuous lips.

"May the dust not clog your nostrils, magnificent Gateway to the—"

"And may the grass not and so on and so forth." The Gateway yawned.

Cal smiled gamely. "May you live longer than the—"

"Do get on with it, will you, disgusting outsider?" said the Gateway, shifting his weight onto his elbow. "What is it you want to pester me about?"

"Well," Cal began, "I came to inform you that a shipload of . . ." Cal hesitated, not sure how to render *actors* into Depasian. "Um, representers, um, has arrived from my planet, and to invite your glorious Dey to a performance by these same—"

"What is a representer?" Again the Gateway yawned.

"Well, that is not precisely what they are. There is no word in your language for this thing. They are men and women who represent an event before an audience of observers. They convey the event by pretending to be, um, participants in it."

"You mean like a public beheading?"

"Um, sort of."

The Gateway smiled hugely. "Well, the Dey is very fond of beheadings. So am I. We would be eager to attend. Would you be beheading a nomad, or one of your own people? We have never seen anyone from Earth beheaded. It would be extremely agreeable to the spleen of His Ineffability. And considerably more instructive than your demonstration of the internal combustion engine, which covered the Minister-Cousin of State with soot."

"This would not, ah, be a beheading, necessarily."

"A hanging then? Very good."

"Nor a hanging." Cal wished now he'd had Grober's classical education. He had no idea what happened in most of Shakespeare's plays. "I don't think. But even if it were, it wouldn't be a real one."

"Not a real one?"

"No."

"Why would you only pretend to cut someone's head off?" asked the Gateway. "What would be the point?"

Cal tried to imagine what Grober might have said in such a situation. "Because, uh, much can be learned from the representation of an event. The representation can, uh, in some ways be *truer* than the event itself might have been."

"Might have been? When did this thing actually happen?"

"Well, Reverend Excellency, these things probably never happened quite in the way they will be represented."

The Gateway waved his bowl boy away. "You would wish my beloved Dey to come to witness an acknowledged falsehood?"

"But—"

"No matter. You will perhaps be surprised to learn that word of these seditious representers has already reached my Benificent and Glorious Dey, and he has expressed interest notwithstanding. As he was pleased to observe to me, poor and humble thing that I am, though hardly so execrably wretched as those such as yourself who come from beyond the stars, on Depaz, either the Moonface gobbles the little moons or it does not. Which is to say, either a thing happens or it doesn't. He would be interested to see something that happens and yet does not."

Cal drove his nails into his palm to keep from screaming. "The representation, Magnificent Gateway to the Even More Magnificent Dey, will be at eight o'clock, just before moonrise."

"The representation"—the Gateway smiled—"will be when His Ineffability arrives."

"Yes," Cal nodded, driving his nails deeper. "Of course."

By the time his audience with the Gateway was over and Cal was outside securing his face net and swinging up onto his hoverbike, he decided not to go back to the chancery. For one thing, it was later than he'd thought; the evening's line of darkness was already gathering on the eastern horizon. For another, there was a lot at risk in having the Dey physically present when he knew so little about the players and there was so much to be suspicious of. Maybe it wouldn't be such a bad idea to follow Hara out to the players' ship and see what he could see for himself.

He swung around in front of the Gateway's palace and tipped back down the Street of Robbers toward the Elik Gate and the prairie beyond.

It was a relief to escape into the sawgrass from the importuning hands of the beggars and the shrill, jabbering cries of the street merchants. A thunderstorm boiled along the western horizon, black clouds rolling and piling themselves into fantastic shapes. Such storms weren't uncommon, though the rain invariably evaporated before it hit the surface.

It was already dusk when Cal arrived. Against the red glow of the western sky was a great circle of flat white light like a fallen moon, and in the center of it the ship that had come from the heavens that afternoon. A large grandstand had been erected on three sides of the lighted circle, and Cal could see players bustling in and out of the light, spindly shadows with insect limbs against the brilliant floodlights, carrying props and costumes, arranging, preparing. No sign of the one who'd called himself the First Player, and no sign of Hara. He dismounted from his hoverbike and leaned it against the back of the grandstand.

The change from Kabugar was marked. After being

tugged at and poked, Cal had trouble adjusting to the way the players ignored him absolutely. Not one said hello, not one so much as looked up when he passed. He crossed into the light and clambered up onto the stage, turning to look back out past the blinding lights to the dimmer but fiery red sky in the west. A man wearing a donkey's head and carrying a bench stumbled into him.

"Watch it," Cal said.

The man backed up as though nonplussed, turned his body to look out in either direction from inside his false head, and then deliberately walked into Cal a second time.

"What the hell's the matter with you?" Cal snapped, but the man ignored him, picking up his bench and circling around Cal in a way that suggested he hadn't the least idea of the dimensions of the invisible obstacle that had stopped him.

Cal scratched his head. This warranted further investigation.

He walked to the back of the stage, inside the ship. Several players passed him by, but still none appeared to notice him. Idly, he walked the perimeter of the rear of the stage, flicking the curtain in the center as he passed by.

Very good. There was a room of some sort back there.

He circled back, pushed the curtain aside, took a quick look around, and ducked in.

The area behind the curtain was dimly lighted. A tangle of weights and ropes, a chest, a candelabra and several other props. To one side was the small brown bulk of a holographic projector, presumably to create larger props and set elements, and an audiobot mounted on one wall. But these were what he'd have expected. They were of no interest to him. He was far more intrigued by the small crew door to one side. He glanced around quickly to doublecheck that no one was watching, then let himself through the door.

He found himself in a narrow corridor. He turned on his belt light and followed the pale egg of light to the end of the corridor. Another hatch. Stealthily, he put his ear to it to hear what might be going on inside. Nothing. He reached down and touched the release square. The hatch slid open.

This was clearly the cockpit. A variety of junction boxes and all the connections to suggest some kind of navibot, as well as readout maintenance taps. But no accessible readouts themselves. The operation was entirely automated; there was nowhere for a human pilot to interfere with the navibot's course or even feed information in. There weren't even any lights or other status indicators for a human being to check on the navibot's work.

Cal eased himself out of the cockpit again. This time his belt light fell across an alcove in the corridor—several sets of shelves forming little cubicles eighteen inches high, eighteen inches deep, and six feet long. Good God, they were—

"Good evening, Cal," said a voice.

Cal whirled around to find himself face-to-face with Hara. Just slightly behind her stood the First Player.

"Who are these people?" Cal demanded.

"Actors," said the First Player.

"Don't hand me that," Cal said.

"They're not Depasians." Hara smiled.

"I know that. They're not even clones."

"That would be illegal," Hara said, still smiling evenly. "So what are they, my boy?"

"A navigational system with no human accessibility, an undersize starship with no suspension units or cryogenic pumps, shelving here instead of couches to rest on." Cal said. "You're robots!"

The First Player looked embarrassed.

"Well?" Cal persisted.

"Not *all* of us."

"What?"

The First Player cleared his throat. "I said, not all of us. Just the smaller roles." He twisted his hands together nervously. "You won't tell anybody, will you?"

"Then you admit it?"

"Of course."

"Robots that perform Shakespeare?" Cal said, as though suddenly aware of the implications of his discovery.

"Sure," Hara said. "That's the thing about robots—they can perform meaningless tasks that would bore a human cross-eyed, and not complain. Matter of fact, apparently some of the new engineering produces machines that aren't just indifferent to boredom, they *love* Shakespeare."

"Dramaturgbots," said the First Player. "Very latest thing. You're sure you've never heard of them?"

The actor with the donkey's head wandered past and started down the corridor toward them.

"Not tonight, Bottom," the First Player said.

The actor stopped as though confused. A fly settled on the donkey forehead, looked about for a bit, seemed disappointed, and bumbled off.

"But how can you call this live theater when you use machines?" Cal asked. "Doesn't it miss the point of theater, having living actors performing while you watch, the dynamics of audience and performer, that kind of thing?"

"Be serious, Cal," Hara said. "Who cares about crap like that?"

"But weren't there any real actors who wanted to bring Earth's culture to the stars?"

"Of course," said the First Player. "You know how we actors are—we'll do almost anything. But those first all-human companies were disbanded."

"Budget cuts?"

"No. Staff cuts." The First Player fumbled again with his hands. "In the middle of a performance."

"What happened?" Cal asked.

"A company doing Ibsen's *Rosmersholm,*" the Player said. "Someplace on Gamma something or other. Wiped out, every one of them."

"How terrible," Cal said. "Some kind of natural catastrophe?"

"Stoned to death."

"An avalanche?"

"No, the audience threw whatever they could find, and on Gamma, that was stones."

"My God," Cal said. "Had they violated some kind of Gamman taboo?"

The First Player looked sad. "Only the Gammans' low boredom threshold."

"I see."

"At least the Gammans spared the technical people," the First Player said. "It could have been worse, you know. They might have been doing Gorky's *Summerfolk* and lost the backstage crew, too."

The donkey-headed player stumbled back into the corridor.

"*No*, Bottom," the First Player said. "How many times must I tell you, you're the doctor tonight." He turned back to Cal and Hara. "It was quite a scandal, and the Home Office decided it couldn't risk losing entire companies of actors in outer space or people might start to complain. That's when it was decided to substitute dramaturgbots in the minor roles. They'd been a big flop with the general public back home, and there were lots of them available. The government was delighted that the Home Office found a use for them."

"Well, so much for our plans for an endless round of dinner parties," Cal said. "But I suppose the machines are more efficient in some ways. I'm glad it's worked out."

"It has," the First Player said. "Generally speaking."

"What do you mean 'generally speaking'?"

"Well, there is the occasional icicle out in the depths of interstellar space that gets lodged in someone's circuitboard, that sort of thing. I say, Bottom, will you change heads? The doctor, I tell you. We had an unfortunate incident just last stop. Lost Claudius in a minor explosion."

"But everyone's functioning properly now?" Cal asked a little nervously.

"Indubitably," the First Player answered. "Indubitably. But as I said, I would appreciate it if you'd keep this little secret of ours to yourself."

"Why?" Cal asked.

"Well, it's the original problem with audiences on Earth—people don't like robots doing Shakespeare. They feel silly watching machines emote, if you know what I mean, even though, as I say, they're only in supporting roles and they're programmed for the most exquisite sensibilities. People feel unfulfilled at the end of an evening, uncatharticized, if I may say so, begging Aristotle's pardon."

There was an ear-shattering hoot from somewhere off in the distance.

"What the hell was that?" asked Cal.

That moment, Bascomb appeared at the far end of the corridor. *"There* you are!" she called. "Thank God! That was the Dey's steam tractor. His whole procession's just about here!"

"Holy sh—" Cal began.

"Everything about the Dey is holy," Hara said, pushing past Cal and making her way toward Bascomb. "And I suggest we go meet him. The Dey must never be kept waiting."

"Right," Cal said. "Right. By the way," he added, turning to the First Player, "what's the play we're going to see tonight?"

"Macbrutus," said the First Player happily.

"But isn't that the one where an ambitious man murders his king?" Cal asked.

"Macbrutus murders King Coriolanus, yes," said the First Player.

"Whose idea was it to do a play like that?" Cal asked.

"Make way!" came a distant shout. "Make way for his Miraculous and Holy Ineffability, Monarch of the Sawgrass, King of the Prairie, who laughs at the daggers of his enemies! May the Gobbling Moonface keep him from harm!"

"Why, the older lady I was talking with, sir," said the Player, "what's her name—Hara?"

"Holy shit," Cal said.

CHAPTER SEVEN

OUTSIDE, A CROWD of Depasians had already gathered, straining for a first sight of the Dey. Eyes sparkled, slack mouths grew taut, leathered hands tugged anxiously at fingers in anticipation. Among the dirty faces, Cal suddenly saw clean ones, Grober's, then Mary's. Cal began to edge his way toward them.

The skull-splitting steam hoot again. Several tractors were visible now, massive machines glowing fire-red at the grate ends and belching worlds of sparks into the blackening sky.

First came the lesser tractor of the Gateway to the Dey, shuddering through the gloaming toward them. The Gateway reclined on an open *mels* beneath the flare of torches held by his huddled houseboys, who clung to the rocking cart for dear life. They were obviously only just recruited from among the nomads.

Next came the Dey's tractor and glittering, gem-encrusted, enclosed *mels*. Cal had seen the Dey himself only a few times before, and never outside his palace. He was surprised to observe that around the royal *mels* was a continuous circle of cloth perhaps fifteen meters in diameter, mounted on poles carried by dutiful slaves gasping for breath as they jogged to keep it a constant distance from the Dey's conveyance, like a ring of Saturn. The smokestack belched another shower of cinders bright enough for Cal to see through the cloth. On the side facing the Dey was painted a crude but verdant landscape of trees and grass and even two or three circles on edge, which Cal took to be freshwater versions of the Marood.

"What the hell is that?" Cal asked.

"No one ever told you about the Dey's peculiar travel arrangements?" Grober laughed. "That's his cyclorama."

"His what?"

"His view of Depaz. Can you imagine, dear boy, the pain of being reminded every time you look out your window that the world you're absolute master of is the most wretched wasteland in the universe?"

"I guess it would be depressing."

"Depressing? That's not the half of it," Grober said. "You know how desperate it is just living here. Think of being responsible for it! So he's had his court painter supply him with an appropriately Edenic worldview. It has the advantages of portability and predictability—you can take it wherever you go, and no matter where that is, you always know what you're going to see out the window of your coach."

By now, the Gateway's tractor had drawn up beside the grandstand. One of the houseboys leaped to the ground and knelt, offering his back as a step to the ground. Two more houseboys held the Gateway's hands as he let himself down.

"May the dust not clog your nostrils," Cal said, bowing.

"And so on and so forth," returned the Gateway.

"Please convey to His Ineffability, Incarnation of Sky and Grass and Special Concern of the Gobbling Moonface, our hope that this evening finds him in good health and good spirits," Cal said.

The Gateway slipped his head in a convenient slit in the cyclorama as the Dey was being lifted from the *mels* by five adult slaves while yet other slaves hurried ahead to construct a ziggurat of pillows for him in the center of the grandstand. Cal caught just a glimpse of him over the Gateway's shoulder, the same round, soft face as the Gateway, but a body bloated into caricature with self-indulgence.

"The miserable off-worlder in his indescribable wretchedness has the audacity to hope that Your Highness is in the best of health and spirits," said the Gateway.

"Unh-nh-nh-nh," said the Dey as he was bounced by his slaves toward the pile of cushions.

"His Limitlessness is pleased to return your compliments twelvefold in his unparalleled graciousness." The Gateway smiled.

"Gently, scum!" shouted the Dey as they heaved him into the pillows.

"Is his Limitlessness ready?" Cal asked.

The Gateway paused to look. "He is. Follow me. The Dey wishes you nearby to answer any questions that may arise."

"Then tell the Player we can start the play," Cal said to Hendrix, who happened to be nearest. Then he followed the Gateway inside the cloth world and up the steps to seats just below the Dey's pile of cushions. A trumpet fanfare cut through the night.

"Please inform His Graciousness that we will be able to observe the representation more effectively if he has his cyclorama opened on the side facing the stage. Otherwise we won't see anything."

"I will tell him," said the Gateway. "If he wishes to see anything, he will see it. He *is* the Dey."

"He is," Cal agreed.

"Have the one called Grober stay near," said the Gateway. "We are told he understands these things."

"Oh, please," Grober whispered from the seat behind, craning to see over the cyclorama, "don't let anything spoil the performance tonight. Do you realize how long it's been since I've seen live theater, Cal? Please let the stupid creature exercise common sense just this once."

With a great rustling of cloth, the slaves opened a flap in the cyclorama, revealing the stage beyond flooded in an eerie green light. Three figures were crouched there.

"When shall we three meet again,
In thunder, lightning, or in Gloucester?"

Cal was surprised to hear the words spoken in Depasian. Earplugs located every half-meter also fed the same lines in English. Grober had opted for the original English, and

Cal was just trying one out for himself when he felt someone slide onto the grandstand bench beside him. It was Bascomb. Immediately, Cal felt uncomfortable. He had to fight the urge to move down to preserve the space between them.

"Fair is foul, and foul is fair.
Hover the frog through filthy air."

"Is everything all right?" she whispered.

"How can everything be all right when we haven't found the Ambassador and I have to sit with Depasians at the theater?" Cal shot back.

"The regulations say we're supposed to cultivate relations with the local population."

"The regulations never met a Depasian."

"Anyway, I mean between us. Is everything all right?"

"Of course."

She glanced away toward the stage without seeming to look at it.

"Unh!" protested a loud voice. The Dey was leaning toward his Gateway.

"My Most Gracious Lord and Sovereign wishes to know what they are doing now," said the Gateway.

"Macbrutus has defeated some of King Coriolanus's enemies, but one of Coriolanus's own nobles, the Thane of Cawdor, has proven disloyal," Grober said.

"Always kill traitors," rumbled the Dey. "Reward the loyal. That is the duty of the monarch."

"No more that thane of Cawdor shall deceive our bosom interest," said King Coriolanus. "Go pronounce his present death, and with his former title greet Macbrutus."

"Good, good," boomed the Dey. "A fast learner."

"His Limitlessness, my master," said the Gateway to Cal, "is pleased with the willingness of this king to profit from my master's great wisdom."

Cal wondered whether King Coriolanus was one of the living actors or not.

"Are you *sure* there's nothing wrong?" Bascomb whispered.

"Of course not."

"But you seem to be avoiding me."

"Where hast thou been, sister?" one of the witches asked.

"Nonsense," Cal said.

"Killing swine," answered the second witch.

Bascomb bit her lip and was silent a moment. "If you don't like me, say so. I can take it."

"Bascomb, this is an official event," Cal hissed, just barely able to keep himself from screaming. "Let's not keep injecting our personal lives into it."

"So fair and foul a day I have not seen," Macbrutus said.

"Does he mean the Dey my master is fair and foul?" bristled the Gateway.

"This is very confusing," the Dey muttered loudly. "First he says one thing, then another. Am I insulted or not?"

"Shh," Grober said.

"Shh?" asked the Gateway, astonished. "Is my glorious master a servant to be shushed when he is called foul by a wretched off-worlder?"

There was a moment of unbearable tension, and then the slow, rhythmic rumbling of snoring. The Dey had dropped off to sleep. Cal felt a kind of relief; perhaps His Ineffability would sleep through the entire evening. The Gateway shrugged and turned his attention to the play.

"You're right," Bascomb said a little later. "I'm the last person to ignore my duty. I grew up with duty. But I can't help how I feel. I'm a woman."

". . . unsex me here," Lady Macbrutus declared. "And fill me from the crown to the toe top-full of direst cruelty!"

The Dey's snore caught halfway, and he opened his eyes.

"My dearest love," Macbrutus was saying, "Dunking comes here tonight."

"And when goes he hence?" asked Lady Macbrutus.

"Tomorrow as he purposes."

"O," said Lady Macbrutus, "never shall sun that morrow see!"

"It is all very murky," said the Dey loudly. "What does the woman mean? Who is Dunking?"

"His Highness the Endless Dey is graciously pleased to wonder," said the Gateway, "what the female representer is saying."

"For heaven's sake," Grober said under his breath, "why can't they just watch the play?"

"I did not hear the answer which I was to convey to my Dey," said the Gateway.

"Dunking's a what-do-you-call-it?—epithet, another name for Coriolanus. She's saying she hopes the King doesn't live to see another morning."

"What?" said the Gateway.

"She's hoping the King dies during the night," said Grober.

"Such a wish would, of course, be treasonable," gasped the Gateway, horrified.

"On Earth, too," Cal said. What the hell could Hara have been thinking of to have requested *Macbrutus*? And why didn't Grober have the good sense to lie on tough ones like this? The truth only made things worse.

As if on cue, Lady Macbrutus asked in the next scene: "What cannot you and I perform upon the unguarded Coriolanus?"

"Again, it is murky," said the Dey. "My spleen is troubled."

"His Ineffability wishes light shed by the off-world scum upon the meaning of the woman representer's last statement," said the Gateway.

"God, what could be clearer?" Grober grumbled, then more loudly, "She's saying to her husband that there's nothing to stop them from murdering the king."

Oh, no, Cal thought.

There was a long pause. "Is this Macbrutus the King's son that he dares to undertake plotting the death of the King?"

"No," said Grober.

"Only an heir apparent has the right to plot such a thing, as my master undid his father. I cannot report such an unprecedented act as this to my Dey," said the Gateway. "It is unheard of. It is—"

"What is it?" insisted the Dey.

"Your Limitlessness, forgive one so unworthy as myself, but I cannot bring myself to say the words."

"What do you mean, fool? Tell me."

The Gateway leaned over and whispered to the monarch.

"Treason!" shouted the Dey. "My bowels cry out against it!"

"Tell His Ineffable Limitlessness that all will be well," Cal said to the Gateway. Cal leaned down toward Hendrix. "Go around back and tell them to stop the murder."

Grober looked over as though someone had slapped him. "Change the play?" he asked.

"Why not?"

"But it's Shakespeare!"

"But this is a diplomatic emergency!"

"You can't change Shakespeare," Grober said. "Have you no sense of honor, man? No decency?"

As Hendrix rose, Hara slipped out of the shadows and grabbed him by the arm. "Don't worry. We're doing fine."

"What does he mean?" the Dey was bellowing. "Any fool can see there is no dagger before him! Talk, talk, talk—these representations are worse than Privy Council meetings! Has he no liver to say truth to him? Has he no bladder?"

Hendrix wavered, uncertain whether to go forward or stay where he was, and then it was too late. Macbrutus reappeared, covered with blood.

The Dey rocked back silently, too stunned to speak. At last he found his voice and turned to the Gateway. "Can this be?" he asked.

The Gateway turned to Grober.

"Has he murdered King Coriolanus? Yes. You ninny," Grober added under his breath.

"No!" said the Gateway. "Majesty, I shudder to—"

"He has killed the *king?*" the Dey demanded. "These hopeless vermin have undertaken to represent the unthinkable? Stop this at once! I refuse to watch another moment of such treason! Such sedition! Such blasphemy!"

"Stop the play!" screeched the Gateway. "His Ineffable

Limitlessness demands that the wretched play of the wretched off-worlders stop at once!"

"Get somebody to turn on the lights!" Cal hissed at Hendrix. His eye caught Hara, smiling happily as though everything were going according to plan.

Pandemonium had broken loose. One of the Dey's guards began firing his flintlock into the air. The sudden shots startled the *eliks* of the cavalry detachment, and the armed riders, trying to calm their bucking mounts and thinking they were under attack, began firing back. There was an explosion and shower of sparks from under the top of the stage door of the players' ship, and tinkles of lute music four times faster than normal began tumbling out into the night. Apparently, one of the shots had struck something vital.

"But your worship," Cal was saying desperately. "Please explain to His Ineffability that—"

But the Gateway to the Dey swept off in the wake of his master, already being borne by his slave toward his *mels* while his crew of slaves huffed and jogged to keep him surrounded by his cyclorama. Then one of them stumbled, caroming into a fellow bearer, both going down and dragging most of the others with them. The Dey's crude but beautiful dream of Depaz collapsed around him. "Agh!" he cried. "Agh! Agh! I am beset by fools! Take it away! What's happened to the world?"

"It'll be all right," said Bascomb's voice behind Cal, sounding very small and a little frightened. The Dey's bodyguards were reerecting the cyclorama and helping the bearers up as the Dey was heaved onto the *mels*.

"All right?" Cal exploded, relieved to have someone to vent his fury on. "All right? I've lost the Ambassador, and now I've alienated the monarch of the planet this Mission is supposed to serve, and it's going to be all right? The only way this could be all right is if the sun supernovaed and swallowed Depaz, the Dey, you, the Legation, and especially me before word about this gets back to the Home Office!"

Bascomb shrank back, but before he could say more, Cal

heard the clank and hiss of the steam tractors lumbering in a circle to make their way back to Kabugar.

"Don't worry about it," Grober said. "We can still enjoy the play." He tugged Cal gently by the arm, leading him back toward the grandstand.

"Are you crazy?" Cal said.

"What's done is done, Cal. No point spoiling the whole evening. Worrying won't help."

"But what am I going to do?" Cal asked, shaken. "What am I going to do?"

"Outlive the scandal. Remember, by the time you've traveled to your next assignment, most of the people in the Home Office familiar with your dossier will have died of old age. You're an immortal, man. Pull yourself together."

"I guess you're right," Cal said. At that moment, out of the corner of his eye, he saw Hara deep in conversation with the First Player. She was handing him something, and the next moment the First Player had pulled on a cloak and was wrapping a red scarf around his forehead. It wasn't precisely nomad clothing; it was a costume of some kind. Yet it could pass as nomad dress, at least at night. A moment later, the Player had slipped off into the shadows. Hara turned, smiling, and then looked in Cal's direction. Their eyes locked in mutual recognition; she knew that Cal had seen, and Cal knew that she knew. Her eyes were cold, hard, deadly. Then she, too, disappeared into the shadows.

"Come on, come on," Grober was saying. "How often do you get to see live theater? It'll take your mind off your troubles, Cal."

Too numb to care, Cal allowed himself to be dragged back to their seats. A stray shot had gone through several of the Dey's pillows, and fluffs of *pulgarg* hair still floated lazily above the grandstand.

On stage, the dramatic lighting had come back on, and Lady Macbrutus was standing in a holographic projection of a castle corridor while a man and woman watched. The man had on a donkey head.

"Yet here's a spot," Lady Macbrutus said, studying her hands, then rubbing them.

"Zounds," mumbled the donkey-headed man through his mask, "had a but piled velvet, 'tis haddock pricks me on't."

"What?" Grober said, leaning forward. "Are my ears going bad?"

"I think its's a deep-space icicle," Cal said.

"Out, damned spot! out, I say!" Lady Macbrutus continued, rubbing her hands together vigorously. Sparks leapt from between her palms. "One: two: why then 'tis time to do't. Hell is murky! Fie, my lord, fie! a soldier, and afeard? What need we fear who knows it, when none can call our power to account? Yet who would have thought the old man to have had so much blood in him?"

Cal winced. She was trying to wash her hands clean of murder. Murder. Drofsko, the Depasians. But what choice did he have now? For better or for worse, he was wedded to Hara and the course they'd marked out, willy-nilly, that day of the shootout. Like Macbrutus, he had stepped in so far that, should he wade no more, returning were as tedious as go o'er.

"Worship mark that?" the donkey-headed doctor asked a bomb-shaped fire extinguisher he'd apparently carried in from backstage under one arm.

"The thane of Fife had a wife; where is she now? What, will these hands ne'er be clean?" She began to turn her head. It reached her shoulder and continued to turn.

Cal shook his own head sadly.

"No more o' that, my lord, no more o' that." Her head had completed a 180-degree arc, looking straight backward, and was still going.

"Do you have any idea what's going on, Cal?" Grober asked, bewildered.

The donkey-headed doctor dropped his extinguisher, grabbed Lady Macbrutus, shook her, and then tucked her, feet up, under his arm as though she were a two-by-four.

"She has spoke what she should not," said the gentlewoman. "Heaven knows what she has known."

"Here's the smell of the blood still," Lady Macbrutus said, still head down, her face hidden by the cascading folds of her gown. "All the perfumes of Arabia will not sweeten this little hand. Oh! Oh! Oh!"

The doctor with the donkey head carried her off the stage.

Grober stared speechlessly. "I think," he managed at last, "that this may be the low point of my entire career. Where the hell's that First Player or whatever he called himself?" His face grew flushed.

"Take it easy, Frank," his wife soothed.

"Gone, I think," Cal said. "Maybe Hara knows."

"She should have died hereafter," Macbrutus said.

"There would have been a time for such a word.
Tomorrow, and tomorrow, and tomorrow
Creeps in this petty pace from day to day
To the last syllable of recorded time;
And all our yesterdays have lighted fools
The way to dusty death. Out, out, brief candle!
Life's but a walking shadow, a poor player
That struts and frets his hour upon the stage
And then is heard no more."

Macbrutus lowered his face into his hands, and his shoulders heaved with a silent sob. Lady Macbrutus appeared in the doorway.

"—unsex me here," she said, "And fill me, from the crown to the toe, top-full of direst cruelty! Make—"

Cheerfully, two servants strode in, grabbed Lady Macbrutus, and carried her off like a bench. Macbrutus did not raise his head. Grober let his head sink into his hands.

"I, ah, I think maybe one of those stray shots must have hit some kind of control center," Cal said.

Grober said nothing.

"Well, what can you expect?" Cal said. "A lot of them are robots."

Grober looked up. "Robots?"

"Uh, yeah."

"I've been watching robots do Shakespeare?"

"Sorry to be the one to tell you," Cal said. "The Home Office—"

"Thank God," Grober murmured, letting his head sink back into his hands. "At least that explains it. It's a relief to know human actors wouldn't mess up quite that way. And it's a relief Shakespeare's been dead for so long."

Suddenly, there was the distant bass rumble and a flash in the sky. Cal turned to look. The entire heavens in the direction of the capital glowed a fiery yellow, and a column of flame and smoke billowed upward.

"What the hell is that?" Bascomb cried, leaping up.

"Do you think the Dey . . . ?" Cal couldn't bring himself to finish the sentence. "Come on!" he shouted. "Grab a hoverbike!"

"And let the angel whom thou still hast served tell thee," a voice was shouting from the stage, "Macfudd was from his mother's womb untimely ripped!"

The streets of Kabugar were choked with terrified citizens. Merchants, children, cossacks, bureaucrats, the lame and blind, the infirm and incontinent all poked and punched and gouged each other to clear a way to the nearest city gate and the putative safety of the night-dark prairie.

Cal and the others parked outside the Elik Gate, leaving a Marine to stand watch while they followed a wedge of the remaining Marines, struggling to make their way through the waves of anonymous faces black against the firelight.

"It looks like it's over near the palace!" Cal shouted.

"You know," Grober shouted back over the heads of the crowd surging past them, "I think maybe Hara's been right all along!"

"About what?" Cal had to dodge a particularly frightened young butcher wielding his cleaver.

"About the existence of—well, you know." Grober gave a lift to his eyebrows as though Drofsko's altered Depasians were all around them.

"You mean, she told you?"

Grober shrugged. "The point is, if all these years nobody's ever even made an attempt on the Dey's life and now somebody does, then something's changed drastically around here! And I think we know where that change occurred—in a specific segment of the population! With outside help!"

Around the next corner they found themselves up against the wall of the Dey's palace. Scraps of fire-blackened sod still burned, curling in the heat, casting a ghastly light over the bodies scattered the length of the street. A Depasian man sat stupefied near two corpses, staring with one eye. The other eye socket gaped bloody and empty, from it, dangling by the clotted cord of the optic nerve, the eyeball itself, like a pendant jewel. An old man staggered up against a nearby wall and then sagged down unconscious, his face scraping along the hard, dried mud of the bricks.

Suddenly from nowhere appeared the Gateway to the Dey. His rich robes were disheveled, his face blackened with soot.

"The Dey," Cal called. "Is he—"

"His Ineffable Limitlessness is well," the Gateway said, "thanks to the grass sea and the sky. And no thanks to you. It is fortunate it was a nomad that did it."

"A nomad?" Cal asked. "How do you know?"

"Anyone who has been in Kabugar even a day would know that his Marvelousness lives in the central tower. Only a bumpkin would have planted a bomb on this side of the palace." The Gateway gestured, and one of his houseboys ran up with a fresh cloth to pat his master's face. "Only a nomad."

"Yes, quite right, quite right, my friend," Hara was saying. Cal wasn't sure whether Hara had been there all along or whether she'd just arrived. "The nomads have always been a menace to the right-thinking and loyal subjects of His Ineffability."

"We are going to have to do something about them," the Gateway said emphatically.

Cal had crossed the body-strewn street to the palace wall. There in the mire of the lane he found something. A red scarf. It was nothing like the coarse weaves typical of Depasian weaving. In fact, it didn't look at all like anything made on Depaz.

He glanced up. Hara was looking straight at him with the same cold, hard eyes she had fixed him with before.

"Yes," she was saying as she looked at Cal. "I think you should do something about them. Perhaps it is time for that little meeting we were discussing before?"

The Gateway to the Dey did not hesitate or condescend. He seemed to know exactly what she was talking about.

"Yes, of course. The afternoon. Come tomorrow afternoon. And you'll bring the others?"

"Everyone you might need." Hara smiled.

Cal rubbed the material between his thumb and forefinger. Yes, he thought. It was very much like something that might have been made on Earth.

CHAPTER EIGHT

"HOW I SUFFER," the Gateway to the Dey remarked casually the following afternoon. The skin at the end of his nose was red and peeling, and he held up the first three fingertips of his left hand. They, too, were burned and raw. "There was at one time, so they say, a religion on Depaz which taught that the greater one's virtue, the more one suffered. I wonder now whether the illustrious predecessor of my beloved master so many generations ago was wise in launching a holy war to exterminate those fanatics. I perceive there was some truth in their teachings. Bring the wretched *miship* closer, dolt," he said to the houseboy, steely voice cloaked in velvet. "Of course," he added, "my tongue does not mean by this any disrespect or, by my lungs, criticism of His Limitlessness's ancestors."

He lay sprawled on a pile of pillows at the foot of the platform where the Dey himself reclined on an even deeper pile of pillows. Several plump houseboys shuttled between the two men and the kitchens far below, bearing plates of steaming babygrass, seedlings, and *galba* nuts, *elik* kabobs, *pulgarg* in aspic, goblets of green sawgrass whiskey, and even a bowl of *miship*. The *miship* was not for these refined palates, however; a houseboy held a shallow dish of it near the Gateway so that he could dip the three burned fingertips into it at regular intervals.

Cal, Hara, Major Sedewski, Hannibal Myers, and Leon Baum lay on rugs somewhat lower than the Gateway's seat, and below them the two FSS technicians who'd brought the portapik. Cal had been too exhausted to offer any resistance when Hara had insisted he come. He had even been too tired to be curious.

"I hadn't been aware that such a war had ever occurred," Hara said, leaning forward with obvious interest.

"Eh?" said the Gateway, glancing up to see what, if anything, the Dey required, but the Dey had slipped off into one of his dozes.

"The holy war you mentioned, against the religious fanatics."

"That was many years ago," the Gateway said. "Far beyond the memory of any now living, or even the memories of those dead we once knew. Too long ago to think on."

"But I had not known," Hara persisted, "that there had ever been war on Depaz. I did not know that there had been opposition to any of His Ineffability's predecessors."

"I did not say that there had been," said the Gateway.

"Of course not, of course not," Hara said. "But what was the cause of the war, then?"

"I do not know," said the Gateway with a stony look. "But it *cannot* have been rebellion."

"Ah." Hara smiled. "No doubt you're right."

The Dey stirred, and his head rolled back. He began to snore.

"Still," Hara continued, "one cannot help recalling last night's performance."

The Dey's head slipped off its pillow, and he woke with a start. "What? What?"

"The miserably unimportant off-worlder wishes to know if Your Limitlessness has in mind the representation of the other off-worlders but one evening past?"

"Sedition," said the Dey. "An invitation to every ambitious hothead across the grass sea to try to put his knife to my throat. And did you not see? Even before it was over, an attempt had been made on my life!"

"I saw, I saw, My Ineffability! These very fingers were scorched beyond recognition."

The Gateway held his fingers up, but the Dey didn't look. The Gateway turned to Hara.

"My master says—"

"Alas," Hara sympathized.

"And my stomach tells me *it's their fault!*" the Dey said petulantly. "Convey that to them, if you will."

"His Ineffability should not blame us for telling the truth," Hara said.

"The wretched insect claims to be telling the truth," said the Gateway to the Dey.

"The truth?" thundered the Dey. "My liver says to have you all beheaded and then castrated." He paused. "Or castrated and then beheaded," he added thoughtfully. "Perhaps that would be better."

"Please convey to His Limitlessness," Hara said, "that it was our wish simply to warn him of the existence of such ambitious, dangerous persons. They are common on our poor planet. Thanks to His Limitlessness's enlightened rule, they have been hitherto rare here. But they existed in last night's representation, and they existed on this planet in the past. And His Limitlessness should be aware that there is every reason to believe that outside meddling by unnamed persons from the stars may have caused them to exist here again."

The Gateway to the Dey repeated to the Dey what Hara had said.

"It is irresponsible to countenance such treason by portraying it in a public place. If a thing is wrong, then it should not even be spoken."

The Gateway to the Dey reported the Dey's feelings.

"How can an enemy be fought if his name cannot be mentioned?" Hara asked. "Is it not more irresponsible to ignore that enemy?" Hara paused while a houseboy with freshly steamed seedlings passed in front of her on his way up to the Dey. "Rather than finding offense where only loyalty and admiration were intended, His Ineffability should instead consider the fate of King Coriolanus as a kind of object lesson."

"A what?"

"A warning."

"Is she threatening me?" growled the Dey.

"You dare to threaten the Dey?" demanded the Gateway.

"That would be the last thing I would wish to do," Hara said.

"It is the last thing that anyone ever does on Depaz," said the Gateway.

"But things do change," Hara went on. "All is not as it was. Once, for instance, off-worlders enjoyed absolute safety as the adopted second cousins of His Limitlessness. His word alone protected them. Yet only a few days ago, our Ambassador was kidnapped."

"We also know how unhappy our beloved master's vitals became," sniffed the Gateway, "when he heard the insinuations that he was in some way responsible."

"The Acting Chief of Mission was understandably upset," Hara said.

"And most apologetic later," Cal added.

"He did not mean what he said at the time."

The Gateway to the Dey sniffed again in a kind of acknowledgment.

"He and I, recognizing His Limitlessness's innocence in all this, subsequently went in search of our Ambassador," Hara continued. "But we were not able to find him."

"This also we know," said the Gateway.

"But we did find something else," Hara said. "Something of vital interest to His Limitlessness."

"Here, dolt," the Gateway said to the houseboy. "Your mind wanders more than an *elik*, and your body is always mooning after it. Get back here!"

"We found a group of nomads," Hara said.

"Yes, well, the prairie is full of scum like that. It's terribly depressing. Hold still, you vile little creature. Oh, my fingers!"

"But these were not just any nomads," Hara went on. "They were . . . how shall I say it? Their stomachs were not true."

"Your meaning is like the wind, impossible to lay hold of," said the Gateway.

"They were of questionable loyalty to him to whom all loyalty is owed by grass and sky," Hara said. "They were untrue to His Majesty the Dey."

"Impossible," murmured the Gateway. "It is from him

that all blessings flow. All rational creatures delight in their obedience to his Ineffable Marvelousness."

"Except," Hara said coolly, "the one who exploded a bomb outside the palace last night."

"The fool in a red scarf?" the Gateway said.

Cal was startled. "There were descriptions?"

"Two beggars saw him," said the Gateway. "Utterly inexplicable. No doubt an off-worlder."

"But what if it were not?" Hara nodded. "There is a story told on my planet of a perfect world where two beings dwelt in peace and harmony and every want was fulfilled as long as they refrained from eating the seedling of a certain plant which the lord of that place had forbidden them. He was," Hara added, "in many ways like His Limitlessness, except not so magnanimous or powerful."

The Dey smiled with pleasure and leaned closer.

"A creature entered that place from another world, and beguiled them, tempting them through their stomachs until they ate that forbidden seedling and were thus driven from that place."

"How foolish," the Dey rumbled to his Gateway. "Such a thing could not happen here."

"Even if some outside force coaxed and coerced a few of your people into disobedience?" Hara asked. Her voice had become soft and low. She thrust her head forward, smiling coldly, and plucked a seedling from the bowl proffered by one of the houseboys. She pressed it into her mouth.

"All children are born loving the Dey, my master," said the Gateway.

"Without exception?"

"Without exception."

"Then perhaps I was mistaken," Hara said.

"I am sure of it," said the Gateway.

The Dey smiled and leaned back.

"Still," Hara said, "have you ever seen a white fly?"

"A worm-fly?"

"No, a six-winged fly, but white."

"Such things have been known. They are accidents of the grass sea."

"They are accidents of birth. For every million right

flies, a wrong one is born, for every million black, a white. Consider that in the same way, it *could* be possible that there *perhaps* can be born among those millions of loyal subjects a single nomad who might be *susceptible* to voices not from the stomach."

The Gateway looked up to the Dey. The Dey looked grim.

"My Dey will entertain the theoretical possibility without accepting it as proven fact."

"The Acting Chief of Mission and I found such people. They had been corrupted by the Ambassador from Si."

"The jelly in a tube?"

"The same."

The Gateway smiled. "We never liked that one."

"We believe him to be dead," Hara said. "And we were careful to kill the corrupted nomads."

"They killed them," said the Gateway. "Of course."

"For the sake of Your Limitlessness."

"In the name of Your Limitlessness," said the Gateway.

The Dey smiled broadly. "It is well," he said. "Thank you."

"My Dey says it is well. And thanks you."

"But none of us can relax our vigilance," Hara said. "We found one nest of them. There may be others."

"What?" demanded the Dey, thrusting himself directly into the conversation.

"I mean—"

"She means—"

"I *know* what she means!" the Dey thundered.

"What is needed," Hara said sweetly, "is a holy war, a war of extermination like that I learned of just a little while ago against the heretics."

Cal's mouth dropped open.

"No doubt you are right." The Gateway sighed. "But our cossacks are *so* unreliable. They are with us a few weeks, and then poof! They are gone for the *galba* harvest. They are back a few more weeks and poof! Gone again."

"Ah"—Hara smiled—"I believe I may have a way to make up for some of the deficiencies in your manpower and even speed up your eradication of the spreading plague of rebellion." She snapped her fingers and motioned for the FSS technicians to come forward. Quickly they carried the imaging elements of the portapik unit forward and set them down before the Dey's platform.

"I have here," Hara said, signaling the technicians to turn on the machine, "several items which might be of interest to you."

"We have seen your devices and we are not interested in them." The Gateway yawned. "Very tame, very useless. You show us conveyances that cause dust storms and must be fed more often than a herd of *elik* and require a nobleman to give up his steam tractor and *mels*. You show us communications devices that obscure a man's rightful rank because he would no longer need his slave runners. You—"

"That was when we were showing you simple domestic devices," Hara said. "That was when His Ineffability had no known enemies." She pointed to the three-dimensional image that appeared before the Dey's platform. It was an armored hovercar with a ball turret sporting three cannons. The cybot controller simulated rotating the huge vehicle in space so it could be admired from every direction. "When it comes to problems such as this," Hara continued, "I think you'll find the kind of solutions we offer much more interesting than the hovercar and telephone."

Cal found himself speechless. Hara was unilaterally offering them weapons. Yet Federated Earth was a cosignatory to the convention voluntarily prohibiting the introduction of sophisticated weaponry into the Depasian sociosphere by any of the advanced planets, except for sidearms issued to mission personnel for defense of each embassy. What the hell was she trying to do, get Earth into a war? Even OWS Regulations restricted weapons to Earth-born staff except in the case of overwhelming political or military necessity.

"What are the stalks on top?" the Dey was asking.

"Those are not stalks. Those are guns."

"Guns?"

The Dey pretended not to be able to hear directly, but his

eyes widened with interest and he propped himself up on his elbow.

"Extremely powerful guns. Powerful enough to level all of Government House with a single shot." Hara's eyes narrowed into cunning slits. "I am not talking about potassium nitrate devices."

"Your Illimitability, it is powerful enough—"

"Oh, shut up!" the Dey snapped. "It could do the same to people?"

"Unquestionably," Hara said.

The Dey's eyebrows butted with the intensity of his excitement and interest. "You mean your light-stalk guns?"

"Lasers, yes," Hara said. "For your holy war to eradicate the nomads who plot against you."

"But we can't give them stuff like that!" Cal finally managed.

"I should have known," the Dey sulked. He let himself sink back into his pillows.

"What my Acting Chief of Mission meant," Hara said affably, "was that we are prohibited from supplying such devices to you directly."

"Heh-heh-heh," Baum laughed. "That's not the half of it."

"It is always the same." The Dey sighed, staring at the ceiling of the room. "The off-worlders make promises and then break them."

"But you wouldn't want us to make them for you," Hara said. "We have no facilities to manufacture them. We would have to send back to our home planet and have them shipped out. It would take many years."

"The one thing the wretched vermin always have enough of is excuses," rumbled the Dey.

"My Dey says—"

"By then," Hara continued, "it could be . . . too late. I do not wish to say anything more specific, but I beg your Ineffability to recall what happened to King Coriolanus in last night's representation."

The Dey looked up angrily.

"I don't see how any of this is going to help," Baum said.

"These things are all antiques, and a lot of them aren't even from Earth. We couldn't supply them if we wanted to."

Hara's eyes flashed. "You seem to forget," she said, "weapon collecting is my hobby."

"A hobby is one thing," Baum said, "but actually—"

"I don't just collect a few sidearms or interesting holos of weapons," Hara said evenly. "I collect *ideas*. I collect the essence. And I collect engineering specifications and drawings." She turned to the Dey. "We could show you how to make such things for yourself."

The Dey yawned.

"Perhaps we might even help you."

The Dey yawned again.

"But perhaps His Holy Vastness would like to see some of the other devices?" Hara signaled again, and the armored car faded into a tribot with a ring-mounted laser cannon. The laser cannon swiveled and fired. The Gateway ducked involuntarily as the semitransparent phantom beam stabbed over his head.

"Or what about this?" The tripod dissolved into a bipedal machine seated rakishly on canted legs with three wrecker-ball fists located equidistantly around the circumference of its trunk. Then it, too, dimmed as it rotated, becoming a gigantic, balloon-tire troop carrier with segmented units like a caterpillar bouncing directly toward the Dey's platform. But even before the Dey could react, it had metamorphosed into a lower-atmosphere delta-wing studded like a pin cushion with laser cannons. The Dey was all attention. So was Major Sedewski, his face wreathed in a huge smile.

"As we've often told you," Hara said, "your planet is an untapped treasure trove of natural resources."

"We know, we know," the Gateway said. "But the coal mines are family affairs, and those who dig in them have them by right of the status they surrender by their willingness to grub in the dirt that others may heat their palaces and fire their tractors."

"Of course, on their world it seems women grub in the dirt, too," the Dey was pleased to observe to his Gateway with a low laugh. He was referring, Cal recognized, to the archaeologist Weston. For a fleeting instant he thought again of the plastic fragment. He'd have to ask Hara what had happened to it.

"I am not talking about coal," Hara said. "I am talking about iron ore for steel, titanium for airframes—"

"Wait a minute," Baum said. "Are you going to let her get away with this, Cal? We're supposed to help them develop their economy through peaceful diversification. She's talking about imposing a complicated system of production devoted to a single product—armaments. She's talking about a war economy."

"How else are they to rid their world of seditious vermin?" Hara asked. The reflections of the holographic war machines flickered across her face. "And what more effective, proven way to stimulate economic growth than through the demands of wartime production? Anyway, compared to mining coal for steam tractors, this qualifies as significant diversification. And as Attaché for Development, I believe I'm empowered to employ a certain amount of discretion in implementing the Home Office's directives."

"What else is there?" asked the Gateway.

"Sounds more to me like you're trying to destroy the economy. Next thing, you'll be wanting to help them develop tactical nukes!"

Hara licked her lips. "Who says that's such a bad idea?"

"This is going to help them develop their natural resources to draw outside investment from other systems?" Baum asked.

"I never mentioned nukes," Hara said. "You did. But even a puny conventional war's going to make an enormous difference in outside development. The sooner His Majesty has cleaned out all these dangerous, destructive rebels, the sooner we can in good conscience help him develop Depaz's natural tourist potential."

"Tourist potential?" Baum said. "Cal, are you hearing this?"

"You certainly couldn't, in good conscience, encourage

THE TIMESERVERS

outside development with assassins running all over the place," Hara said. "Depaz needs to be pacified first."

"What tourist potential?" Baum said. "This is a planet with nothing on it."

"Gentlemen, *please,*" Cal said, anxious to cover any cracks in their rulebook united front. The Dey looked annoyed. His brow furrowed.

"Of course there's nothing on it." Hara said. "That's its great virtue." There was an almost messianic fervor in her voice. "We'll make Depaz famous as a place to get away from it all."

"But this is light-years—"

Myers looked rhapsodic. "Do you think we could make it a beach resort?"

"Perfect!" Hara said.

"A *beach?*" Baum said. "Where, for God's sake?"

"The Marood."

"The Marood? That mudhole?"

"Technically," Hannibal Myers observed, "it's a closed-ended high salt-density aquatic ecosystem—"

"That's twenty meters wide," Baum interrupted. "You're going to make that a tourist attraction?"

"It's just amazing what you can do once you industrialize," Hara said.

"Cal," Baum said. "You're Acting Chief of Mission. Are you going to let her get away with this?"

Cal hesitated, and suddenly Hara's eyes locked with his, and that same hard, cold force bore down on him.

"What was that?" the Dey shouted, starting up and pointing at the holo flickering in the space before his platform.

"Eh?" Major Sedewski said. "Oh, you wouldn't want that."

"But I *do* want it! See, my Gateway, there are more guns on it than on any of the other vehicles."

Myers's eyes filled with tears. In their glazed surface Cal saw the prow of a full-sized antique battleship bearing down on them. He turned to look directly at it, its banked turrets of nine-inch guns and antiaircraft batteries stretching back into the foglike walls of the palace room.

Arms of spray shuddered up against it as it sliced through the misty ocean of another world. Waste water spilled from vents along the side. Hannibal Myers was wracked by a huge, silent sob.

"Your Majesty," Major Sedewski said, "it just wouldn't work out."

"Why not?"

"A battleship requires . . . well, tell him, Hannibal, will you?"

Myers struggled to get hold of himself. "Our word for it is . . . oh, God!" He burst into fresh tears.

"Ocean," Cal said.

"I see. And what is this ocean?"

"Water. Lots and lots of water."

"Ooooh," moaned Myers.

"Like the Marood?" asked the Dey.

"Please explain to his Majesty," Cal said to the Gateway to the Dey, "that a battleship requires many times that much water." He felt relieved. This impasse might be a simple way to sabotage whatever it was that Hara was up to.

"Your Ineffability—"

"I don't want to hear it! Don't tell me!"

"Explain to his Majesty that on our planet," Cal said, "the land occupies only a small percentage of the surface, and all the rest is water."

"Here it is the opposite," Cal continued. "There is no place a battleship could sail."

Myers burst into fresh sobs.

"I insist on having one anyway, or I will have nothing to do with any of your plans," the Dey said.

"Please, Your Limitlessness," the Gateway said, "let me—"

"Never *mind,* Cal," Hara said. "We'll be happy to show him how to build one."

"Build a battleship? How?"

"On wheels, my boy. What's the difference?"

When Cal got back to the chancery, he left the others and went straight to his office. Bascomb was waiting for him.

"We've got to talk," she said.

"I-I'm afraid I can't talk much right now," Cal said.

"Are you ever going to talk to me again?" Bascomb asked.

"Of course I am," Cal said. "It's just that this afternoon—"

"Because I couldn't stand it if you kept on hating me for what happened. We've got to live in this Legation—we can't not talk. Honestly, I couldn't help it. Working beside you, I was drawn to you. You seemed older, more experienced."

"The hell I was. I was just as green as you were."

"I know that now. So I'm a jerk. Maybe it's what I told you that day, you reminded me of my father."

"That's what we all need," Cal said, sinking exhaustedly into a powerchair. "Fathers. I wish I had one."

She was silent a moment. "Anyway, I wanted you to know I realize you were right."

"About what?"

"Regulations. It would have complicated everything too much. It's better this way." She paused again. "I mean it," she said. "I really do. But you've got to stop avoiding me. You have to be able to look me in the eye. If nothing else, we're colleagues, professionals."

"All right," he said.

"So," she said, trying to be relaxed. "What, ah, what happened at the big meeting today?"

"Oh, nothing. Hara just talked the Dey into launching a genocidal holy war against people who probably don't even exist except in Hara's imagination. You know—the usual."

"You don't have to be flip. She had a reason, I'm sure."

"For mass murder? No doubt. But it does bring up again the nagging question of why a reserve rating assigned as Attaché for Development is involved in organized genocide."

"For someone so interested in regulations," Bascomb said, "you don't seem to have much faith in your fellow OWS officers or the system that selects and approves them."

"And she's just doing her job the best she knows how." Cal drummed his fingers on the desk. "I wonder how you find out if someone's in Intelligence."

"Ask."

"You can't ask someone a thing like that."

"Yes, you can."

"And if the person says yes, it's fine, like Townsend," Cal said. "And if the person says no, it's either true or the Home Office has a good reason for ordering him or her not to tell anyone."

"Right. Either you believe in the system and trust it, or you get out. That's what my father says."

"It's not quite that simple," Cal said. "Anyway, even you must be wondering how it is we've given up trying to find the Ambassador."

"If you're ACM, isn't it up to you to see we keep at it? Issue the orders."

"I wish I thought I could," Cal mused.

"You're blaming even what you do yourself on Hara?" Bascomb asked. "What would you do if Hara turned out to be Intelligence after all?"

"I'd feel better," Cal said.

"Why?"

"I'd finally know what the score really is."

"Well, I've got work to do," she said. "Regulations."

"Well, I'm going for a walk," Cal said. "Indigestion."

"Hey," she shouted after him, "if you're going for a goddamned walk, why the hell are you riding in a powerchair?"

As it happened, Cal went for more than a walk. Unable to concentrate, he rode restlessly along the corridors, wound up finally on the garage landing where he took one of the hoverbikes and headed out for the prairie. He had no particular destination in mind, so it was with some surprise that he found himself approaching the players' ship. The players seemed busily lugging equipment inside their ship.

"What are you doing?" Cal asked when he'd found the First Player.

"Our revels now are ended." The Player smiled sadly.

"You're leaving?" Cal asked.

"These our actors as I foretold you, were all spirits, and are melted into air, into thin air." The Player shrugged and did one of his little capers.

> "And, like the baseless fabric of this vision,
> The cloud-capp'd towers, the gorgeous palaces,
> The solemn temples, the great globe itself,
> Yea, all which it inherit, shall dissolve;
> And, like this insubstantial pageant faded,
> Leave not a rack behind. We are such stuff
> As dreams are made on, and our little life
> Is rounded with a sleep."

Cal felt himself seized with a kind of melancholy, as though this were more than a simple actor taking leave of them, as though this were an important link with Shakespeare himself and the Earth that spawned him. As though all he knew and loved were saying good-bye forever. "You never came to dinner," he said, trying to express what he felt but coming up only with what had become on Depaz the touchstone of ultimate value.

"Yes, well, never had the time," he said uneasily. "Working too hard to make a go of this. But it's a failure. No one comes."

"I tried to warn you."

"I wish I knew what we'd done wrong. Do you?"

Cal shook his head. "Nothing. It's just the nature of Depaz."

"A few of the nobility came to see today's matinee. They even cheered at the end."

"*Macbrutus?*"

"*Hamlet.*"

"Ah. It was the body count, then."

"I beg your pardon?"

"The body count. That's what they were cheering."

"Goodness. If we'd known that, we could have done *Duchess of Malfi*. But I suppose there still wouldn't have been enough interest."

There was a breath of prairie wind, and wisps of dust streamed between them.

"Are you really determined to go?" Cal called. "Maybe we could help get you some publicity, drum up interest."

"Well, actually, I couldn't, anyway."

"Oh?"

"Orders."

"Orders?"

"Unexpectedly." The Player looked down. "Came through on the high-speed coder."

"Oh?" Cal said. "Hara tell you?"

"Yes, I think it was her."

"Tell me something," Cal said. "Did you go into Kabugar last night?"

"No, of course not."

"And that red scarf you had on—do you still have it?"

"It's packed in the wardrobe section."

"I'd like to see it," Cal insisted.

"My friend," said the Player, "let this go. We are kindred spirits, you and I. I sense it."

Cal regarded the Player for a moment. "Yes, I think you're right."

"You know where the red scarf is," said the Player. "Let it lie."

Cal nodded. "Perhaps someday we'll meet again."

"Perhaps, indeed," said the Player.

"One of the sad things about interstellar travel is how seldom we do manage to come back," Cal said. "We're forever doing things one time only. We never even get a chance to savor the anticipation of something, because we've never done it, never known it before. And all the time there's the gravity, pulling you down."

The Player looked puzzled.

"Well, never mind," Cal said. "But good luck."

"Indeed," said the Player. "And to you, luck as well. 'Forever, and forever, farewell, Cassius. If we do meet again, why, we shall smile. If not, why then, this parting was well made.'"

Cal stayed long after the Player had disappeared into the ship, until the side of the ship had folded up and the ship itself had rotated in its carriage. He watched the engines ignite, watched as it rose atop its tail of flame, slowly at first, then faster and faster, rising into the darkening sky.

Watched as it exploded into a fist of flame and arms of smoke.

CHAPTER NINE

THERE WAS NO time to mourn the loss of the Players' ship. And with the exception of Grober, no one mourned the loss of the Players at all. To a man, the potential supper hosts of Embassy Row felt they'd been had.

"Not once," Leon Baum said at a diplomatic dinner not long after, "not once did one of those bastards bother to take five minutes out and come in here for so much as a sandwich and the least little distraction, let alone a whole evening's dinner and some decent entertainment."

"Death waszh too good for them," buzzed the Albarian Public Affairs Trainee.

"A lot of them weren't even human," Grober said. "Dramaturgbots, or whatever he called them. But whether they entertained us at dinner isn't the point."

"It is, if you haven't heard a well-told anecdote since that jar of silicon jelly disappeared," Baum said. "Heh-heh-heh. Whatever happened to Drofsko, anyway?"

"The point," Grober said, "is that we could have seen more Shakespeare. Shakespeare, Baum! Drama! Doesn't that mean anything to you?"

"Drama," observed Baum, "was born out of the bloody sacrificial rites of Dionysus in ancient Greece, and I for one am thoroughly sick and tired of all this mimetic crap. And I think we owe Hara here a vote of thanks for getting us back to real death, in drama and out of it."

"Yeszh." The Albarian Public Affairs Trainee grinned with relish, not quite getting the allusion.

And, anyway, there was so much to be done. There were

mine shafts to sink for the additional coal and the new ore. There were holes to be drilled from crude oil derricks. There were fabricatories to be raised where the machines of war could be erected. At night the squalid capital was a hell-scape of belching catalytic crackers and steel-mill smokestacks, flames glittering in the fingers of sewage that poked in every direction into the prairie.

The Industrial Revolution had come to Depaz.

The brief truce between the embassies of Earth and Albar ended. When the Albarians saw what was happening, the Albarians filed a formal objection to the violation of the mutual noninterference pact. Nargom sent home for instructions. And Hara had Cal sent out for any available technical or military experts from Federated Earth missions in neighboring systems.

"Is this going to help us find the Ambassador?" Cal asked.

"Cal, I think we've got to face the probability that the Ambassador is gone for good." Hara did not look upset; something very like a smile tugged at the corners of her gray lips.

"Jesus."

"All we can do is make sure he didn't die in vain."

Cal blinked. "Come again?"

"His death, my boy," Hara said, "provided a timely warning about the Superdep menace."

"What's a Superdep?"

"The Super-Depasians Drofsko created."

"We haven't even seen real proof they exist. How are they a menace?"

Hara smiled. "Have you forgotten the attempt on the Dey's life?"

"No, I haven't forgotten it," Cal said. "I also know that no Depasian had anything to do—"

"We've invested billions in the present government," Hara said. "We're associated with it in the Depasian public mind. If this revolution succeeds, everything we've done is down the crapper."

Half an hour later, Hara sent over a poster for Cal's wall. It showed a disembodied finger held against a pair of lips to enjoin silence. "Watch Your Mouth," it read. "Superdeps are everywhere—and they don't look any different." Across the bottom were the words "PROJECT NIMROD—everybody's job." When Cal left the office in his powerchair for lunch, he found copies of the poster all over the chancery.

The biggest problem was constructing the wheeled battleship for the Dey. To the south of Kabugar, the ribs of the great ship rose from a cacophony of clangs and wreaths of smoke beneath the low black clouds pumped from the neighboring steel mills.

"The other day Myers and I hopped over there and had a tech X ray the welds," Baum chortled. "You realize there's not a sound weld in twenty on that thing? Not one. Well, after all—you know these people. Lazy down to their dirty fingertips. The minute they try to shift that thing into first, its going to shake itself into the galaxy's biggest jigsaw puzzle."

Sedewski laughed. "And then they'll blame it on their stomachs or something."

"Heh-heh-heh, glands," Baum said. "They're always misled by glands."

"We're all misled by glands," Bascomb said, glaring at Cal. Cal tried to look as though he were staring at the Nimrod lips poster.

"What's this, Cal, you randy beggar? Heh-heh-heh!"

The next biggest problem was the aircraft. Major Sedewski and the metallurgical engineer from Hara's Development Office kept finding gaps in their lists of ingredients when they tried to fabricate parts for the delta-wing the Dey had been promised. A bauxite mine had been discovered, but no one could be found willing to lose status by digging in it. The rutile mine where they'd expected to extract titanium from the ore had caved in after a prairie fire following a lightning storm destroyed the supporting sawgrass root structure overhead. And there was no steel for the engines because the entire outputs of the new drop forge and rolling mill were needed for the battleship.

"Well, you've got to expect shortages," Hara said. "These people are in the throes of a desperate war."

"I don't see any evidence that it's all that desperate," Cal interjected.

"Survival depends on our aiding them in the development of the kind of air mobility they need to combat these vicious nomads."

"Maybe we should give up on the idea of metal aircraft," the metallurgist said thoughtfully. "Go back to basics."

"How do you mean?" Sedewski asked.

"Well, I was looking through some histochips on the early history of flight. Nobody knows much about original aircraft, of course, but the very first planes developed after the Social Security Wars were wood and fabric, and apparently they were based loosely on what was remembered of the very first aircraft, generations prior to the war."

"Well, we don't have much wood on Depaz."

"No," said the metallurgist, "but we've got sawgrass root, which is what the Depasians use for everything. It can be worked when it's green, but it hardens virtually strong as steel when it dries out—and there's certainly plenty of sources for fabrics."

"Cloth and sawgrass planes?" Sedewski said.

"They're only fighting a bunch of nomads on *eliks,*" Cal said. "What more do they need?"

"Good point," Hara said. "You're absolutely right. And even better, it'll look like something the Depasians *could* have developed by themselves if the Albarians continue to protest."

"What about a power plant?" Sedewski asked.

"Well, there's that internal combustion prototype we were going to mount in the hovertank," the metallurgist said. "Assuming those oil wells actually start producing in sufficient quantity, it could easily be adapted to heavier-than-air flight."

"That'll get us operational," Hara said. "Later we can worry about coming up with an engine that looks like something the Depasians could have thought up."

In the end, they developed two airframes—a one-man craft for reconnaissance and quick thrusts, and a slower, larger ship, rather like a huge canoe slung under a double set of wings with two engines facing backward, which carried assault teams of ten soldiers, a pilot, and a bombardier. Sedewski insisted on class designations for both; the one-man fighters were *misha* class scouts, and the larger craft were *elik* class dreadnoughts.

Both were fitted at the prow with deadly watercooled machine guns in gleaming brass casings. The Dey, through his Gateway, expressed considerable displeasure that they had not been fitted with the promised light-stalk guns, but in the first and only field test of lasers by the Dey's Own Regiment of Cossack Lifeguards, three *eliks*, a sod stable, and two noncommissioned officers had been burned to the ground, and it was decided that improved versions of existing Depasian weaponry could be handled more effectively than unfamiliar devices by native troops.

"The whole thing gets crazier every day," Cal said.

"I don't see how," Bascomb said, looking up from her soup. Cal had moved down to the Ambassador's office on C-level, making his relations with Bascomb even cooler and more distant, but today Cal and his Executive Assistant, Gondolphi, who came with the Ambassador's office, had happened into her in the chancery cafeteria and taken a table with her, ostensibly to catch up on developments in the Political Section since she had taken over as acting section head.

"Did you know that yesterday the Dey's troops staged two attacks on suspected encampments west of the city?" Gondolphi said.

"Real fighting?" Cal asked. "Already?"

"The Dey's government is fighting for its life," Bascomb said. She blew on her soup to cool it.

"Against a handful of mutants that may or may not actually exist? Bullshit, it's political necessity. It's Hara exploiting the traditional hatreds between the city people and the prairie nomads."

"I don't think you're qualified to make that kind of judgment," she said.

"Why the hell not? I thought I was Acting Chief of Mission."

"Have you tried the salad?" Gondolphi asked nervously. "Steamed baby sawgrass shootlets in pepsin marinade with *galba* nuts. It's to die."

"Because you haven't been in your new job long enough to see the big picture," Bascomb said, ignoring Gondolphi. "You don't have the perspective."

"Who *has* got the perspective? Hara?"

"A good ACM learns to trust his subordinates. She certainly seems to know more about the political situation on Depaz than either of us."

"Don't make me laugh."

"It's so easy, isn't it?" she said, leaning forward. "So easy to find fault. But she's been a lot more help than you ever since I had to take over the section. And as far as I can see, she's doing most of your job for you, as well."

"I don't think that's quite fair—" Gondolphi began.

"The hell she is," Cal said.

"Well, I don't see you taking on any of the things she's had responsibility for. You ought to try being in her shoes a few days and see what it's like before you criticize."

"Jesus."

"No, really. I've never known a woman who worked as hard as she does at her job."

"Every day, day after day," Gondolphi added. "We certainly have to grant—"

"And accomplished nothing."

Bascomb pushed the empty soup cup away and pulled the steamed salad toward her. "As a matter of fact," she said, "you don't even have the small picture."

"Isn't it good?" Gondolphi asked.

"I most certainly do," Cal said.

Bascomb was busy for several minutes trying to chew her salad.

"We really ought to get rid of that Depasian chef," Cal said. "Nobody can eat this stuff."

"Stop changing the subject."

"I'm not changing the subject. I was simply say—"

Bascomb fixed him with a cold, hard look. Cal was startled to be reminded of Hara. "Have you been on any of these missions you're so ready to criticize?" she asked.

"No." He looked down, trying to drive his fork into one of the baby sawgrass shoots. "Why should I?"

"I don't see where you get off criticizing when you don't have any firsthand knowledge of any of it."

"I have reports from the Marine NCOIC, reports from Major Sedewski—"

"It's not the same," she said. "If you're going to criticize the work of loyal officers, the least you can do is know what you're talking about."

"Do you know where the name Project Nimrod comes from?" Gondolphi asked brightly.

"No."

"It's Biblical. Nimrod was one of the sons of Cush. He's described as a mighty hunter."

"Just like Hara to pull a name for genocide out of a holy book," Cal said.

"I suppose that's all you need to know for an informed opinion," Bascomb said. "Where the term came from."

"You think I should go out with Sedewski or somebody on one of these missions?" Cal said.

"I didn't say that."

"But that's what you think."

"I'm not sure I have the clearance forms for that," Gondolphi said.

"You seem to forget," Cal said. "I was there when we discovered these—whatever they are."

"Superdeps," Gondolphi said.

"And they didn't strike me as much of a threat."

"Tell me about it," Bascomb said.

"I can't. It's a security matter."

"Ha!" Bascomb shrugged. "Regulations again. What would you do without them to blame for everything?"

"All right," Cal said, slamming his fork down. "I'll go on one of those goddamn missions! And then we'll see!"

Gondolphi insisted that Cal not ride with the cossacks. He was better off, Gondolphi said, with the Air Corps.

The burgeoning Royal Depasian Air Corps was headquartered at the autoshuttle's burned-off landing field. The next morning, Cal, Sedewski, and the Marine NCOIC, whose title "Gunny" was by force of tradition rather than rank, since he was actually a master rather than a gunnery sergeant, donned face nets and headed for the field on hoverbikes. Another storm was brewing to the west, and the sky at the horizon was smeared an unhealthy yellow-black, like an old bruise.

When they arrived at the fire-blackened runway, they found the *elik*-class assault bomber shaking with the torque of its twin motors, propellers kicking up a great column of dust as the ten cossacks clambered up the rope ladder and over the side into the gondola body. Cal was the last aboard, dropping down into the tawny, raddled sunlight cast through the translucent canvas wings and interlace of struts. The Depasian gunmen hunkered down, backs against the gunwales, meditatively chewing *galba* nuts and spitting. The floor slats were slippery with saliva and *galba* juice.

"Unbelievable, isn't it?" Sedewski grinned.

The cossack nearest Cal spit into the backwash of the propeller, and a fine spray swept back over them all.

"Unbelievable," Cal said glumly.

"Why, in just a matter of months," Sedewski continued, "we've brought them from the most primitive level of machine culture to the age of flight."

A fine spray of *galba* spittle wafted over them.

"Of course, there are areas that could use improvement," Sedewski said.

The ground crew pulled the chocks from in front of the wheels. The bomber shook itself like a wet hound and began to lumber forward down the field. Cal had never flown in an open craft before, and he watched the fire-blackened stubble moving faster and faster under them.

"Which areas are those that could use improvement?" he asked as casually as he could.

The Depasian pilot stood in the bow of the gondola gripping the tiller and grinning maniacally.

"Well, the pilots could really use a little more training," Sedewski said. "Smooth a few rough edges."

Cal steadied himself on the gunwale and watched the Gunny standing at the pilot's elbow to oversee his flying.

He couldn't recall ever seeing the Gunny look frightened before. The bomber began to pick up speed.

Cal gripped the gondola railing tighter. The burned grass raced past on either side, faster and faster. A slow fly smacked with a wet splat across his face net; another struck his shoulder with the force of a thrown pebble. The pilot, vacant-eyed and grinning, looked away to spit; it spattered all over the forwardmost gunman hunkered behind him.

"You're sure this is safe?" Cal shouted to the Gunny.

"Sir?"

Faster, faster, faster.

"Is this thing safe? Will it fly?"

"Usually, sir. We lost one last week, of course."

"Oh?"

"Yes, sir. Hopped up too soon, lost power, came down in the sawgrass up there."

"Any survivors?"

"After being thrown into killergrass at better than a hundred key an hour? Are you kidding?"

The thundering of the stubble under the wheels suddenly stopped, and the bottom dropped out of Cal's stomach. The floor under his feet was tipping, shuddering as they dipped and wobbled inches above the runway. Gravity, Cal thought. It was everywhere. The tall, deadly blades of sawgrass were still rushing toward them at eye level as the end of the runway approached.

"When do we start to climb?" Cal shouted to the Gunny.

"About fifty meters back," the Gunny said. "Pull up, you ninny!" he called to their pilot. "Pull up!"

"What's the matter?" Sedewski asked.

The sawgrass raced closer, closer. The pilot was pulling back on the joystick like a man wrestling an alligator, his face still set in a trancelike grin.

"Is a control surface jammed?" yelled Sedewski.

"The engine speed!" the Gunny screamed. "That's it! He hasn't increased the speed!" He leaned forward and pulled the throttle all the way back. The motor roared with extra effort. The razor-sharp blades suddenly fell away.

"Hai, hai!" the pilot exulted. Again he spat all over the lead gunman.

"Made it again!" The Gunny grinned with relief. "Easy on the tiller, now," he shouted to the pilot. "He's one of the ones has trouble remembering whether the plane goes left when he swings the tiller to the left or whether it's right."

"Minor details," Sedewski assured Cal.

"Minor," Cal agreed. For several moments he watched the lazy progress of their shadow over the flat expanse of yellow-green grass. "What's the agenda today?" he asked at last.

Sedewski shrugged.

"We got to do a sweep over the Randon trade route," the Gunny yelled over the throb of the motors.

"Oh?" Cal shouted. "Isn't that to the southeast?"

The Gunny glanced down at his wrist compass. "Yeah, guess it must be."

"I thought all Drofsko's altered Depasians were supposed to be toward the west."

"I wouldn't know. I just follow orders."

"But—"

"It's a decision of the Depasian military," Major Sedewski said. "We're just advisers."

"You can't take any chances, right?" the Gunny said. "There's a report of a nest six key out from Beta-five-oh. That way, Chas."

The pilot swung the tiller to the left, and the plane banked right.

"What the hell's the matter with you, nitwit?" the Marine shouted. "Beta-five-oh's that way!" He pointed. "Can't you read a map?"

"It's that tiller problem again," Major Sedewski said.

The Depasian grinned hugely and pulled the tiller to the right. The plane shuddered around to the left.

Major Sedewski shook his head and turned back to Cal. "At least there aren't any flies at this speed," he said.

"Every cloud has a silver lining," Cal said.

"Hai!" cried the driver. He was pointing excitedly. Far off in the prairie was one of Weston's partially overgrown pits, Beta-five-oh. And beyond, a cluster of tiny black shapes moving ahead of a plume of dust.

"You said it, pal." The Gunny grinned, unslinging his laser rifle from his shoulder. "We got 'em!"

"Wait a minute," Cal said. "All you've got is a sighting of some nomads, right?"

The Gunny glanced past Cal toward Major Sedewski. "Right."

"So now you have some way to check if they're Superdeps or not?"

"Well, uh . . ." The Gunny again looked to Major Sedewski.

"They're nomads, aren't they?" Sedewski said.

"Of course they're nomads," Cal said. "What's that got to do with the price of eggs?"

"Think about it. I mean, these Superdeps look just like normal everyday nomads. You can't tell one from the other."

"So?" The wind was hard against Cal's cheeks.

The Gunny folded his hands and looked over the gunwale. Beside him, the brass casing of the machine gun gleamed as the pilot banked, and a shaft of sunlight slashed between the planes, wings. He seemed to be trying not to hear the conversation.

"So you . . . don't take chances," Sedewski said.

"What's that supposed to mean?"

The Gunny turned back and saw Cal's troubled expression. "We never attack unless we have some indication, of course, sir."

The pilot banked and came in low, his face aglow with another huge smile. The tiny figures scrabbled frantically to get away, whipping their *eliks* and turning to look up and back at the airship bearing down on them. Cal could make out their faces now, white with fear. Among them were two or three women, one carrying a baby. Others were children, two to an *elik*. The airship's shadow swallowed them, and then they seemed to flow under the craft as the pilot overtook and passed them.

"Looks like they're just running 'cause they're fright-

THE TIMESERVERS 151

ened," Cal said. He felt an inexplicable pressure inside his chest, a pounding in his ears.

The Marine said nothing. He nodded to the pilot. The pilot banked and came around. Cal looked out at the nomads still fleeing just off their wing. A moment later they were again coming up behind the nomads.

"What are we doing?" Cal asked. "Double-checking?"

"Right, sir," the Gunny said. "Got to be absolutely sure."

They were lower this time, low enough to see the grass tips streaking under them. They overtook the terrified Depasians, swooped past them. Two of the cossack gunmen were leaning over the gunwale, waving their weapons. The ship banked away. Cal felt the pressure in his chest beginning to subside.

The Gunny and Sedewski exchanged glances, then the Gunny leaned over and said something to the pilot. They arced out over the empty prairie and swung around to come in a third time. Again Cal saw the frightened white faces emerge from the fleeing shapes huddled on their galloping *eliks*. But this time, one of the mounted men below raised his weapon and fired. Cal couldn't hear the report, but he saw the puff of white smoke.

"That's all the proof I was looking for," the Gunny said. "Take us in." He signaled to the gunmen behind.

"What's going on?" Cal asked.

"Confirmed hostiles down there," the Gunny said.

"What are you talking about? You buzzed them again and again till they were so terrified, they didn't know what else to do. They thought they had to shoot back to protect themselves."

"I'm sorry, sir, but you know perfectly well we've just been fired on, and I have my orders."

"He's absolutely right," Major Sedewski said.

"Whose orders, you want to tell me that?" Cal shouted.

Now all the soldiers were crowded at the gunwales, rifles ready. When they fired, the sounds of their weapons were distant champagne corks over the roar of their engines. As they swept over, Cal saw the man who'd fired fall from his mount into the grass, a glimpse of bloody grass stalk suddenly emerge from the center of his back, a severed arm flop to one side. The others were too desperate to stop for him, racing on to nowhere. For where in the endless grass sea was the safe harbor? No hiding place, no escape.

They banked and came in again.

This time Cal saw among the upturned faces, like flowers along a bough, a boy's, his hands clinging desperately to the pommel of the saddle inside the circle of an older sister's arms, an older sister who did not look up. And then the features gone suddenly slack, the least puff of smoke at the temple, a wisp of atomized brain. The child flopped back against his sister so hard, they both plunged into the grass. A woman—the mother, perhaps—reined her mount to go back when several Depasian bullets found her. Her arms flew into the air, her head jerked, and she slumped forward across her pommel. The wing sliced off Cal's view of her for an instant, and when he could look back, her empty *elik* was standing quietly in the grass munching at the sawgrass with its bone-hard lips, and the woman had disappeared among the roots.

It took two more passes before there were no riders left. The pilot made one last, lumbering pass so the gunmen could be sure. They fired at whatever bodies they could see. The corpses twitched and flopped among the puffs of dust when the bullets hit them, and the soldiers laughed.

"It's insane," Cal said.

The Gunny shrugged. "Well, our guys are city types. They hate nomads."

"But these people were innocent. There was no proof they were Superdeps. They hadn't done *anything*"!

"They shot at us."

"They were provoked."

"Look, be practical," Major Sedewski said. "As far as our guys are concerned, they don't care which kind they find, innocent or guilty. They hate them all. We have to adapt to that, adjust to local needs. Be flexible. We can't be imposing our point of view on them."

Cal glanced behind them where the cluster of the two or three *eliks* the gunmen had missed stood witless and confused by the bodies of their masters hidden in the grass. The first of the moons had just risen above the horizon, a blank white circle.

Cal thought of Drofsko's sphere. Drofsko had been right, in the end. Whatever meddling he had done in Depasian biology had been benign compared to what Federated Earth had accomplished since his death.

CHAPTER TEN

"CAL, ARE YOU all right?" Mrs. Grober asked.

He was still smeared with a paste of gunpowder and atomized oil from a leak in a fuel line, streaked where trickles of sweat had cut clean paths like cracks in a mask. "I need to find Mr. Grober," he said.

"Well, he's not here right now, I'm afraid, dear. He went out first thing this morning. It's the wind—it stirs up those white worm-flies down by the Marood. Slows them down, makes them easier to capture. He has this theory that they're actually a stage in the development of the black flies, but they're even rarer than the white mutants, and he's never actually been able to catch—"

"The Marood, you say?" Cal said. "I'll look for him there."

The prairie wind hissed through the sharp-bladed marsh grasses, clattering them against one another like knives at a banquet. Cal found Grober crouched at the far end of the Marood, face net half untied, a neuron-jammer and a scoop under one arm.

Cal waved when he spotted him. "Any lu—"

"Shh," Grober warned, finger to his lips. His eyes were focused on an arch of marsh grass several meters beyond him. All at once he lunged forward with the jammer buzzing. A speck of something looped around and winked off into the brilliant sky.

"Damn it," Grober puffed, waving his arms to try to regain his balance, then giving in and letting gravity drop him into the mud on the seat of his pants. He draped his arms over his knees.

"You ought to get into better shape if you're going to do all this jumping around," Cal said.

"Who's out of shape?" Grober said. His face sparkled with sweat.

"Nobody, of course."

"There's nothing wrong with me that a dry pair of pants wouldn't cure." Grober heaved himself up and struggled into a standing position, the seat of his pants black with moisture that had seeped up through the spongy soil. "What brings you out this way, Cal? You taking up entomology?"

"A little conscience trouble, I guess."

"Again?"

"I went on a mission this morning," Cal said. "A military mission with the Dey's troopers."

"You didn't!" Grober said.

"In one of the *elik* assault bombers."

"Jesus."

"Do you know anything about what goes on during those missions?"

"How many times do I have to tell you, Cal? The best thing you can do is know as little as possible about these things. What the hell got into you, actually going along? Why can't you be satisfied reading the reports from the NCOIC, the advisers, whoever?"

"You're missing the point," Cal said. "We're sponsoring murder!"

"Don't overdramatize things." Grober puffed and slapped the mud off the seat of his pants, already cracking in the dry air. "Life's grim enough as it is."

"I saw a child shot down in cold blood this morning," Cal said. "A child—do you understand? How can you overdramatize that?"

"Cal—"

"They're not running military missions, they're just slaughtering civilians," Cal continued, shaking his head. "I don't know which it is, whether our money and equipment started this, or we've just stumbled into an old feud between the city people and the nomads."

"Well, I think there's always been bad blood—"

"But it doesn't matter. Whatever it is, Federated Earth has gotten itself into a partnership to turn Depaz into an abattoir."

"We've been in worse," Grober said in a prairie-flat voice. "We've been in much worse."

"You mean the atomics on Avvanos?" Cal rubbed his hands together nervously, pulling at the fingers of his left hand with his right. "That's exactly my point. What if back there somebody who was against it had said something. It might have averted . . ."

For a moment Grober said nothing, waiting tight-lipped. "Look, Cal," he said at last. "We're professionals. We don't have the luxury of liking a policy or not liking it."

"It's one thing to talk about war at policy level, but to see it translated into . . . into murder . . ."

"Cal, you can't understand policy if you get hung up on the little details—"

"Details? That kid is a detail?"

"I didn't mean that."

"Anyway, I thought I was ACM here. I thought I had the last word on policy."

Grober shrugged. "A good ACM listens to the specialists from each area. Hara—"

"Should be deferred to?" Cal jammed his thumbs into his belt and sighed. "If I'm really ACM, then the ultimate responsibility for what happens is mine. I don't know why I let Hara get away with this for as long as I did. But no more. I'm going to put a stop to it."

Grober looked genuinely frightened. "Cal, you can't."

"Watch me."

"At least talk to Hara before you do anything."

"What for?"

"Simple courtesy to a fellow officer." Grober sucked in his cheeks and stared off toward the horizon somewhere to the west.

He was an old man, Cal thought, older than he'd realized. Burned out.

"Maybe you haven't really understood what she's trying to accomplish," Grober said. "Planetary development's a tricky business. She's bound to have solid reasons—"

"Development? Since when is war a form of development?"

Grober shrugged. "Why don't you at least find out her game plan?"

"I think that's clear enough. She's trading the lives of the nomads to stay on the Dey's good side. She's decided the Dey's where the profit is."

"Profit's not a fair word. Nobody ever accused Hara of being interested in profit."

"Not personal profit, no."

"All she's got is that weapon collection of hers."

"I said I wasn't accusing her of having a personal stake in it. Matter of fact, I'm not even interested in motivation. I'm interested in a kid who got his brain vaporized this morning. A neat, clean incision drilled his life out the way you'd knock a nail all the way through a board with another nail. I want to make sure it never happens again."

"It's all right, Cal. Calm down."

"You know what happened after we landed? I vomited. Threw it all up."

Grober was silent, picking the caked mud out from under his fingernails with a thumbnail. "So are you going to talk to Hara?"

"No."

"If you're not going to follow my advice, what did you come out here for?"

Cal looked down at his feet. What had he come for? Because he wanted it to be somebody's fault. He couldn't see a child die, even a Depasian child, and not be able to hate someone for it. Always before there had been higher-ups to blame. Now he was the higher-up, and he wasn't used to it. He didn't want to be at fault. Anybody else—Hara, Townsend, Baum, even Grober. Yes, he wanted to rub Grober's nose in it. He wanted to hear Grober admit it was his fault for misleading Cal. He wanted Grober to save him from himself.

"All right," Cal said. "Let's go talk to her."

* * *

Cal followed Grober's hoverbike, behind but slightly to the left, hoping to avoid most of the dust wake, but he could feel it settling on his sweaty skin, collecting on the hairs in his nostrils, covering him like a shroud. They found Hara back at the chancery, in her office. A Watch Your Mouth poster had been taped to the wall just outside her door, and another to the front of her desk.

"Cal," she said. "Just the man I wanted to see."

Cal blinked. "How's that?"

"Well, my boy, there's been some grumbling."

"Grumbling? Who's grumbling?"

"Among the Dey's troops—you know how they are, never satisfied. But the feeling at the court is that they could really do the job if they just had the hardware."

Cal glanced over at Grober. Grober raised his hand ever so slightly, signaling Cal to watch himself.

"They don't think they're really doing the job already?" Cal asked.

Hara's eyes widened with surprise. "Cal, my boy, have you talked to Townsend recently?"

"No."

"Then you have no idea how bad things are. When we got involved in our little firefight with that nest of them, we'd just scratched the surface. It was one out of thousands, maybe tens of thousands of pods. Like that Wailing Place—probably a hidden nest of them."

"What's the Wailing Place?"

"Oh, a spot on the west road where the natives claim they hear voices sometimes. Think it's haunted, but it's more likely a guerrilla base. Townsend estimates a possible Superdep population of—"

"Whatever it is," Cal said, "he can revise that estimate down by a good dozen after this morning."

"How's that?"

"Never mind," Cal said. "Just how is it that Townsend knows which are Superdeps and which are just plain Depasians?"

Hara knitted her brows together and looked thoughtfully at the ceiling. "My boy, you ought to trust your subordinates more. Honestly, Grober, sometimes you wonder what the Academy teaches our boys and girls these days."

"Do you think we could cut the crap?" Cal said. "We all know that."

"Uh, Cal had a couple of things he wanted to discuss," Grober interrupted. "Didn't you, Cal?"

Cal was about to wave Grober off when he caught Grober's eye. "Yes, I did. Look, I flew on a mission with your Royal Depasian Air Corps today," he began, "and what I saw—"

"Was that these people don't have the equipment, right, my boy?" Hara smiled hugely. "Then you agree it's time to give these people the weapons they need to do the job."

"I thought we'd given them everything they needed," Cal said.

"Peashooters and brickbats."

Grober looked uncomfortable. "Look, Hara, we've got to be a *little* more reasonable. Just last week I saw some kind of combot with a cannon for a head and a rocket launcher for a right arm. Are you telling me it was a peashooter?"

"I'm just telling you what the Dey made clear to me. He wants these weapons so he can finish this job once and for all. He's a very dedicated monarch, you know. He feels this sacred obligation to guarantee his peace for a thousand years."

"You mean his liver told him to," Cal said.

"I don't think we need to worry about the mode of expression," she said.

"So what are the weapons these people need to do the job?" Cal asked. "Nukes?"

Hara was silent a moment. "You have some objection to that?"

There was another ominous pause. Grober cleared his throat. "I don't think I quite heard that," he said.

Hara kept her massive gray head immobile, eyes on Cal. "Nothing."

Cal in turn was startled by the transformation in Grober. His hands trembled, and he had to clutch the edges of the table to steady them. "It sure as hell *isn't* nothing. Are you saying you're planning to let these barbarians have nuclear weapons?"

"What's the difference?" Hara asked, still not looking.

"The difference!" Grober shouted, flushing. "On a world where there's almost nothing left of the ecosphere? You want to risk poisoning the little that's left?"

"You're worried about sawgrass and flies?" Hara sneered.

"I'm worried about people," Grober said.

"I didn't know you thought the natives were all that human, my boy."

Another red flush suffused Grober's face. "Look, Hara," he said, his voice tight, sweat standing out in diamond-beads across his forehead. "We're old-timers, you and I. We've seen some pretty low things. We've gotten used to things we wouldn't have dreamed of Earthside, and let them pass. But there's a line somewhere, a moral bottom you can't fall through. That was where we were when we *started* supplying the Dey with technical help. But if we give them nuclear weapons technology—"

"Why do you say weapons?" Hara asked. "It has peaceful applications, too. Why, with the energy generated by only two atomic power plants, they could—"

"The hell you say!" Grober shouted, smashing a fist on the table. "What the hell do they need atomic power for when they've got enough coal to satisfy their needs for generations? They need atomic power like they need more flies. What the hell's happened—have we gotten more depraved than even the Dey and his cronies?"

"What the hell's gotten into *you* is a better question," Hara said.

Grober seemed to lose his balance momentarily. He tightened his grip on the table to steady himself, squeezing until his knuckles whitened.

"Take it easy, sir," Cal said. There was a small knot of fear at the pit of his stomach.

"Look, this is technically a development project. Isn't that correct, Cal?" Hara asked.

Cal nodded.

"And that makes me officer in charge," Hara continued. "According to Home Office policy, any OIC has the right to carry an approved project to full implementation without further recommendations or judgments or second guesses unless Cal here as ACM and chief administrator overall decides to relieve me of duty. To do that, he has to be prepared to prove negligence, incompetence, or moral turpitude, because they're the only grounds for relieving me. Again, correct me if I'm wrong, Cal—you're the resident expert on regulations."

Cal bit his lip. He felt trapped. "No, you're right," he admitted. "Absolutely right."

"And are you prepared to relieve me of my duty?" Hara asked.

Cal hesitated for an instant, glanced at Grober, then back to Hara. "No."

Grober sagged, shook his head, then pushed against the table, letting his powerchair float him away. "I'm afraid I can't continue under these conditions," he said.

"What do you mean, continue?" Hara said.

"I mean I'm resigning."

"Frank," Hara said calmly. "We're in the middle of a crisis. You can't just walk out on us like this. You're an old-time team player. Not a quitter."

Grober puffed through his lips the way he always did to calm himself. "Every man has limits. Cal, you'll have my resignation on your desk in the morning."

"And where were you planning to go afterward?" Hara asked.

"Out of this place on the next available freighter. And until then—damn it, I'll go hunt flies and white worm-flies!"

"You'd give up a few months before your full pension?" Hara asked. "What's the matter with you, Grober? You were always levelheaded before."

"I can't be levelheaded about nuclear weapons."

Hara raised her eyebrows. Behind her eyes Cal could almost see the sorting and connecting of a good cybot going on. "Ah, yes. You were on Avvanos, weren't you?"

There was a long, electric moment of silence.

"Yes," Grober said. "I was posted on Avvanos."

"I see," Hara said. "But this is nothing like Avvanos."

"Like hell," Grober said. "That's exactly what they said on Avvanos. And this is *exactly* how it started there. I ought to know. I was coordinator for the military assistance group. And that time, I let the military attachés talk me out of filing a minority report. After all, we were going to *help* the Avvanes against a rebel population on one of their moons. And we were going to steal a march on the Albarians—all at the same time. But the Albarians had been stealing a march on us all along, doing the same thing for the other side. What's to stop them from helping these Superdeps of yours, Hara?"

"Technically, nothing. But—"

"In fact," Grober went on, "if these Superdeps are as super as you say, what's to guarantee they haven't invented such weapons on their own, and if you try nuking them, they'll fight back with whatever they've got—a disastrous retaliation?"

"We have Intelligence. They're clean."

"Oh, Intelligence, is it?" Grober said, his voice quavering with emotion. "In*tel*ligence. Oh, well, now we'll be all right. Of course we had Intelligence on Avvanos, too. And Intelligence didn't have the foggiest idea the other side had nukes. It was just luck Mary and I were up on the orbital station to welcome in some more visiting military brass when it started. Just bad luck."

"Don't you mean good luck, sir?" Cal asked.

"It wasn't any kind of luck," Grober said. "Just the same luck that made us leave Sarah down below with the Avvane housegirl."

"Who was Sarah, sir?" Cal asked.

Gober sighed, a long, punctuated breath like whispers of old sobs strung together.

"Their daughter," Hara said.

"I never knew—" Cal began.

Hara put the tips of her fingers together. "Go home and sleep on it, Frank," she said. "Then come back in the morning. We can pretend this never happened."

"I swore I'd never let myself be fooled again. I swore I'd never get involved no matter what." Grober gave the floor a slight scuff, and his chair tipped toward the door. "And I won't. I just wish there were some way I could stop it completely."

"Is that a threat?" Hara asked.

"No," Grober said. "I'm too old. Too old and too tired. That's what the years do to you, Cal. Back on that transfer station, looking down at Avvanos puking its guts out, dying under my feet, I was so sure I'd do anything, whatever had to be done, to stop such a thing from happening again. For Sarah's sake. And now look at me—too scared to do a thing."

Grober sighed again.

"If you'll be in your office later, Cal, I'll bring in all my eyes-only classifieds and my sonikey."

"Please reconsider, sir," Cal said.

"And don't call me sir," Grober said. "You're ACM. I should be calling you sir." He gave a more vigorous kick, and the chair accelerated through the door and was gone.

"I've never seen him like that," Hara said.

"I just hope he'll change his mind once he's calmed down," Cal said.

"I don't think he will," Hara said.

"You've got to admit, it's understandable," Cal said. "Considering. Their only child . . ."

"Understandable but dangerous." Hara touched one of the squares on her desk.

"You calling someone?" Cal asked.

"No, no," Hara said. "Just sending for someone to see to the air conditioning. Doesn't it strike you as a little hot in here?"

"I hadn't noticed," Cal said. "How do you mean dangerous?"

"If he does something to screw up Project Nimrod or hamper the Depasian war effort, we could all wind up being slaughtered in our beds some night when the Superdeps take over Kabugar."

"You really believe they could take Kabugar?"

Hara looked him in the eyes. "They're going to take everything. Unless we stop them."

"But I don't think Grober would ever do anything that might hurt the Mission," Cal said.

"I wouldn't count on it. But the real danger he poses is to himself."

"How do you mean?"

"What if the Dey were to find out? Things could get very sticky for Grober around here. The Dey's not the type that worries over little details like the occasional political murder. And once Grober resigns, he loses his adoptive second-cousinship."

"I hadn't thought of that," Cal said.

"Hmm," Hara said, biting her thumbnail. "Maybe that's the point."

"What's the point?"

"Maybe the Albarians are behind this."

"Behind Grober's resigning? Impossible."

"I don't mean Grober's a conscious agent for them. But there's always the standard mind-drugs. And just the other day Townsend was talking about some kind of advanced neuron-jammer that could be used selectively. That kind of thing could possibly be adapted to turn an unsuspecting dupe into a kind of agent—agent enough to get us into hot water with the Dey and come up with egg on our faces."

"Ridiculous," Cal said.

Hara shrugged. "Then maybe he's just getting old. You notice his eyes?"

"No."

"Pupils contracted. Not a good sign. His health is lousy these days. Frankly, I worry about him—we go back a long way. But the real question is, what are we going to do about him?"

"Do about him? Nothing."

"Cal, that might be all right in another situation. Obviously, he's not fit for duty, and it would be better for everyone if he resigned. But he can't."

"Why not? It's his right to resign his commission."

"Technically, yes. Practically, no."

"You're not making sense."

"This is a war we're in, my boy." Hara closed her eyes partway, as though she were seeing something a great distance away. "If word of this defection gets out—"

"It's not a defection," Cal protested. "It's a matter of conscience."

"My boy, in wartime, a defection's a defection, no matter how you slice it. It's going to undermine your credibility with the Dey—he's going to think you aren't able to control your subordinates. It could even undermine your credibility here among the junior staff."

Cal hesitated.

"And consider," Hara went on, "it could compromise more than Nimrod if we lose the Dey. It could queer Earth's entire Mission to Depaz—hand everything to the Albarians on a silver platter."

"We've got no proof they're involved."

"We've got no proof they aren't. In point of fact, I didn't mention it because I'm not sure Grober has the proper clearance, but the fact is, it's believed that the Avvanos accident was actually an Albarian plot, that the MAAG group Grober headed was maneuvered into holding off using their nukes till the other side had them."

"That's hard to believe."

"You can believe it or not," Hara said. "But that could be what we're dealing with. So my advice is to go and get Grober back into the fold before he does damage. Real damage."

"Okay, I guess you're right." Cal kicked away, felt the familiar lightness of the chair's sensors triggering a centimeter's lift off the floor. The more he thought about it, the more sense Hara seemed to make. "I'll go check on him."

"Good," Hara said.

Cal tipped at the door to swing down the west hall toward B-level and the Consular Section. He saw one of the Depasian OWSLEs hurrying along the hall in the direction of Hara's office. Another day he might have stopped to check, but he was preoccupied with Grober.

He didn't find him right away, however. An OWSS-3 with a fistful of authorizations caught him, and it was a good hour before Cal tracked him down at the long table in the Consulate's conference room, his face startlingly pale. Baum had apparently happened by and was seated to his left, chin in his hands. A Depasian houseboy was clearing away the lunch dishes onto a servobot. Cal couldn't tell whether Grober had told Baum he intended to quit.

"Must be some wind out there," Baum said. "Weatherbot's predicting a three-day blow. Grober was just saying how his face is still tingling from the Marood earlier."

Cal glanced at Grober, but Grober seemed to be looking elsewhere. Obviously, he hadn't said anything. He shouldn't have doubted for a minute that Grober would be too much the professional to talk when he shouldn't. Now it was just a matter of quietly getting him to take back his threat to resign. "Really," Cal said, making conversation as he eyed Grober expectantly. "I was out there myself, and it didn't seem that windy to me."

Grober seemed to mutter something.

"What was that, sir?" Cal asked uneasily.

Grober said something again, louder, more urgent, a kind of grunt.

"How's that?" Baum asked.

"Yeszh, uh . . . iszh."

Baum looked puzzled. "Come again?"

Grober opened his mouth, but the sounds that came out were guttural, almost animal lowings.

"Is anything wrong?" Cal asked.

Grober seemed to be looking at something distant through the tinted glass. No, that wasn't it. His eyes were glassy, unfocused, like the puddle of Drofsko at the bottom of his sphere. And the irises were now dilated, huge and black.

"Grober?"

A bubble of spittle had formed between his lips, and his jaw dropped slowly open. The pearl of saliva trembled on the lower lip and then drooled downward in a thin, silvery cobweb strand that reached to his thigh. A dark spot of moisture appeared on the pant leg. His tongue was a blunt pink stub slipping slowly out of the mouth.

"For Christ's sake, Grober, what's the matter?" Cal stood up and shook him by the shoulders. Suddenly, Grober sank forward. For an instant Cal was paralyzed by the flash of wide, staring eyes, tongue lolling out, then he caught Grober in his arms. For another instant they were frozen together, Cal struggling to push the dead weight back into its chair.

"Say something, damn it!" Cal felt his own face flush. "Say something!"

The powerchair slipped out from under Grober's sagging body and bobbed away, dipping to a stop a few feet distant when its sensors registered no weight.

"What the hell's the matter with him?" Cal said, easing himself onto the floor to cradle Grober in his arms. Out of the pale, incredibly pale face, the fish eyes stared dully up at him. It was funny how heavy dead weight could be. Somehow gravity pulled at it more than anything else Cal had ever tried to hold. Like it wanted to swallow the thing in Cal's arms.

"Looks like a stroke," Baum said, tapping one of the wall squares by the door. "I'll get the Med section."

It seemed forever before Cal heard the medibot purring down the hall on its cushion of air. Its snakehead sensor peered around the door, triangulated the distance to Grober, and dragged its padded stretcher body into the room. Multijointed arms slipped under Grober's back and scooped him out of Cal's arms. Without a pause it transferred Grober to its padded top and backed out without looking along its memory track of the way it had come.

"It's all right," Baum said. "It's going to be all right."

"Yeah," Cal said. It was his fault. He'd driven Grober to this. He'd made him a stalking horse for his own doubts because he'd been too afraid to challenge Hara himself. And this was the result.

"I guess one of us should tell Mrs. Grober."

"Tell her what?" Cal said. His own voice sounded startlingly sharp.

"Just that, uh, he's down in the infirmary, but everything's going to be—"

"I'll do it," Cal said.

A fly had somehow gotten past the grids and the fountains of insecticides at every door. Having come all this way, it now buzzed at a tinted window on the far side of the room, trying to get back out, persistently, stupidly, endlessly.

"And then, I think, maybe I need to go somewhere quiet."

"What for?" Baum asked.

"To pray."

CHAPTER ELEVEN

CAL HAD BEEN KNEELING reverently in the MUDD room's white-noise hush for what seemed like hours, his face a kaleidoscope of colors from the squares glowing nearby. He had not touched any of them. Nor had he been able to pray.

The pager on his belt squealed, a sudden, annoying intrusion. And then Cal realized what it had to be. He waited impatiently through the microsecond while the pager determined that he was in a secure area and opened a noncoded channel.

"Is it about Grober?" he asked anxiously. "Is he all right?"

"No, it's not," said Bascomb's voice over the pager in clipped, businesslike accents. "The starship *St. Ulfilas of the Goths* has just locked into a transfer orbit."

"What?"

"*St. Ulfilas of the Goths.* The Papal Nuncio!"

"St. Ulfilas of the Goths," MUDD began, "was a missionary to the German barbarians about—"

"I *know* that," Cal said, whirling angrily on the machine.

"Haven't you been checking the daily calendar and fact sheet Gondolphi and I prepare for you every morning?" Bascomb's voice said. "We've been expecting it for—"

"Damn it, you don't have to be snippy," Cal said. "Any word on when the shuttle's due in?"

"I had a little trouble with their starpilot's English, but I gathered it was an hour."

"Jesus," Cal said.

"Baptist, Church of Christ Scientist, Church of England, Congregational?" said MUDD, beginning to rotate. "Presbyterian, Methodist, Holy Catholic Church Roman Rite, Greek Rite, Russian Rite, Ukranian Rite—"

"Would you shut up?" Cal said.

"Who shall I send?"

"I'll have to go myself," Cal said. "It's an ambassadorial courtesy."

"Do you want . . . someone to go with you?"

Cal knew what she was asking. Did he want her? "Tell Gondolphi—"

"Gondolphi's at court with Major Sedewski," Bascomb said crisply.

"All right, ask Hannibal Myers to meet me around front."

"Shall I call the driver, then?"

"He's probably drunk. Just send down a Marine, if you would."

"Major Sedewski and Gondolphi are also setting up a reception to share the wealth."

"Pardon?"

"Share the new face with Embassy Row. You know, party?"

"Ah, party." Cal looked down at the pager. "Is there any word on Grober? Any change?"

"I would have told you if there was," Bascomb's voice said.

Cal ticked off the pager. MUDD was still revolving and softly listing religions utilizing Jesus.

"You'll have to excuse me," Cal said to MUDD. "Looks like I'm on duty. But keep an open channel—I'll be back as soon as I can. And if you're programmed to pray automatically . . . well, it couldn't hurt, could it."

MUDD blinked silently at him and coasted toward a stop.

Cal and Myers didn't speak much on the way out after the garage door had reminded them to take their face nets and salt tablets. Myers was by turns morose and catatonic, and Cal had given up worrying much about it.

"I wonder," Myers said at length, "if this Nuncio character comes from anywhere near one of Earth's oceans."

"I wouldn't know," Cal said. Outside, the sawgrass undulated, stood and fell, stood and fell in the dying breaths of wind. The expected three-day storm had nearly petered out two days early. Even Depaz's liabilities were predictable disappointments.

As they approached the landing field, Cal saw that the inevitable crowd of the curious had gathered among the aircraft, the tents of the soldiers, and crated supplies, along with another Minister-Cousin and the ragtag band of musicians with blowguns he'd seen when the players landed. He couldn't help remembering how happy those Shakespeareans had made Grober. But now the field was ringed with armed troopers, and at the far end an *elik* assault bomber studded with cossack rifles lumbered down the runway and lurched into the sky. At least there weren't any personnel from the other Legations.

Cal put on his face net, unpacked a spare for the Nuncio in case he hadn't known to bring one—the last thing they needed was a Papal Nuncio in the clinic for six months with fly-bite poisoning. Then he hopped out through the squirts of insecticide and crunched across the stubble to the Minister-Cousin, followed by Myers and the Marine. Possibly a new one, he thought. He expressed the hope that the dust would not clog his nostrils, and the Minister-Cousin hoped in turn that the grass would not cut Cal's feet.

"Do these ship bring more weapon?" the Minister-Cousin asked.

Cal flashed a pained smile and glanced around to be sure no Albarians were lurking within earshot. "I'm sorry, no. This is a religious leader coming to visit our Mission."

"A grave disappointment," said the Minister-Cousin. "I had hoped this would be the promised shipment of weapon for the Royal Life Guards."

Cal smiled again. He still hadn't gotten used to the number of Depasians who were fracturing English these days, though it was a natural consequence of the increased number of natives dealing with Earth's Military Assistance

Advisory Group. "Tell me, how did you know a ship was coming in?" Cal asked.

"Even the stars have no secrets before His Ineffability."

"The Dey told you, then?"

"Not directly, no. But who else would know such thing?"

"Who else indeed?"

"There it is!" Myers shouted. "The autoshuttle!"

It was only a matter of minutes before the autoshuttle was settling into a cloud of retro dust. The band played "Hail to the Chìef."

There was a pause as the motors whirred off, and then a figure emerged coughing from the swirls and streamers of dust. It was the Nuncio, his black cassock flapping, a small, frail man leaning to one side to counterbalance a heavy, clanking bag. He stopped short, startled, as though he somehow recognized Cal from somewhere, then waited awkwardly for the Minister-Cousin so Cal could translate the exchange of papal and Depasian greetings.

The Minister-Cousin was still sulking about the lack of weapons, and his obligatory wish that the Nuncio should live longer than the *elik,* but more cleanly, was delivered with as much surliness and insincerity as the man could muster. Suddenly, the Depasian crowd began to surge forward, a small herd of children scampering in front. Cal reached instinctively behind his back for his pistol, then caught himself. Not again.

"This way to the bitch!" the children shouted raggedly in English. They pointed excitedly toward the west. "This way to the bitch!"

"Scusi?" said the Nuncio, nervously licking his thin lips.

"The *beach,"* Cal sighed with relief. "The Marood—a mud hole on the other side of the capital. I'm afraid one of our people got it into the Dey's head to make it a tourist attraction. We can't seem to explain there isn't a prayer—so to speak. But we'd better get to the car before we're trampled." He hurried the Nuncio into a half-run.

"This way to the bitch!" hooted the disappointed children after them.

Cal clambered into Moby Dick behind the Nuncio and

his clanking bag. As the door slicked shut, he hit the button for an extra burst of insecticide for any flies that had gotten it, then slid into his seat and signaled the Marine driver to turn on the engine. He had to crank it for several anxious minutes before it caught, the crowd milling around outside the craft.

"Always that is the problem," the Nuncio said, hacking on the perfumed mist. He had delicate features and pale, almost translucent skin. He shot Cal another covert, curious look.

"Beg pardon, Your Excellency?" Cal was watching the Marine carefully, intent on not running down any beach promoters. The Nuncio made him uneasy. Humans fresh from Earth always seemed strange, even alien to him. It was as though he'd lost his own link to humanity.

"The terrafication of the planet," said the Nuncio. He was looking across the prairie to where a nest of oil derricks stretched their necks like fledgling birds. "We always tempt others into imitating us. We are serpents in a universe of gardens."

"As a matter of fact, we're very strict about noninterference," Cal said, eyes on the dusty road.

"But we cannot help wanting to be attractive," the Nuncio said, "wanting them to imitate us. It's hardest in a place like this, where the population is vaguely humanoid. Ever we would make them in our image."

If only you knew, Cal thought. To think what he'd done to save these people from real meddling, only to sit through this stupid lecture. It was so easy for outsiders to feel smug and morally superior. They didn't have to dirty their hands with the day-to-day realities. What choice had any of them had once Drofsko had interfered? They hadn't *wanted* to get involved in changing the sociosphere. But of course it wouldn't do to try to make the Nuncio understand such subtleties. In fact, keeping their involvement here a secret from him posed some real difficulties. Cal thought again of the puddle of dead, dull glass somewhere out on the prairie, unhoused and unannealed, of Grober lying broken in his infirmary float.

"But aren't you in the missionary business yourself?"

Cal spoke carefully and slowly to hide the anger in his voice.

The Nuncio shrugged. "We hold some great truths universal. We believe it is our duty to spread the Good News. But we try to walk a very thin line. We try not to make the mistake of the priests who converted the ancient Aztecs."

Cal decided to change the subject. "They tell me there's a reception tonight."

"That's right," Myers chimed in in a rare burst of enthusiasm. "Most of Embassy Row will be there."

"I guess I don't have to warn you some of the personnel from other legations will be in pressure suits, that kind of thing," Cal said. "And we've got a Tsaulian here who tends to perch on chairs and—"

"If there is time," the Nuncio said carefully.

"Excuse me?"

"I may not be able to attend."

"But you've *got* to attend," Myers protested. "Everybody's been looking forward to meeting you. I mean, it's so boring here, we'd kill just for a new face at dinner."

Cal gave Myers a sharp look.

"Uh—just a figure of speech, of course," Myers said, collapsing into his customary gloom.

"I regret that I must first attend to a matter of some spiritual urgency. Then we will see."

Cal raised his eyebrows. "No one on the staff, I hope?" He spoke lightly, hoping his twinge of fear didn't show. "If you're thinking of missionary work, they don't really have an idea of gods, and the Dey wouldn't allow it, anyway. He bills himself as the incarnation of the spirits of sky, grass, and fl—"

"I wish only to see your Multimodal Unitized Devotional Device."

"MUDD?"

"You have one, correct?"

"Of course," Cal said brightening. "You planning a mass? A little human-run service would be a welcome change."

"Perhaps later." The Nuncio patted the black bag on his lap. "I must see to the machine itself."

"Making some kind of modification?" Cal wondered.

"In a manner of speaking."

"It seems to work fine the way it is."

"A matter of opinion. Your Home Office—"

"It's your home, too," Cal corrected.

"Not spiritually. As I say, your Home Office distributed the MUDD machines throughout the Off-World Service like entertainment units. Vatican approval was never secured. Your people seem not to understand what means thorough consideration."

"Sure, but when it takes six light-years just for instructions to get here, you've got to get these things into the pipeline right away."

"Convenience has never been a priority with Mother Church," the Nuncio said. "How did your people think a machine could be a priest, Christ's own representative?"

"But if you programmed in the right formulas—"

"The miracle of the mass is not just so many formulae," the Nuncio said. "Could a machine judge the sincerity of a sinner's confession or assume that awful burden of guilt before passing it on to Him? No, my friend, the Church has held firm through the centuries—only a human is capable of the priestly life's love and suffering."

Cal shifted at the mention of sin's burden. "So what is it you want to do?"

"Transfer the machine's data banks to a dump box so I can review them and speak with those who believed themselves absolved of mortal sin. They must be told so they can make valid confessions."

Cal froze. The Nuncio would hear *his* confession! Security would be compromised! His career—

But before he could ponder the matter further, something pinged off the hovercraft's hull. He looked up to see twenty or thirty mounted bandits charging across the prairie. If it hadn't been for the second puff of smoke, Cal might have thought they were having a harmless race.

"Full speed!" he barked to the Marine. "Lose the bastards!"

"What is it?" the Nuncio asked as the Marine floored the pedal and the hovercraft listed to one side.

"Primitive projectile weapons," Cal said.

"Someone is shouting at us?"

"Shooting, Your Excellency."

"With guns?"

"You could say that. We'll lose them in a second." He checked the rear screen to see their dust-wake roll over the pursuers. "What can I say?" he added as he felt Moby Dick pulling well away. "The only law on Depaz is family ties. In order to survive here, we've had to have the entire Mission adopted as second cousins to the Dey. And as you can see, not even that's a guarantee anymore, at least not since this civil war broke out."

The Nuncio chuckled. "My diplomatic passport would have been the birth certificate, then?"

"It still is, most places. Some of these people hunt each other for sport, and to them we're not even that, well, human. Why, just a few weeks ago our own Ambassador was kidnapped." Cal scowled. He'd never heard of bandits attacking a hovercraft. Obviously, Hara had been right. There was no other explanation than that these were more remnants of Drofsko's experiments.

"He is all right now?" the Nuncio asked. "You found him?"

"What?" Again it all played through Cal's head, the Ambassador, the Depasians, the flies . . . and Drofsko. "Uh, no. No, we didn't. But we haven't given up hope."

"And this civil war you mentioned. What started it?"

"Some kind of regional dispute," Cal said hastily, before Myers had a chance to speak.

Cal brooded silently the rest of the way, bypassing the official Legation entrance for the protection of the garage. It was already late afternoon, and the grids under the dome had come on. Cal squinted against the surges of harsh, purple-white light of flies bumbling into the grids as the Marine maneuvered them to a stop. The garage was empty. When Cal led the Nuncio up the steps and through the door's spurts of perfumed insecticide, the Nuncio refusing any help with his heavy bag, Cal found Hara. Her gray face was puckered in a more sour look than usual.

"I need to see you when you've got a minute," she whispered. Then she was gone. Cal waited for the Nuncio to finish hacking on the insecticide.

"You get used to the stuff eventually," he comforted, wondering what Hara wanted. "How about if Myers here takes you to meet some of the staff?"

"The MUDD, yes, please?" the Nuncio managed, trying to clear his throat.

"Okay, MUDD first, staff later." Cal shrugged. "Hannibal, can you take care of that, show His Excellency where MUDD is? I've got a meeting." He watched them go, the frail Nuncio and Myers himself, thin and spindly, like two spiders. Then he took out his pager and called the infirmary. The medibot reported no change. Grober was still in a coma, suffering from a cerebral hemorrhage.

Cal headed for Hara's office. Aside from Grober, the thing uppermost in his mind was the idea of the little man's prying Cal's secrets out of MUDD. It was worse than being spied on. It was indecent.

By the time he'd reached Hara's door, his fear of discovery had given way to anger.

"Look," he said, touching the square to make sure Hara's door shut securely behind him, "before we get to whatever it was you wanted to say, there's something else we should discuss."

The door jammed halfway. Hara picked up a club of dried sawgrass root and gave the door a sharp rap a third of the way up. It shut. Then she solemnly gathered the folds of her Depasian robe and sat down. "All right, my boy, shoot."

Cal glanced uneasily around the room. He didn't come here often, and it always had the disquieting, threatening air of the unfamiliar. Against one wall was a little shrine of mementoes from earlier posts—strange wisps of arterial metalwork, squat idols, flashes of mineral samples, and exotic weapons. In the center loomed the rough, cruciform shape of an alien crossbow.

"I don't want to compromise your cover or anything," Cal began, "but—"

"Cover? What are you talking about, Cal?"

"Look, you're the only person I can talk to about this, and I've got to be candid."

Hara sighed and looked off into space for a moment. "Is it about the Nuncio's dismantling that prayer wheel downstairs?"

Cal raised his eyebrows with surprise. "Where did you hear—?"

Hara shrugged. "Townsend's the Intelligence Operative, not me. He passed it on to me in case it related to my project."

"The Nuncio's planning to listen to all the confessions," Cal said, "and . . . well, I don't know how to say this, but I—"

Hara's lip curled with the slightest smile. "You're worried that there might be something incriminating in MUDD, my boy? Something one of our officers might have said? Something you might have said, even?"

Cal looked shocked. "Have you tapped MUDD?"

Hara looked back expressionlessly.

"Outrageous," Cal said.

"I'm not interested in arguing who tapped MUDD, Cal. I know you won't believe me no matter what I say. But what's the difference how I found out? Didn't you come here to confess all this to me, anyway?"

"I came to tell you because I decided to. It was a matter of free choice."

Hara shrugged and leaned back, her face almost disappearing in the gloom. "The results are the same. You're here."

Cal sank lower in his chair. "Well, maybe the Nuncio will consider the machine a temporary surrogate or something, and honor its pledge of secrecy."

"I wouldn't stake my Annual Evaluation on any priest who had a voice print of my murder confession," Hara snorted. "You and I may understand that this business has its own morals, and selective elimination can be a valuable tool to—"

"Drofsko was an accident!"

Hara looked up at the ceiling. "Suit yourself, my boy, but the Home Office is six light-years away, and they don't care how we do things as long as we get them done and don't get caught and embarrass them. So if this priest comes down with a bad case of moral outrage and blows the whistle . . . well, you were political officer before your emergency promotion, Cal. Do I have to draw you a picture?"

Cal's forehead was icy with sweat, his fingers cold. "What do I do?"

"Glad you asked. Not too much, in fact. Townsend's had the Nuncio's tickets lifted."

"His diplomatic passport?"

"I don't really understand these things—they're out of my bailiwick—but apparently Townsend has someone in Grober's office who could take care of it while you two were en route."

"I see."

"Townsend says it's going to take time to set things up," Hara said. "You know these locals he has to work with— you can't get one of them to take a leak without fifteen relatives to back him up. That's why he wanted me to let you in on this."

"What's he planning to do?"

"Does it matter?"

"Of course it matters. Is he going to have someone jump the Nuncio and grab the dump box?"

Hara looked toward her tinted window.

"Is that it?"

"Sure, Cal. That's it."

There was something about Hara's voice. "You're lying."

"What makes you say that?"

"Never mind. You're going to have them kill him, I know it."

Hara sighed. "Jesus Christ, Cal, how many times do I have to tell you it's Townsend, not me? But give him a break, will you? It's hard enough for him to explain to these people what a dump box looks like, let alone complicate things by telling them not to hurt somebody."

"So you want me to play Judas and set him up to be murdered?"

"Townsend, Cal. And he's not asking you to stay. He's not asking you to hurt anybody yourself. He's not even asking you to risk getting hurt. He's just asking you to withhold certain information, kind of play footsie for sixty minutes or so before you let him go up to his room. Isn't that what diplomacy's all about, not telling the other side everything?"

"You're missing the point. I'm not worried about my personal safety."

"Whose, then? Bascomb's?"

"It's got nothing to do with her. I just don't want my hands bloodied with another murder."

Hara sighed. "I thought you showed real promise at the shootout. I had genuine hopes when I heard you went along on that sweep over the trade route. But I guess I should have drawn you that picture after all, the part about your career."

Cal felt suddenly cold and clammy. "What are you trying to say?"

"Just that I wouldn't want the End User's Report you're going to have in your file if the Drofsko business gets out, you know? I like looking forward to retiring at full pension, myself."

Cal shook his head. "Maybe I can learn to live with knowing what the Depasians are doing to one another, but when it comes to fellow Earthlings—"

"There's something else, Cal," Hara said.

"What's that?"

"Grober's condition. Townsend tells me he's seen cases like this among the native population."

"Strokes? Sure, why not? We all know they're physiologically similar, so of course you'd expect them to have strokes, too."

"No, he was talking about artifically induced states."

Cal started. "What do you mean?"

"You remember I was talking about drugs not so long ago?"

"You mean Grober's condition was caused deliberately?" Cal said.

"Sawgrass has lots of strange uses."

"Is there an antidote?"

"Townsend might know of one," Hara said. "But he's a busy man. If you want him to use his contacts to dig up an antidote, I think you ought to be willing to offer something in return."

"The Nuncio's life for Grober's?"

Hara raised her eyebrows but said nothing.

Cal's mind raced desperately. "Look, give me the hour and let me see if I can get the dump box away from him without any rough stuff."

"Why?"

"Why? You've got to ask why I wouldn't want to waste a human life if it could be avoided?"

Hara shrugged. "You're softer than I thought."

"Look, yesterday I saw a lot of people killed and my best friend collapse. And I know that friend would want me to try to save this priest's life. Would you call off your people if I can get the box my way?"

"How many times do I have to tell you?" Hara said slowly. "This is Townsend's operation. But all right, I'll talk to him. But you'd better do it *without* letting that priest know what's going on here. Otherwise, Townsend's probably going to have to eliminate him anyway. And remember, Cal."

"Remember what?"

"Somebody will be listening to every word." Hara leaned back. "Someone is always listening to every word."

CHAPTER TWELVE

CAL MADE HIS WAY toward the MUDD room on foot, nervous and sweating. Hara wasn't joking; the whole Legation was probably bugged. But whether or not he believed her story about Townsend—and he didn't—how was he going to get the Nuncio to hand over the dump box without telling him the real reason?

Halfway down the hall, Cal began to hear strange whirrings and clankings ahead.

"Sir?"

Cal turned. From behind, a Marine swept toward him on a powerchair and tipped to a stop.

"Officer Bascomb would like you to stop by her office when you get a chance," the Marine said.

Whrrr went something farther down the hall. *Clank.*

"Pardon?" Cal asked, preoccupied. What could the Nuncio be doing in there?

"Officer Bascomb asked me to ask you—"

Clunk-crash THUMP!

"—if you'd stop by her office when you get a chance."

"Yes," Cal mumbled, hurrying on. *Thwack*! "Tell her as soon as I can."

Cal reached the MUDD door and stepped inside. He froze openmouthed on the threshold. The room was a shambles. In the center the MUDD polyhedron leaned at an insane angle. Gears and bits of hydraulic linkages lay everywhere as though a deranged squirrel had been throwing parts out of the mechanism in a search for nuts. The Nuncio was nowhere to be seen. Absently, Cal palmed the Roman Catholic square, and the machine began to wobble on its axis, then lurched to a stop at the Hindu face.

"Once to every man and nation," the soundwands blared, "comes the moment to decide. . . ."

The polyhedron rumbled on, then stopped a second time, revealing a huge gap like a Gouda cheese with a wedge sliced out of it. In the empty space crouched mouselike the dark shape of the Nuncio, outsize power wrench in one hand.

"In the strife of Good with Falsehood, For the good or evil side."

Whrrr, said the powerwrench.

The Nuncio looked up and waved the heavy tool. "Some minor difficulties." He smiled.

"By the light of burning martyrs," burbled the machine ever more slowly, winding down into deeper and deeper registers until it was inaudible. For another moment Cal felt the lowest frequencies reverberate through his chest like subsonic engine rumble, and then it stopped.

"You killed it!" Cal gasped.

"Eh?" the Nuncio said. "Oh, I shall restore most of the functions, my son. But one cannot kill something created by mere man."

"But the cybernetics laws—"

"A thing cannot have life without a soul," the Nuncio went on, not listening. "And only God can grant that."

"But you said you were just going to tap the memory."

"That was one of my purposes, yes. But I assumed you understood when I told you the machine never received Vatican approval, it would have to be removed." He reached into the tangle of conduits and wires that formed the machine's center. "Why, the altar isn't even consecrated." Back out came his hand with a small black box that had been clamped to the metal trunk of the axis like a maple-sugar pail. "So light for something that ought to be so heavy with sin, yes?" The Nuncio frowned. "One wants to believe that only this few have gone astray, but it's like this at every Embassy." He shook his head.

"Pardon?" Cal had been looking at his watch. Fifty more minutes. His palms were slick with sweat. Only a priest could have killed a computer with so little concern. So damned smug and self-assured.

"Would you assist me?" the Nuncio asked. He was gathering the odds and ends of machinery into the overturned casing of the ruined interface, like returning deformed peas to their pod.

It occurred to Cal he might try blackmail. "Wouldn't that make me an accessory to a crime?" Cal asked sweetly.

"Your cybernetics law again?" said the Nuncio. "Of course, they must be especially important out here to people like you."

"What's that supposed to mean, people like me?"

"We try to observe all laws, of course," the Nuncio continued, ignoring Cal's question, "but when there is a conflict, God's law takes precedence over man's. It must."

Damn, the man was more persistent than a Depasian fly. "But if clones were still legal, your rule about artificial life not having a soul would mean I could shoot as many as I wanted."

The Nuncio looked startled. "Strange," he said.

"How do you mean?"

"That you should pick that example," the Nuncio said.

"I don't understand."

"Never mind. Mother Church condemned cloning from the start, but when in doubt, she has always erred on the side of caution—assuming the existence of a soul, just in case. The papal bull *De Homunculus* teaches that clones were a real—if unnatural—extension of the donor's soul. Just as, if I found you dying, I would administer last rites without asking if you were Catholic. For the sake of the immortal soul, better safe than—how do you say?"

"Sorry."

"Yes, sorry." He straightened, looked down at his greasy hands, shrugged and wiped them on his black robe. "It's the same principle."

Something told Cal to stop, but he found the idea of beating this priest with his own churchman's logic irresistible. "Still," he said, "inside this Legation is Federated Earth soil, and what you've done is a crime. I could have you arrested."

The Nuncio smiled. "You couldn't even if you wanted to. I have diplomatic immunity. By the same token, it would be impossible for me to bring you back to a Vatican tribunal."

Cal started. A Vatican tribunal? Had he already listened to the confessions? Did he *know?* "But, morally," he went on lamely, "there are, uh, well, for instance silicon life forms that operate on the same principle as the thing you've destroyed here. Are you saying you have the right to kill them?"

"A mechanical pump and a human heart operate also on similar principles, but that makes them not the same. This MUDD unit is a cousin to talking doors and floating chairs, not to man. Your silicon alien is another matter."

"My alien!" Cal sputtered.

The Nuncio seemed to study Cal for a moment. "Is there something you wished to speak to me about?"

"Of course not."

"Come, come, my son, we both know that representing a secular government can tempt one to impose an alternative morality to allow one to manage a morality of compromise."

Cal said nothing.

"I have no idea what your religion is. If you are a Catholic, I do not have to remind you how confession can lift the burden of guilt. If you are not, still I will help you if I may."

Cal remained silent. How much he wanted to have someone lift from his shoulders not only the weight of Drofsko's death and Grober's stroke, but also the responsibility for the bloodshed since and bloodshed yet to come. But he could think only of Hara listening from everywhere, like a disembodied spirit. To say even one word could destroy him and his career. It might even mean the difference between life and death for Grober. "I can't."

"Then there is something?"

"I didn't say that." Cal bit his lip. "But if there were, it would be a security matter anyway."

"I see. But in such a situation, you would be contrite?"

"Sorry I did something wrong? Of course."

"Though perhaps not for the right reasons," the Nuncio said. "Off-world diplomats tend to form an exclusive club, protective of its members and contemptuous of the planets where they serve."

Cal thought of the terrified nomads riding through the sawgrass, the shadow of his biplane swooping after them like a great, ravenous bird.

"You even have a term for yourselves," the Nuncio went on. "Immortals, I think."

"We don't really think we're literally immortal," Cal protested. "It's a joke about the time we spend in suspension traveling between posts. We wind up with more chronological years than people back home. It's a technicality, that's all."

"But there is an element of pride, also, yes?"

Cal shrugged.

"Do you regret breaking a divine commandment, or are you only disillusioned that not all members of your club observe the same rules?" When Cal hesitated, the Nuncio gave him a kindly smile. "It must be hard for you," he continued. "Here you are in deepest space, and instead of the spiritual help you need, you deserve, they send you a misprogrammed machine. MUDD is good enough for them, they say. It is an insult."

"If it's such a big deal, why don't you send out your own priests?"

"I'm afraid we couldn't."

"Why not?" Cal asked. He didn't like being told he'd been insulted when the insult was invisible to him. It made him feel stupid and foolish.

"For one thing, the Holy Father has forbidden it."

"And so the Home Office came up with a perfectly acceptable substitute, which you want to deny us. You won't do anything about it yourselves, but you refuse to let anybody else do anything as well? You know what I think? I think you don't care what the hell happens to us!"

"That isn't true."

"Don't hand me that," Cal said. "Here we are, up to our elbows in the dirt, trying to keep a home planet that we'll probably never see again safe for people like you, just so you can go around feeling morally superior."

"Have you ever wondered how you chose this life of voluntary exile?"

"Because I happen to love Earth and because I believe in its values. At least I used to."

"Patriotism, then," said the Nuncio.

"I guess you could call it that."

"Do you remember how you actually reached that decision? The precise moment?"

Cal thought for a moment, but he could find nothing but a dull and empty ache. "Sure."

"Describe it to me."

"I . . . it was about . . ."

"As predicted," muttered the Nuncio to himself. "You don't remember, do you?"

"Why should I?"

"Don't you think that's the sort of decision that would stick in a person's mind?" asked the Nuncio softly.

"Maybe I always wanted to be in the OWS," Cal said. Through his thoughts flitted like a creature amidst forest trees the image of his father. He remembered how it had sprouted tentacles and extra heads in his dream. "I just grew up wanting it. So there's no single moment." Cal glanced down at his watch. Forty-five minutes. "Does that make me a freak?"

"Hardly," said the Nuncio.

"Next I suppose you'll ask if I'm some kind of robot," Cal said.

"Not a robot, no."

Cal paused. The possibility of the unthinkable dawned. "What, then—a clone?"

The Nuncio shrugged. "Did you know there are rumors that many Home Offices maintain their deep-space off-world staffs with clones?"

"You hear things like that from time to time," Cal said. "But not Federated Earth."

"Of course not. A massive deception like that would not be possible, I am sure."

Cal eyed the Nuncio suspiciously. "But that's exactly

what you're implying, isn't it? Well, look—cloning's been illegal since the Social Security Wars. And not only that, but I remember everything else about my life on Earth before I joined the Off-World Service perfectly well."

"Yet a clone could be fed his donor's memories—with modifications," the Nuncio said. "Do you miss Earth?"

Cal hesitated. "You get used to being away." He cast a covetous eye on the black dump box. The irony, he thought. Here he was trying to save the life of this man who seemed to take genuinely perverse delight in tormenting him.

"You don't miss it, then."

Cal shook his head.

"I have never gotten used to the isolation and loneliness of being so far from my birthplace. But you accept it—and most other aspects of this job. Almost as if you had been programmed for it."

"Stop it!" Cal shouted furiously. "Just stop it!"

"Still, you might yet find your human origins."

"I'm perfectly human!"

"You could confess," the Nuncio went on.

"What is this, the Inquisition? I have nothing to confess!"

"There is clearly something troubling you, my son," the Nuncio said quietly. "If you cannot confess it to me, then perhaps a public disclosure might relieve this burden you carry. Who knows—the right kind of revelation might inspire a reform of your entire service."

Cal was silent, his brain whirling. Not genuinely human? A clone? A mere creation? Was such a systematic deception—the deception of every member of the Off-World Service—even possible? And in the teeth of all the laws? Was that the explanation for Hara's indifference to human pain and suffering, the reason for her insensitivity to basic tribal morals? No, it was too horrible. A prickly cold spread across Cal's scalp.

"Well," the Nuncio said, "I can't confess for you." He picked up the dump box. "But however much I may disapprove of MUDD, I think you have made the important beginning to come to it at all. This gives me hope. And

Mother Church's great strength is her patience. I shall try to make it mine."

"You're lying," Cal said.

"I know how difficult a thing it must be for you to admit, even as a possibility. The idea of our ultimate humanity is at the heart of our consciousness. Now to face the idea that your Home Office has chosen to fight its battles with a race created to live in perpetual exile. In effect, a race of slaves. Because if you are made to act through manipulation, through being kept in ignorance of the truth—then, indeed, you are in chains worse than any that can be forged of steel. And then to accept that you might be part of that race—"

"Do you seriously believe the Home Office would ever sponsor such an affront to human dignity?" Cal wiped his sweaty palms on his thighs, trying to calm himself. "Do you believe that I'm not a man but a *thing?*"

"I hardly think you're a thing," said the Nuncio. "A clone is a human unnaturally conceived, but it is not a thing."

"And I'm a clone? What proof do you have except your damned Jesuitical suspicions?"

"Have you ever met me before?" asked the Nuncio quietly.

"Of course not!"

"And have you ever been on Coracesium?"

"Our Embassy there? Never."

The Nuncio regarded Cal sadly. "I have been on Corecesium, my son. And I have met you—that is, a duplicate cloned from the same genetic materials. I knew from him those very doubts you, too, are facing."

"You presume too much," Cal said, striding toward the door. "How the hell do you know what doubts I'm facing?"

"Your double," said the Nuncio, "had murdered."

Cal slapped the square to slick the door shut as he lurched into the hall. Not real? Not real? Impossible. He stepped around a parked powerchair. He *was* real, he *was!* And he would goddamn well walk on his own two legs just to feel the goddamn human muscles working! Who the hell did the man think he was, slandering other people, making them doubt their own connection to Earth? It was insufferably pompous and presumptuous. How could a good man like Grober believe in the same tripe this . . . this . . .

Cal was startled by the beeping of his pager. He found himself at the metal landing of the stairs leading down into the garage bay.

"Yes," he said.

"I have a message to relay," Bascomb's voice said. "Hara wanted me to remind you about some job you're doing or something. She didn't explain, but she said to tell you to get back to it because there are still almost thirty minutes—"

"Tell Hara to get stuffed!" Cal barked. He threw his pager down onto the landing. It let out an ear-piercing squeal as it flipped up and skipped, clattering down the stairs.

"Mr. Troy? Cal?" called Bascomb's insect voice.

Wordlessly, Cal clanged down the metal steps after it. The hell with it. If there was only one way to get some peace and quiet, then that was the way he'd take. He mounted a hoverbike and touched it on. The motor rattled to life and lifted him an inch above the tarmac of the garage floor. He would ride somewhere—anywhere. He pulled the utility face net out of the compartment under the seat and tugged it on. He'd feel the rush of wind, the vibration of the hoverbike, he'd taste the dust. He'd be *alive!*

"Don't forget your salt tablets!" thundered the door as Cal's hoverbike slid out into the baking sunlight. He glanced over at the chancery, at the dusty explosions of flies disintegrating against row upon row of grids by the door.

If this man was going to denigrate Cal and all the other OWS officers who'd risked their lives and would go on risking their lives . . . the hell with him, that was all. The absolute hell with him. Whatever Hara did to him was better than he deserved.

He looked back to the road, his eyes slicing through the miles to the edge of prairie, stark against the horizon.

THE TIMESERVERS

Where would he go? What did it matter? As long as it was away from the Nuncio, from Hara, even from Grober.

It was nearly sunset when he found himself tiring. He eased back on the stubby handles, letting the hoverbike gradually right itself as the speed dropped. He'd been following one of the prairie roads—the west road, as a matter of fact. Stupid of him—this looked pretty near the airfield. Exactly the kind of area that would attract Superdeps looking for a military target. Place was probably crawling with them. He was just asking to be ambushed. He got ready to accelerate out.

"Anon, Francis?" said a voice.

Cal tensed, waiting for the report of a rifle. Nothing.

"No, Francis," said the voice.

Cal twisted to the right, then the left, trying to see who had spoken, but there was no one in sight. Had he stumbled on the Wailing Place he'd heard about?

"But tomorrow, Francis."

Wait a minute—that was English. Would even a Superdep call out in English like that? It didn't make sense. "Hello?" he shouted.

"But tomorrow, Francis."

Cal backed off on the idle to hear better. There was something terribly familiar about that voice.

"Or Francis, o' Thursday."

Cal put the bike in hold and dismounted. It was hard to tell direction because the wind kept shifting and the walls of sawgrass tended to soak up sounds in funny ways, like fog back on Earth.

There! Another Earth memory!

"Or, indeed, Francis, when thou wilt."

He had it now, a little to the left, apparently lying among the sawgrass roots just off the road.

"But, Francis . . ."

He still couldn't see anything. He knelt by the roadside, terrified that any second a dagger would thrust out from between the stalks. He reached gingerly amongst the deadly grass blades and felt around. His gloved fingers touched something hard.

" 'Wilt thou rob this leathern jerkin, crystal-button, not-pated, agate-ring, puke-stocking, caddis-garter, smooth-tongue, Spanish-pouch . . .' "

He pulled whatever it was out. A fire-blackened chunk of metal, perhaps from some kind of machine.

"Why, then your brown bastard is your only drink," the voice continued from the grass roots. "For look you, Francis, your white canvas doublet will sully. In Barbary, sir, it cannot come to so much."

Cal leaned in and pushed the stiff blades aside. There! It looked like . . . a face!

"I am now of all humors that have showed themselves humors since the old days of goodman Adam to the pupil age of this present twelve o'clock at midnight."

It was the face of the First Player that stared back at him from between the yellow stems. But one eye socket was black and empty, the other eye dark gray and glassy. And there was no body. The chunk of metal had been part of his ship, and here was the man's head. . . .

"Faith, if 'a be not rotten before 'a die . . ."

Talking? Yes, the jaw was unmistakably moving! Horrified, Cal reached in and slipped his hands under the head to draw it out. It was cold and leaden in his palms, and where he'd have expected blood about the torn flap of skin at the base of the skull, he saw instead a strange glint.

". . . as we have many pocky corses nowadays, that will scarce hold the laying in . . ."

Cal almost dropped the head in his fright when the jaw moved in his hand. And then he saw that the glint was a metal joint plate at the base of the skull, and the skin was egg-smooth and perfect. Plastic.

". . . 'a will last you some eight year or nine year. A tanner will last you nine year."

And by holding it at an angle, Cal could see into the mouth to make out the metal soundwand at the back of the throat. A robot, a goddamned robot! Not just the bit players—they'd *all* been robots!

For a moment he held the metal skull at arm's length. The sunlight bloodied one side of it.

"You poor jerk," he said. Then the anger, the resentment, the humiliation flooded through him. He cocked his arm and pitched the gruesome thing into the grass. It soared away like a basketball, clattered among the brittle stalks, was gone. If it spoke again, Cal didn't hear it.

All robots, created and programmed to lie about themselves, and sent out to . . . to entertain their near cousins.

The clones of the Off-World Service.

So the Nuncio had been telling the truth.

"Jesus—the *Nuncio!* He'd left him in the MUDD room to be killed! Suddenly, he hated it all: the OWS, the rulebook, the Haras and Townsends that poisoned everything. He was damned if he'd help them. He would save the Nuncio. He would stop him before he went back to his room. He would save him from Hara. And save Hara from herself.

If it wasn't too late.

He hopped up onto the hoverbike and gunned the throttle. It roared to life, smoked down the dirt road toward Embassy Row.

All the way back, Cal's mind buzzed with the welter of thoughts. Robots, clones, semiconductors, the creatures that had made up Drofsko. It was all one, wasn't it? All a single piece that distinctly wasn't what life on Earth was like. Aliens to deal with aliens—was that the Home Office's plan?

The hoverbike was overheating by the time he got to the garage. He tipped in so hard, he nearly lost control, skidded across the broad tarmac floor, killed the ignition, and hopped off just before it sailed into a pile of fuel drums. He ran up the stairs, leaped through the puffs of insecticide, charged full-tilt down the hall. No point in a powerchair—they had governors on them. He was faster on foot.

A sentribot swung its laser head around to deal with the intruder.

"Official business!" Cal shouted. "Official business!"

Reluctantly, the sentribot let him pass. He hopped into the elevator, drumming his fingers nervously on the door as it took forever to carry him down to the basement. Then out again and down the corridor to the doorway of the MUDD room.

The polyhedron leaned as it had before, but there was no sign of the Nuncio. Cal was too late.

CHAPTER THIRTEEN

CAL STOOD in the shadows of the MUDD room, staring at the wrecked machine. It took him a stunned moment to realize that maybe the damned priest had just left a few minutes ago. It might not be too late. He might still be able to catch him before he reached the death trap in his room. Cal spun on his heel and ran back the way he'd come, swung into the elevator, and palmed the fourth level for the tube to the guest quarters behind the chancery. The elevator did a kind of sideways leap into the tube, sliding swiftly across the space to the neighboring building and opening to deposit him in the foyer.

The mechanical eyes of a sentribot twisted on their stubby stalks to look at him balefully.

"Good evening, Mr. Acting Chief of Mission. May I be of service?"

"The Papal Nuncio," Cal said. "Has he come this way?"

"Checking, no."

"Is there any other way in? Would he have to come past you?"

"Affirmative."

Then he was still somewhere in the chancery. "Can you run an INT through the other sentribots for any sign of him?"

The machine floated impassively before him, giving no outward sign that it was checking in with each of its fellow sentribots. It was an incredible antique, all business in its machinish way. Didn't even have one of the more efficient turret heads. That was the problem with travel times measured in scores of years; the equipment in the places farther out was apt to be hopelessly outdated, like everything on Depaz. The newer bots acknowledged you with something a little more helpfully human, such as, "Excuse me," or "Just a minute, please," while they rotated through the strict protocols and priorities of their subroutines.

More human.

"No traces recorded, Mr. Acting Chief of Mission," said the sentribot a millisecond later.

"All right, then inform all guard posts that the Nuncio is to be detained if he's seen, and his safety secured. Make that a class-one voice order." That would keep Hara from countermanding it; only cancellations or modifications in Cal's own voice would be accepted. "And see that word gets to the Marine NCOIC."

Cal hurried back to the elevator. There was one other possibility—the Nuncio had gone to the reception after all. He glanced at his timepiece. It would be already beginning in the main hall of the chancery. He would try there.

When he reached the foyer, the change-hungry delegations from the other Embassies had already begun arriving, and the huge room was pungent with insecticide from the doors. Officers and OWSS clerks were laughing and joking among themselves, eager for this break in the dreary routine.

He saw Hannibal Myers by the buffet table. And Bascomb beside him. He looked away quickly, scanned the rest of the room for the Nuncio. No sign of him. If he wasn't here, where could he have gone? He had to get hold of himself. Hara had been quite clear about the trap being set up in the Nuncio's room, and Cal could count on the sentribots following his voice order to the letter. He looked back to find Bascomb stealing a glance at him. He decided to meet the challenge head-on. He headed toward the buffet table.

"Where iszh he?" hissed the Albarian chargé d'affaires, intercepting him halfway.

"The Nuncio?"

"I waszh never given a name, only that a new faszh had arrived. Where may I szhee it?"

Cal obligingly scanned the room a second time. "Doesn't seem to have got here yet," Cal said.

"Haszh anyone yet extracted from him the promiszh of dinner tomorrow night?"

"Not that I know of," Cal said.

"Thank Godszh. Another day I do not have to commit szhuiszhide."

"Nice weather, though," Gondolphi said, stepping up to join them.

A look of puzzlement spread through the Albarian's lizard face. "The weather haszh not changed for szheveral hundred year."

"Ah." Gondolphi nodded. "Lucky it's not raining then, eh?"

Cal excused himself and headed on toward the buffet. Myers was mournfully watching the ice transmute itself into rusty water under the dish of pseudoshrimp. Bascomb was still next to him.

"You seen the Nuncio?" he asked.

Bascomb flipped her hair back, a calculated gesture to show she didn't much care whether Cal had finally spoken to her or not. "No, did you lose him?"

Cal smiled gamely. "Just a little."

The conversation thrashed and rolled dead over in the water.

"So, how's everything been with you?" Cal said at last.

"Busy."

"Same here." She stared into her drink. "Air conditioning broke down in number two section of the compound, my section."

"Everything's always breaking down."

"Yes," she agreed. "Always."

And sank like a stone.

"I didn't mean it that way." He smiled to himself. Imagine a little artificial human like him, a mere mock-man, worrying over morals and emotions as though what he and Bascomb did or didn't do mattered any more than what the Ambassador's dog Trixie did. He knew he ought to move on, keep looking for the Nuncio, but suddenly he wanted her to know what he knew about both of them. He wanted to hurt her with it. He wanted to know they could both *feel*, even if it were pain.

"You remember home?" he asked abruptly.

"I beg your pardon?"

"Earth. You remember much about it?"

"Of course. What's got you on this kick again?"

"Curiosity. Tell me what you remember."

She pursed her lips thoughtfully. "You mean like where I grew up, who my parents were, where I went to school?"

"Sure."

She shrugged. "The usual, I guess."

"More specifically."

"Then name a topic."

"Parents."

"We've been over this. My father was an OWS officer with training in hydroponics engineering, and—"

"Did you go back to Earth for vacations?"

"What? I . . . I don't remember. Yes, a few times."

"What did your grandmother's bedroom look like?"

"I . . ." She looked confused.

"Never mind," Cal said, turning back to stare out into the blackness beyond the floor-to-ceiling windows. His arms felt heavy as lead; his eyes stung. He didn't want to hurt her after all. He didn't have the energy. "I guess it's no wonder."

"What's no wonder?"

"Never mind." He had to find the Nuncio.

"Are you still harping on that Nimrod mission?"

"I said never mind. Is there any word on Grober?"

She shook her head. "No change."

Nargom hopped onto the back of a straight chair and ticked his head in greeting. "I was told your Consul was taken ill."

"Yes," Cal nodded.

"If there is anything we can do . . ."

"Nothing, thank you," Cal said. "Your concern is appreciated, of course."

Suddenly, across the room, Cal saw the small, dark figure of the Nuncio. Under his arm was the black dump box. Wherever he'd been, he'd never gotten back to his room. Thank God. Mary Grober was with him, looking haggard, older than he'd ever seen her.

At that moment Baum appeared. "I need to talk to you," he said.

"Don't mind me," Bascomb said.

Cal watched the Nuncio anxiously, now deep in conversation with Mary Grober. "Can't it wait?"

"Not really. It's about Grober." Baum looked worried.

Cal excused himself and crossed with Baum along the arcade of floor-to-ceiling windows. "Any change?"

"It's not that," Baum said. "I just got a medibot report."

"And?"

"Well, for one thing, they want to do laser surgery to relieve the constriction of the blood vessels to the brain."

"Has there been permanent damage?" Cal asked. He felt a hope rising inside himself that the answer would be yes. He felt confused.

"They won't know till they go in." Baum paused, looked to either side, then up, as though he expected to find a listening device overhead. He moved closer to Cal. "They also sent a readout of the blood workup they did."

"They found something unusual?"

"Possibly. Traces of sawgrass toxins, a few other things, mainly supercoagulants, all native-grown."

"What do they make of it?"

"Well, heh-heh-heh, you know medibots. They aren't much on interpretation or analysis, but it sure looks like this seizure was, well . . ." Baum leaned even closer. "Artificially induced."

Cal leaned against one of the floor-to-ceiling windows, his face pressed against the cold glass to stare into the endless prairie night. The fly-grids by the outside ramp were on; through the glass he could just hear their crackling, see their brief burning in the dark, like fireflies over a blackened meadow back on Earth. Where'd that memory come from? A fake, he supposed. Angrily, he cleared it from his thoughts.

So Hara had told the truth. To a point. It *was* a Depasian

poison. Possibly she was also telling the truth about an antidote. In that case, if he helped the Nuncio get away, he could be condemning Grober to death. It was the kind of question a mere homunculus shouldn't be expected to have answers for.

Except he had to. There were no excuses, no ways out, no choices, except this overwhelming choice between one life and another. A friend and fellow golux versus a stranger and real human. Now he understood the strange feeling of hope that had crept into his voice when he'd asked about permanent damage. He'd been hoping he'd be spared the choice. He choked off his self-loathing. It was remarkable he'd been as concerned as he was. Remarkable for a simulacrum. Funny, back when he'd been . . . grown, he hadn't been programmed automatically to favor the human in the case. But of course, the OWS must never have expected any real humans ever to come in contact with him. Trust the Church to insist on the real McCoy, like the Nuncio. Trust a secular government to opt for counterfeit people.

"Okay," Cal said. He moved on, slowly, not quite in the Nuncio's direction. What would he do? There was still a chance, the least chance, that getting the dump box would be enough. He would try that.

He approached the Nuncio, smiling broadly. "I tried to find you, but you'd left the MUDD room and you weren't in your room."

"Ah, yes." The Nuncio smiled back. "The elevator was at the time—how do you say? On the freeze?"

"Fritz."

"Bless you. Anyway, I could not get to the room, and I was looking for the back stairs when I find myself here."

"This is the reception, Your Excellency. The one in your honor."

"Yes, I guess that. I see you are not so angry at my words as you were before."

Cal squeezed his hands together and forced another smile. "No, of course not."

"None of the hard feelings?"

"None, Your Excellency. I realized the answer is unknowable, so there is no point distressing ourselves seeking it."

"The possibility is perhaps a hard thing to accept."

"I'd rather not talk about it." Cal looked about nervously. Still no sign of Hara. "You, ah, still have that dump box, I see."

"What?" The Nuncio followed Cal's eyes to the black box under his arm. "Oh, yes, yes." He shook his head, his face a mixture of sadness and anger.

"Is anything wrong?" Cal asked.

"Oh, no, I suppose not. In one sense I should let them decide to come or not, but those who confess thinking true absolution was obtain may not know how grave their risk. I must canvass your staff, I suppose."

"I'm afraid I don't understand."

"And then I promise Mrs. Grober I will see the ill husband."

"But what were you saying about the—?"

"Ah, Mr. Nunszhio!" hissed the Albarian, elbowing his way in front of Cal. "Are you occupied for dinner tomorrow night? I wiszh you to know that the Albarian Legaszhion iszh known all over Depaszh for the quality of mealszh and of szherviszh. If you will only—"

"I am afraid," the Nuncio said, "that I can—"

"Aha!" cheeped Nargom, hopping up. "I have been *dying* to speak with you, sir. When word came that you had completed the journey from—"

"But I must see—" the Nuncio was saying.

"Perhapszh a light szhupper—"

Cal found himself being propelled slowly but inexorably away from the Nuncio by the growing circle of diplomats constricting around His Excellency in swirls of colorful and exotic alien costumes like an organic whirlpool.

"Help!" Cal called in a small voice.

And just as quickly, the crowd dispersed. And somehow the Nuncio was gone, too!

Cal caught sight of Mrs. Grober. "Where is he?" he asked.

"Oh, Cal," said Mrs. Grober. "You startled me!"

"Mrs. Grober, it's important. Where's the Nuncio?"

"He's gone down to his room to freshen up, I think. He promised to check in on Frank, and—"

"Damn!" He turned on his heel and sprinted toward the elevator bank. But the elevator was in use. Probably the Nuncio himself up there on it. Anxiously, he waited for the machine to complete its trip and return.

If it could just keep from breaking down this once.

In another few moments, the door clicked open and he skipped in.

"Floor?" asked the machine.

With a series of ominous rattles and sighs, the elevator staggered up and across toward the guest quarters.

A sentribot met him when the door opened.

"I am sorry sir no one is to see the Nuncio."

"Look, I'm the one who ordered the Nuncio protected," Cal said, trying to push past. "Check the voice print with the central securibot."

"I am sorry sir no one is to see the Nuncio," the sentribot repeated, blocking him.

"Check the voice print, you miserable pile of junk!"

The Gunny appeared at the end of the corridor. "That won't be necessary."

"Thank goodness for human beings," Cal said. "You want to let me by?"

"I'm afraid I can't do that, sir," the Gunny said. "I'm afraid you'll have to get back on that elevator."

"What?"

"Sorry, sir, but we've got updated orders from another source, and there're no exceptions listed."

"But I'm Acting Chief of Mission," Cal said.

"Begging the ACM's pardon, but this was command priority Zed."

"I'm countermanding it, then," Cal said.

"Sorry again, sir, but I'm afraid a priority Zed can't be countermanded."

"Jesus," Cal said. "I can't keep track of this goddamn bureaucracy. I never heard of such a code! But look here, something terrible is going to happen if the Nuncio isn't kept out of that room! Are you prepared to take full responsibility?"

A heavy hand closed on Cal's arm.

"That won't be necessary. The responsibility's mine." Hara's eyes glittered from beneath the folds of flesh, her mouth drawn up in a smile that dug up into the heavy gray slabs of cheek.

"I—"

"Don't you think you ought to get back to the guests?"

"I'm here to see about the Nuncio. He *is* down in his room, isn't he?"

"Have you been to see Grober?" Hara said.

"I haven't had time."

"They tell me he's resting comfortably. No change, though." Hara's eyes drifted toward the corridor's line of windows.

"Are you saying you have a way to make a change?" Cal asked.

"Me? I'm no doctor." Hara's face was a mask of innocence.

"Don't hand me that. You're implying that if I go away and pretend I don't know what's going to happen or who's hiding on the roof outside that man's window or whatever it is—"

"I'm saying nothing of the sort," Hara said blandly.

"The hell you're not," Cal said. He stared into Hara's eyes, trying to sort it out, trying to find some tail of a real truth he could grab on to. Was Hara really offering him Grober's life? Did she have that power? And if she were, should he take it or not? In her eyes he saw reflected his own distorted face, swimming in the gold-brown flecks of her irises. And it seemed to him at that moment that his face somehow began to look like hers, old, slabby, gray. If he accepted the compromise she offered, it would be at her altar he would worship. He, too, would become a timeserver.

He rubbed his nose as though to clear the incense of the insecticide from his nostrils.

A sharp cry came from down the hall.

All at once Cal shouldered Hara into the Gunny, yanked the laser out of the Gunny's hands, and shoved them both into the sentribot. The Marine caught the machine on a corner without its airbrakes set, and it spun around wildly as the Gunny dropped past and sprawled on the floor. At the same instant, Cal gave Hara a hard shove and sprinted down the hall and rounded the corner.

There was a second cry just ahead.

Cal put his shoulder to the door and slammed himself against it. It slipped open automatically. Surprised, the Nuncio looked up from the center of the room.

"Oh, excuse me," Cal said, just barely catching himself before he'd lost his balance. "I thought I heard something."

"My mistake—silly of me. For a moment I think I see somebody on the roof outside my window."

At that instant, a wave of window glass spewed into the room, followed by two shadowy figures and a roaring swarm of flies. Cal fired blindly at the first, batting at the swirls of insects to keep his eyes clear.

"Ach!" cried the Depasian, dropping to the floor. The second froze where he landed. Down the hall came the sound of running feet—the Gunny and Hara. Cal fired, and the second Depasian crumpled and dropped.

"You've shot him!" the Nuncio gasped.

"They were trying to kill you, Your Excellency," Cal said. "And now we've got to get out of here! Your life's in danger!"

"Who could believe such a thing?"

Cal swatted at the flies. "Do you believe these two bodies on the floor?"

"Yes, I must. But why?"

"I'm afraid it's that box under your arm."

The Nuncio looked down at the dump box. "But this is the matter of religion. . . ."

There was no time to waste. Cal lunged to the door and shut it, then palmed the lock. "It won't hold them long, but maybe we can get away across the roof."

"You are joking, yes?" the Nuncio said.

A fist hammered at the door. "You'd better let us in, sir. I'm afraid I'm going to have to place you under arrest."

For the first time Cal realized the full enormity of what he'd done. In one moment he'd caught a loose thread and pulled the entire garment of his life apart. He was finished, ruined. He looked unhappily at the little man he'd traded his career for.

"You'd better open up, sir, or we'll have to shoot our way in," shouted the Gunny outside.

"You'd better do as they say, my boy," called Hara's voice.

"We've got to go, sir," Cal said, waving away the flies. The emergency insecticide sprinkler began to mist the room from the ceiling.

"Go?" coughed the little man. "Where?"

"God knows, sir. Maybe into Kabugar, if we can get around to the garage by the roof."

"But I cannot do such a thing. I have made a solemn promise to Mrs. Grober that I would see her husband."

"But we can't."

"We must. The man may be dying. It is my priestly duty to administer the last rites."

"But—"

"A duty is a solemn obligation before God."

Cal thought of his own duty and how he had betrayed it.

"Open up in there!" shouted the Gunny, banging on the door. "We're going to shoot."

"All right," Cal said. "It's possible we can get to the infirmary section by going across the roof here. God knows they won't be expecting us to do anything that crazy. Come on. Out the window."

He whacked several shards of glass out of the way with his fist and stepped through onto the roof and into a storm of flies attracted by the light. Then he reached back to help the Nuncio down. The Nuncio hesitated, then tossed the dump box back onto the bed and stepped onto the ledge.

"You don't need that?" Cal asked, puzzled, puffing at flies.

"Need it? Young man, it is completely worthless. It is empty."

Holy shit, Cal thought. If only he'd known that before he smacked Hara in the mouth.

There was an explosion at the door and a snarl of

buzzing as flies darted away in every direction. The laser outside had drilled into the lock.

"Come on," Cal said. "Unless you want to die of fly bites or laser bolts, we've got to go!"

CHAPTER FOURTEEN

THEIR FEET CRACKLED on the roof's dry gravel and years of fly carcasses as they ran. On either side were sudden surges of purple light from the racks upon racks of fly grids, throwing sudden, monstrous shadows across one side or the other and silhouetting them against the brightness. Behind them was a smash and tinkling.

"They've come through the window," Cal panted.

Pha-zha-zha-ziinng, buzzed a roof-mounted grid just above their heads.

A bright needle of yellow light stabbed through the darkness overhead. Cal glanced over his shoulder to see one of the sentribots already sweeping along the rooftop toward them, nearly opposite the still sizzling grid. Barely thinking it through, Cal steadied his pistol in both hands to aim, and fired at the base of the grid tower. The first support melted, the second popped under the additional stress, and the tower swung back on itself. The sentribot tried to coast over it, but a guy wire looped around its laser arm yanked it back in an arc that swung it head-first into the live grid. There was a horrific buzzing and then an explosion. Fire and debris shot out in every direction.

"That'll slow them down," Cal called to the Nuncio.

He felt odd up here. Giddy. He'd never been on top of the building before, and he had to keep translating the roof shapes into the rooms below. That wing there was likely his old D-level office complex, and there was the skylight over the foyer and main reception area. Occasionally out of the inky dark ahead, an activated grid's purple surge would throw into relief the long arch of the elevator tube running between the chancery and the staff quarters. It would be a hell of a risk, taking the frail Nuncio across the top of that with nothing but empty space between them and the ground four stories below. But that was where they had to go. Not that he had any plan for them once they got there; it was just that of all the places in the compound, that was the least likely to be under heavy guard. His own place would be watched, of course, but maybe the Grobers' . . .

He glanced back. Behind them, flames licked into the sky, and water from the autosprinklers made fanciful arcs in the purple flashes.

"Look, we've bought ourselves a little time. The safest thing would be to head across there to the staff housing and maybe find a way through the fence."

"The hospital is there?" the Nuncio asked.

"Oh," Cal said. "The hospital. No." His eyes picked across the rooftop's odd geometry until he'd found what was the infirmary wing. "But we've got a chance to get away now. Even if they aren't waiting for us in the hospital, the risk would—"

"I am sorry, my son," the Nuncio said. "You go on, of course. But I must keep a promise."

"I can't leave you alone up here."

"Do not be alarm. I am quite happy with the heights. They do not bother me at all. When I was the young man before seminary, I paint the tall building, yes?"

"I see."

"So you go ahead. Just please to tell me which is the place where I go, okay?"

"I can't do that," Cal said. If this man could be so dedicated, then Cal could do no less. "I'll take you."

The infirmary roof was two levels below. The only way down the first was a set of rungs on one of the fly-grids. Cal went first, followed by the Nuncio. Above them the grid buzzed and surged, and wisps of fly ash drifted down like Vermont snow to settle on their shoulders and in their hair. But at least the constant working of the grids kept the number of free flies low, and Cal and the Nuncio were able to keep from being too badly bitten as they made their way across the roof to the last descent.

Cal led them to the edge, then onto a weight-sensitive ladder that dropped them slowly downward to an arm of building sticking into the eastern darkness. A square of light, the skylight, glowed in the center beyond them, speckled with moving flies.

"That's it, Your Excellency," Cal said. "All we have to do is find a way in."

"It is surprise," the Nuncio said. "For a place so concern with security, the roofs is very open."

"That's because to get here, you have to get over a high-voltage fence, and no Depasian has ever done that."

"Except the ones that take your Ambassador?"

"Yes," Cal said. "Except those."

"But couldn't they just have themselves dropped in?"

"Not till we gave them the technology of flight. Now I guess they could do precisely that."

They reached the skylight and peered in. Below them was the infirmary corridor. A medibot floated in readiness by one wall. Otherwise everything was empty. The skylight had been sealed, and alarm tapes ran around the edges of the glass. They could smash it and drop down, Cal thought, but that would only alert the guards. And the flies might harm the other patients.

Somewhere there had to be a maintenance hatch.

It was the Nuncio who found it. Or rather tripped over it. It was locked, but it yielded to the tube of Cal's master sonikey. Cal went down the ladder first, followed by the Nuncio.

"Good evening sirs how may we help you?" asked a medibot.

Cal licked his lips. There must be a lot of confusion topside for the sentribots not to have reported in to the masterbot and had an all-points sent out to all nonhuman personnel. Either luck was finally falling his way or the Nuncio had a real connection to God.

"We've come to see the Consul General."

"There is no change I am sorry."

"We wish to see him, anyway," Cal said. "I'm ACM."

"Yes Mr. Troy I recognize you I will take you to his room."

The medibot rotated and floated noisily before them down the corridor to the third door on the left. It started to slick open, caught on something, jammed.

"We beg your pardon I will notify Maintenance please be patient."

"Don't bother," Cal said, taking out the laser pistol. "I've seen these fixed before. It's just a minor repair."

He melted the door and powertrain, then wrapped some gauze around his hands to protect his palms and forced the door back.

Grober lay motionless on his float in the dim light, a blockish patch of white. His eyes were open, staring up at the ceiling, blank and empty as mirrors.

"Peace to this house," said the Nuncio, "and to all who dwell therein."

"Oh, Father," said a voice. "Thank God you've come. After I got here, I heard there'd been some kind of trouble and—" She saw Cal. "You!"

"Hello, Mrs. Grober," Cal said.

"They said it was you that damaged a sentribot, dragged His Excellency out on the roof—"

"Please, Mrs. Grober," Cal said, taking a step toward her. "Try to calm down."

"Don't you come near me! I know what happened—I know what happened to Frank! It was *you!*"

Cal halted, stunned. "Me? What did I do?"

"As if you didn't know."

The Nuncio looked from one to the other, confused. From a small container he had taken the corporal and spread it on the night table by Grober's head. On this he had placed the Sacrament. "Daughter, son, please. It is not right to fight like this. And in the room of one afflicted where I am to perform the communion of the sick!"

Cal's eyes went back for a moment to the still form hovering on its sheet-covered float, then back to Mrs. Grober. She stood staring at him, trembling, then slowly sank down into an unpowered chair by the window, her face in her hands. "How could you, Cal?" she sobbed. "How could you?"

"How could I what, Mrs. Grober?"

"Demand his resignation! With only a few months to go! No wonder the poor man collapsed!"

"But I never—"

"Don't tell me that, Cal. I just wish that were all. But to actually suggest using nukes when you knew we'd been posted on Avvanos—"

"That's a lie!"

"I'm sorry, Cal, but I know for a fact that you did."

"How could you possibly know something like that for a fact?"

Mrs. Grober dabbed at the tears in her eyes. "I was told by someone who was there."

"Who?"

"I don't think it would be appropriate for me to say."

"Of course," Cal said. "I should have known. It was Hara, wasn't it?"

Mrs. Grober said nothing.

"Mrs. Grober," said the Nuncio. He was standing by Grober's float, a green stole around his neck. He genuflected, then motioned for them all to kneel. From his container he removed a vial of holy water and sprinkled each in turn with it.

"Thou shalt sprinkle me with hyssop, O Lord, and I shall be cleansed: Thou shalt wash me, and I shall be made whiter than snow."

His voice droned on, and Cal's thoughts slipped away to worlds where there were snow, to places where men might be cleansed.

"The confiteor, Mrs. Grober," whispered the Nuncio "You must say it for him, in his name."

And then Cal heard her voice quavering: "I confess to Almighty God, to Blessed Mary, ever Virgin, to Blessed Michael the Archangel, to Blessed John the Baptist, to the Holy Apostles Peter and Paul, and to all the Saints, and to you, Father, that I have sinned exceedingly in thought, word, and deed."

She struck her breast three times, her eyes on her husband's closed eyes.

"Through my fault, through my fault, through my most grievous fault. Therefore I beseech Blessed Mary, ever Virgin, Blessed Michael the Archangel, Blessed John the Baptist, the Holy Apostles Peter and Paul, and all the Saints, and you, Father, to pray to the Lord our God for me."

"May Almighty God have mercy on you, forgive you your sins, and bring you to life everlasting," the Nuncio said. He looked at them expectantly.

"Amen," they said.

"May the almighty and merciful Lord grant you pardon, absolution, and forgiveness of your sins." The Nuncio genuflected. "Behold the Lamb of God, Who takest away the sins of the world. O Lord, I am not worthy that Thou shouldst enter under my roof, but only say the word and my soul shall be healed."

"Thank you, Father," Mrs. Grober said when the Last Rites had been said. "Thank you for helping Frank into the other world."

"He is not there yet," said the Nuncio. "Still there is hope."

"Mrs. Grober," Cal said. "Please believe me that it isn't true, what Hara said."

She looked at Cal for several moments. "No, I guess I knew you couldn't have done such a thing."

"You know I loved your husband. I loved him very much, like a father."

Mrs. Grober sank back into her chair. "Yes," she said. "I suppose you did. I suppose you did."

"We'd better go," Cal said. "They're looking for us all over the chancery. They'll be here before long."

"I will stay with your husband," said the Nuncio.

"No, don't," said Mrs. Grober. "Cal's right—you'd better go. You've done all that can be done."

Cal hesitated, then kissed the old woman lightly on the cheek. He paused to look at the silent form, mouth slightly open, chest barely moving with each breath. "Good-bye," he said.

He led the Nuncio by a back way to a corner near the elevators, then went ahead to check. No watch-standers or sentribots; it seemed every available hand had been called back to the chancery to help with the search. Swiftly, the elevator whisked them over the courtyard to the staff bungalow section of the compound. From there they could see the lights and the silhouetted figures of Marines and sentribots scouring the rooftops.

Cal brought the Nuncio past his own bungalow. The Gunny and one of his corporals were seated on the sofa inside, just visible in the soft light thrown from the bedroom. Cal motioned for the Nuncio to be quiet, then struck out between two other houses to the rear of Bascomb's place. He looked to see if anyone was watching, then drilled through the doorlock with his laser and stepped inside.

Bascomb was seated at the living room window running a brushgun through her hair. Cal stood in the doorway, arrested by the halo of hair streaming out from the gun's fingers of air like tongues of fire.

She looked frightened when she saw him. "What the hell are *you* doing here?" she said.

Cal put his fingers to his lips and moved along the wall to peer out the window. Whorls of resting flies and speckles of fly dirt almost hid the flat, black line of the prairie in the distance. He had to crane his neck to see the chancery from here. Still enough activity to suggest they hadn't yet decided to look elsewhere in earnest. Then he glanced down. He thought he saw something moving in the grass, but when he stared more closely, there was nothing. He slipped an SU into the soundbox and let the music fill the room.

"Isn't that a little loud?" Bascomb asked, trying to be calm.

Cal gestured toward the chancery, did a little dumb show, suggesting everything that was said could be heard.

"Don't be silly," she said. She had recovered enough to nod a good evening to the Nuncio.

"What's happened to you?" she asked, looking at his face.

Cal touched his own cheek, felt the welts. "We were out in the open without protection for a bit," he whispered.

"You're the ones all the excitement's about?" she asked.

"Yes."

"Well, well. I didn't know. I left the party early."

"Bascomb, what would you do if the life of a fellow human being were in jeopardy?" Cal asked.

"Do whatever I could to help him."

"You mean that?"

Bascomb put down her hairgun. "Of course I mean it."

Cal gestured for her to keep it going. "Don't stop, keep brushing," he said. "You're sure you mean it?"

"How could you think anything else?" she said.

"Then help us," Cal said.

She shook her head. "Then why not just ask me? Why this charade about human beings in jeopardy to con me?"

"Because we're wanted by Mission Security."

"What for? Espionage? Criminal activity? Insanity?"

"Come off it," Cal said. "You know me."

"Yes, don't I, though," she said. "You're the one who taught me respect for regulations if I recall, and according to regulations, it's my obligation as an OWS officer to alert security to the presence of any person, thing, or alien life form which is known or believed to constitute a threat to the security, well-being, or success of the Mission."

"Damn you," Cal said.

She smiled. "I think it's about time I called Townsend or the sentribot."

"Please?" Cal said.

"I knew you could be more conciliatory. What is it you want?"

"Two hoverbikes just on the other side of the fence," Cal said.

"That's all?"

"That's all."

"But where would you go?"

"I . . . I hadn't thought about that. Maybe somewhere in Kabugar."

"To do what, join the rebels?"

"No, of course not," Cal said. "Maybe make contact with

one of the other Embassies to help us meet tomorrow's autoshuttle and get the Nuncio back to his ship. After that—who knows?"

"Are you going with him?" she asked.

"I don't know. Right now his safety's my only worry."

Bascomb bit the tip of her thumb for a moment, concentrating. "All right," she said. "I'll arrange to have someone bring them around to the fence down below."

"Do you have two spare face nets?"

"In the locker over there," she said, pointing. Then she pulled on her coat and slipped out the front door.

Cal waited fifteen minutes, then led the Nuncio out the back way and down the slight incline to the roadway. Farther along in either direction twinkled the lights of the other Embassies. There was another possibility, now that he'd had a little time to think. They could go to any one of those Embassies and ask for political asylum. It would delight the Albarians, that was for sure. And it would serve Hara right. At least the Albarians weren't counterfeits.

At least he didn't think they were.

Cal waited until he saw the headlamps of the two hoverbikes, then burned his way through the fence and helped the Nuncio duck under. Above his head the alarm sounded.

"Here you are," Bascomb said. Her mouth was a thin line. On the other hoverbike sat a Depasian servant.

"Look," Cal said. "I'm sorry."

"Sure you are. I guess I'll see you sometime." She dismounted, gesturing to the Depasian to do the same, and stood watching as Cal helped the Nuncio mount, then got on his own.

"You want to double up and ride back?" Cal asked. "I could drop you right in front of the Mission."

"No."

"It's dangerous. There's rebels—"

"Forget it," she said. "Just go. It would be worse if anybody saw me with you. And the sooner you're out of my life, the better."

Cal nodded to the Nuncio and gunned his machine. It tipped forward down the dusty road in the moons' light.

The fantastic shapes of Embassy Row were all around them.

Suddenly, from behind, Cal heard a monstrous *burring*. He looked over his shoulder and saw one of the new armored hovercars swinging out from behind the Embassy, blazing with searchlights.

"Damn!" he shouted. "She's tipped them off! We've got to try to outrun them."

The two hoverbikes skimmed along the roadway, rocking from side to side, barely in control. A second spotlighted hovercar now swung out of the Legation garage behind the first. But at that moment, more lights appeared ahead. A third hovercar.

There was no place to go except into the prairie, a dangerous move at best. Suddenly, Cal noticed the silent black shape of an unlighted building just off to their left. Drofsko's deserted Si Embassy!

"Cut your headlight, Your Excellency!" Cal called.

"Which button do that?"

"On the right above the speedometer. Now cut over toward that dark shape over there."

Cal swung around a clump of sawgrass, blocking the view from the road long enough to give him hope that he would at least confuse their pursuers. If he could just get around behind the building and hide the machines . . .

Moments later they found themselves behind the Embassy. It was like a huge, artificial mountain, undulating with strange knobs and protrusions. Cal couldn't help a twinge at the recollection of Drofsko back at the start of all this. To think how his life had centered around Drofsko and his stories. And then he saw the moons' light shining through some kind of opening. Was he just seeing the moons reflected from a window? No, it was light from a skylight or something falling out an open door. The wretched Depasian servant had obviously forgotten to lock up before the last time he wandered off and got himself polluted with *miship*.

Cal waved to the Nuncio, gunned his machine, and veered over and through the opening. He found himself inside a single, cavernous room that filled the mountain shape, heard a sudden, thunderous echo all around him, and redoubled as the Nuncio followed close behind. He shut down the power as soon as he'd reached the cover of the shadows by the wall, felt his hoverbike clunk onto the hard ground, and the Nuncio did the same. The engine sound echoed away into the desultory buzzes of the occasional flies, which had not yet been rendered immobile by the gathering evening chill.

Searchlights from the hovercars on the road beyond stabbed the darkness outside, swept back and forth, threw up great and terrible shadows on the wall, but no one came near. It was long past midnight when the shouts and sounds finally died away.

"I think we've made it," Cal whispered.

"Yes." The Nuncio smiled. "So far so well."

"Good."

"Exactly."

"There's probably emergency food in the saddlebags on the back of the hoverbike," Cal said. "I think the best thing would be to sit back here and relax till we're sure the Embassy people have gone back inside."

They sucked on the tasteless food tablets quietly. Afterward, leaning back against the stone wall, Cal found himself looking at the Nuncio, wondering.

"Tell me something," Cal said.

"Anything, my friend," said the Nuncio.

"When we got out of your room, you left the dump box. You said it was empty."

"Yes. How will I canvass your staff now?"

"I don't understand."

"For anyone who went to this wretched machine for absolution. One subsidiary reason Mother Church object to this machine is the memory, you understand? It is not right that a confession should be stored. What is said is passed to the priest and then to God; it should not be saved. But given that they were, I thought at least that vice could be turn to the account of good to tell me what was confessed. The confession all be anonymous, but at least I discover the nature of the sin, if any are mortal."

"And you couldn't?"

"Did I not say the box was light? Your MUDD has one of the new zero-access devices."

"Excuse me?"

"When the tap was initiated, all memory was wiped clean."

"What?" Cal said. "The machine had nothing in it?"

"Exactly."

"You mean I've flushed my career down the toilet for nothing? There was nothing in that dump box that could get out?"

The Nuncio nodded. "Nothing."

Cal let out one long, horrible, hysterical laugh, echoing back and forth again and again before it was finally swallowed by the darkness. He lay there, too weak to move, too weak even to speak further. He'd lost everything, absolutely everything.

He felt the Nuncio's cold hand on his arm.

"Mr. Troy," whispered the Nuncio.

"Yes?"

"Open your eyes, please."

"What for? What's to see anymore?"

"Maybe," the Nuncio said slowly, "all the people standing in the doorway."

CHAPTER FIFTEEN

CAL OPENED HIS EYES. The shapes in the doorway were at first indistinct against the night sky outside. It shouldn't have surprised him, though, he thought. He shouldn't have expected to get away with such a half-baked, last-minute plan. Not from Hara or the entire Marine contingent. A pipe dream, that's what it had been. A silly-ass pipe dream. Funny, though, that they should run him to Earth in Drofsko's old Embassy.

"They are here," called one of the silhouettes to the others, "just as it was foretold."

"All right, put the cuffs on." Cal sighed, holding out his arms and standing up.

"Your pardon, please?" asked another of the silhouettes. His voice rang as he came into the room. Several hardier flies looped out, disturbed by the noise.

This time Cal caught something wrong with the sound of the voice, the pronunciation.

"Isn't that you, Gunny?" Cal said. "Aren't you guys Marines?

"What means Marines?"

"Superdeps!" Cal whispered to the Nuncio.

"Scusi, please?" said the Nuncio.

"Never mind. I don't know whether to laugh or cry."

"You will come with us," the man said, coming closer. "It will be necessary to conceal you."

"What do you mean foretold?" Cal asked, again surprised to find a Depasian speaking English.

"This way, please."

"Now wait a minute," Cal said, planting his feet to resist. "I want to get some idea of what's going on."

The man stopped in front of him, his face muffled in the usual nomad style. There was something strange about the way the man acted, a kind of delay, as though his muscles had to hold committee meetings to decide on his next movement.

"They said I might have to reason with you," the man said. Suddenly, his arm arced up with something at the end of it. There was an explosion of light and noise inside Cal's head as the weighted sling collided with the side of it, and Cal sank to the ground.

Cal's head ached. That was the first and central fact he was aware of. Then his eyes opened to a grainy, tannish glow. It took him a moment to realize that he was staring at the inside of a piece of canvas, lit by the sun outside. The air was hot and close. He could feel himself jounced by the movement of whatever he was lying on. His hands were tied behind his back.

Suddenly, there was a shrill shriek somewhere ahead.

He was on a *mels*, lurching behind a steam tractor. The realization had a further significance: *Mels* were reserved to the upper classes; that meant that these people had connections at the highest levels.

He felt something jouncing against his back.

"Is that you, Your Excellency?"

"Yes," came the voice behind him.

"Did they tie you, too?"

"Yes."

"Shit."

"Scusi?"

"Nothing," Cal said. He began to twist his wrists inside his bonds. He found the rope just slightly loose. He tried to collapse his and slip it out of the loop that bound his wrist. It would not. He tugged, stretching the skin on his wrist until it burned.

"How many of them are there?" Cal asked.

"I did not count."

Cal tugged again against the rope. This time it cut the

flesh. It seemed woven out of green sawgrass shoots. A fly that had gotten under the tarp crawled upside down along the canvas, dropped onto Cal's cheek. He puffed at it, but it continued its exploration of his face.

He tugged a third time, and all at once his hand pulled free. Cautiously, he reached out, brushed away the fly, and pushed the canvas aside enough to peek out.

As he'd expected, they were somewhere out on the prairie. The sun beat down fiercely on them.

"Gadzooks!" came a distant shout.

"What is that?" asked the Nuncio's voice behind Cal.

"Your guess is as good as mine," Cal said.

" 'But screw your courage to the sticking point, and we'll not fail,' " shouted a female voice from a different direction.

And suddenly Cal did know.

"Dramaturgbots," he said. "The prairie's full of them."

"Scusi?"

"Never mind. But that must mean we're headed west." He rolled back, exhausted. What good, after all, would he accomplish by freeing his hands? Just another pointless exercise, like trying to stand up to Hara.

He heard something that sounded like the distant drone of an aircraft, one of the *elik* assault bombers. At one point it seemed to thunder directly overhead, but then it swooped off and the sound receded and died.

Cal relaxed his neck, let his head settle as well as it could on the jouncing bed of the *mels*. His forehead pounded with the pain of last night's blow, and he wrapped his ropes around his wrists as best as he could to simulate being still tied, then let himself drift off to sleep again.

When Cal woke again, it was evening; and the tarp had darkened with the descent of the sun. All at once the canvas was pulled back, revealing a swarthy nomad face grinning against the darkening sky. He balanced himself against the lurching of the *mels*, then reached down and pulled first Cal and then the Nuncio into a sitting position. Behind him more nomads, all armed, and still more clinging to the seat and steps of the shuddering steam tractor. The man grinned at his prisoners, opened a soiled handkerchief to reveal clots of what apparently was food.

"Eat?" he asked.

Cal looked at the grime under the man's fingernails. He shook his head.

"It is the fly bites." The man laughed. "You get used to them by and by. What about the one in *pulgarg*-black?"

The Nuncio opened his mouth, and the nomad dropped one of the clots into it.

"How is it?" Cal asked.

"Awful," said the Nuncio. "But it is probably nutritious. *They* thrive on it, at least."

"All right," Cal said to the man, "I suppose I should keep my strength up."

"The Master will appreciate it."

"The Master?" Cal said. "Who's the Master?"

"That is not for me to say," said the nomad. "You will see soon enough."

They traveled all night by the moons' light. When dawn finally came, Cal had stopped trying to guess the miles or the direction. He never had learned the Depasian constellations. The nomad rolled out the tarp and covered them with it again. His purpose was clearly to keep Cal and the Nuncio from being seen by scouts from above.

And then, a little later, he heard the tractor shudder, then felt the *mels* tip down an incline. He managed to peek out. It was one of Weston's excavations.

The grass had been beaten down all around the periphery of the pit by something like a steamroller. But the steam tractor clanged and stammered on, down into the center of the pit toward what seemed to be an opening in the excavation wall. A cave! Into the darkness they lurched.

Every now and then a torch could be seen flaring against the cave wall, held in place by a metal bracket. What struck Cal was the apparent antiquity of the place, a corridor vast enough to accommodate a steam tractor and *mels* hewn out of what he now saw was bedrock, and ornamented, whenever the occasional torch allowed him to see it, with skillful carvings of birds and beasts, which, if they ever existed on Depaz, had disappeared eons ago.

At last the tractor stopped, and Cal and the Nuncio were helped down off their perch.

"Mr. Troy," said the nomad, "there is no longer any reason for you to pretend to be tied."

Cal tried to mask his astonishment.

"Really," said the nomad, "there is nowhere you can go. Here, Your Excellency, allow me to cut your bonds, as well."

Cal let his hands hang by his sides.

"This way," said the nomad, lifting up a torch and lighting the entrance to a small side tunnel. Cal and the Nuncio ducked under the entryway and followed obediently. At last they came to the end of the artificially formed corridor. Beyond, flickering in the light of too few torches, opened a huge cavern. There seemed to be some kind of indistinct shape at the far end, surrounded by a kind of aura or force field or shield. Through Cal's mind flashed the swallowing horror of his nightmare.

"Welcome, Cal, my dear," buzzed a familiar voice. "A pleasure to see you again."

Not a force field but a sphere!

"Come in, come in," buzzed the voice. "And you, too, please, Your Excellency."

"Drofsko!" Cal breathed.

"The same."

"Who?" said the Nuncio.

"But it can't be," Cal said. "You're dead!"

"Apparently not."

"But it was my shot that punctured your sphere. I saw you oxidize into solid glass!"

"Only our outer layer of beings was consumed. They allowed it to happen, knowing it would protect the rest of us within. And they weren't dying, of course, since they were able to transfer their memory units to our inner beings. Later, we contacted those of our friends you and Hara hadn't found."

"Telepathically?"

"Precisely. They carried us to safety and constructed new housing for us." Drofsko humped himself up into his chicken croquette shape. "Not entirely different from what goes on on my native Si."

Cal sat down, stunned. "How's that?"

"We are not blessed with—how would you express it? Nonvolatile memory. Should a volcanic eruption block the sun for a long period, let us say, or dangerous gases like oxygen be released . . . well, you can imagine the effect on photovoltaic creatures such as ourselves, my dear, dependent on light for energy. Our society would be destroyed."

"Has that ever happened?"

"It is happening now, I'm afraid. There is a central coven of us called the Keepers. They have evolved with less mobility in return for expanded memory. When we are threatened, we can transfer our energy to the Keepers, and thus our essence survives even if our bodily form perishes, to be transferred to a substitute form later."

"Like pouring thoughts into a clone," Cal mused.

"But this time the disruption has been massive, I'm afraid. Normally death is unheard of, and there are only occasionally handicapped creatures with impurities in their component materials. But there has been an unprecedented energy loss through huge doses of ionizing radiation on Si. Even the Keepers seem to have lost all but the nonvolatile primal functions. At least I have had no reports from my home since the initial word of the disaster. We may be the only members of our kind still whole. And we must return. If we can transfer data to the Keepers, we may be able to restore them."

"Is that what all this has been about?" Cal asked. "You've been creating Depasians capable of building a starship for you or something?"

"Simply a fortuitous byproduct. No, my research began long before I had heard of the calamity on my home."

"What *were* you doing?" Cal asked. "Amusing yourself with a lower form of life?"

"On the contrary—our interest was entirely selfless. A rapid survey of conditions here made it clear that unless something were done, the Depasians were doomed. The ecological disaster begun by the explosion of their lowest moon has grown worse as the Depasians have grown less able, to the point that they were likely to fail utterly."

"They would have died?" Cal asked.

"According to my calculations, yes. My hope was to reverse, or at least halt, the degeneration caused by a hopelessly inimical environment."

"You've simply made them your slaves."

"Not at all. I have helped them merge themselves into a larger superconsciousness capable of coping with life here."

"You've robbed them of their individual identities."

"No. These peoples' bodies are composed of cells evolved from independent one-celled organisms that grouped into more complex communities for mutual benefit—like yours. The next step in their evolution is obviously forging similar relationships between the resulting separate individuals. Our purpose was merely to offer them the next step in their development a million years ahead of time."

"So you think imposing some kind of synergistic relationship on them is bringing them to the ultimate stage of evolution?" Cal said. "And I suppose you see yourself as living proof it's the superior way?"

"You disappoint us, Cal. We'd thought you could overcome your anthropocentric tendencies. *We* never act out of chauvinistic species pride."

"The hell you don't. That's what the Ambassador meant about you remaking them in your own image. You're playing God!"

"In fact, we are quite capable of admiring the achievements of other species. Understand that mine is a world of unimaginable minds with incredible powers of recall. But in studying your people and the Depasians, we've come to realize that ours is a world of little creativity. There are no leaps of the imagination on Si, my dear. Indeed, we found our study of you fascinating. You can imagine, in fact, what a furor the mere discovery of anything as illogical as *homo sapiens* occasioned back home. Mankind's thought processes are, well, mind-boggling."

"Thanks. And just why were you studying us?"

"We had to understand both you and the Depasians

thoroughly to help them. And of course, there is always the true scientist's fascination with the unknown." Drofsko shimmered with pleasure, and his oily surface flickered with spots of ionized argon.

"This has really been quite an interesting problem for us, though. We spent considerable time investigating and comparing your primitive minds and those of the Depasians." Drofsko shifted his weight, rolling closer to Cal.

"You Earth people have a fully developed consciousness in which you are capable of deciding on a course of action. That is, your brain's dominant left hemisphere, which controls speech, and silent right hemisphere, which categorizes and sorts experience, are connected. But in the primitive, survival-threatening conditions faced by the Depasians, they have evolved backward for protection, creating a less fully developed consciousness in which the authoritative, categorizing, and planning of the right hemisphere is understood as a series of urges they attribute to various organs, as though they had cognitive powers. Eventually, they would have devolved to a state that would have prepared them for absolute control by a single God-directed authority, the complete breakdown of the connection between the left and right hemispheres to create a nonconsciousness receptive to authoritative commands through auditory hallucinations. Like the bicameral minds of your ancient ancestors."

"Not my ancestors," Cal said.

"Still concerned about your true origin, my dear?"

"What would you know about that?"

"Enough. Perhaps you should not be excessively wedded to sexual reproduction, my dear. *We* aren't."

Cal ignored the comment. "What you did to these people is still horrible."

"No. Life on Depaz is bleak, and it will get bleaker. There cannot be any questioning of authority or struggling for power. The Depasians must be subsumed under a central authority if they are to survive. What we recognized was that this would be disastrous, since the Dey hasn't the intelligence to save his people. The only solution was to pool their abilities, forge them into a collective superconsciousness by hastening their devolution toward a bicameral state that was suitably receptive. The gods would simply be a mass projection of their right hemispheres. It was just a matter of utilizing ancient and forgotten cerebral patterns."

"And the Ambassador? Was that part of your research?"

"No, that was something quite different."

"How so?"

"He threatened our entire project here. Weston's report had been processed by your Home Office. In it she theorized that the Depasians were human, survivors of one of those early missions in your first years of interstellar flight whose records were lost. She thought they might even be descendants of clones."

"I'd guessed that much," Cal said.

"And you were partially right, as your Home Office know only too well."

"What do you mean?"

Again Drofsko seemed to flicker with satisfaction. "The records of the Mission the Depasians are descended from have been stored in one of the sub-basements of the Home Office for years and years."

"Whatever for?"

"The Depasians, Cal, were diplomats."

Cal's head snapped back as though he'd been struck. "Diplomats?"

"Yes. Cloned diplomats, in fact, one of the earliest experiments with using clones for deep-space service."

"So it's true," Cal breathed.

"I would not leap to conclusions, Cal," Drofsko buzzed. "As you can see from the Depasians, the plan was not an unqualified success."

"Am I a counterfeit or not?"

"I can't answer that, my dear. My mind operates on electromagnetic energy, unlike your human ESP. I'm limited by distance."

"Then how did you find out about the Depasians?"

"Because, my dear, we are a very ancient people. We visited here long before even the Depasians, your predecessors. We have their full history, fuller than anything that's likely to be in the Home Office. They were simply a race whose flaws had been magnified by inbreeding from an artificially tiny gene pool, aggravated by a hostile world. They were humans, your distant cousins. But your own history is not necessarily theirs."

"So that's why Hara pocketed that piece of—"

"From an entertainment unit," Drofsko buzzed. "Not unlike your MUDD."

"But how did the Ambassador threaten your precious plans?" Cal asked.

"Whether it was the need for secrecy or ignorant species pride, your Home Office decided to stop it—whether or not it meant the Depasians' destruction. Your Ambassador was ordered to arrange termination of my project."

"So you had him killed?"

"I had him kidnapped to try to reason with him. What happened after that was accidental—as you know."

"No, I don't. Where is he now?"

"Dead. He was struck by a stray bolt during the little fight your friend Hara instigated, my dear. Believe me when I tell you we tried every means available in the known universe."

The Ambassador dead, Cal thought. And who was to say that the Home Office had been wrong to try to stop Drofsko from imposing his alien condition on human beings, forcing them to surrender their humanity to him. The threat to them was ultimately a threat to Cal and his home world.

"I'm sorry you feel that way," Drofsko said.

"What?" Cal said. "Oh, yes—I forgot you read minds."

"I had hoped you might stay and help me save the Depasians. But I have no wish to keep you here against your will. Obviously, you pose a threat to us under such conditions, and I have not only the Depasians' survival to worry about but my own people's, as well."

"And if the occasional Ambassador should get in the way . . ."

"Cal, you must understand, it is not easy for me to foresee what your species' reactions will be. There seems no way to reduce human thought to logical patterns or break the code that controls you. Or even borrow a human brain to run trial programs through, perhaps while its owner slept, to forecast probable outcomes. I had no way of knowing that your Ambassador could not be reasoned with."

"Does that mean you're going to kill me?"

"Goodness, no, my dear. I think the Nuncio would be willing to take you along on his ship. I'm sure you would be happier there than here."

"Of course," the Nuncio said.

"We will arrange for the shuttle to appear while everyone is preoccupied with launching their great battleship. They tell me it will be the day after tomorrow."

"It's going to be ready that soon?"

"Preparations have been feverish since the defection of the Acting Chief of Mission," Drofsko purred. "But don't be downcast. It will provide the perfect distraction for your escape."

Cal nodded.

"There is one other thing, my dear," Drofsko said. "Something I would rather not have to tell you."

"What's that?"

"Our old friend Grober. His essence slipped away into the eternal last night."

CHAPTER SIXTEEN

WHEN CAL and the Nuncio awoke in the morning, there was no sign of Drofsko.

"Come," said one of the nomads who had brought them the day before, "we have clothing for you, so that you will be able to pass unnoticed in the crowd."

"At the launching?" Cal asked.

"And more," said the man. "It will be at the landing field."

They dressed hurriedly in the native robes the man gave them, then clambered aboard the *mels* for the day-long trip. Cal chose to sleep most of the way. He preferred not to think about anything.

It was dawn the next day, the day of the launching, as they lumbered up to the landing field. Already crowds of Depasians and flies had gathered, joining the large contingent of soldiers on the field. The burned-off area had gone to seed; little shoots of green peeked from amongst the fire-blackened stubble. But over it all in the center of the field loomed the great hull of the battleship itself.

It was huge and gray, hulking, brooding over the sea of vicious grass. Wisps of smoke from its coal-fired boilers curled from the line of three smokestacks. Its great guns, set three to each house-sized turret, poked up into the sky like racks of pitchforks. Depasians crew members, decked out in the new uniform of the Royal Depasian Navy, swarmed along the railings, waving their visorless caps. The anchor, the size of four *eliks,* dangled ominously from the bow. Almost directly beneath it a huge grandstand had been built of woven sawgrass shoots and draped with bunting, while pennants bearing the Dey's personal crest snapped in the rising prairie wind.

Cal drew his hood tighter to hide his face, glancing this way and that to see if there were anyone from the Mission. The only familiar face he saw was Major Sedewski on the grandstand, waiting for the Dey, and Hannibal Myers, dabbing his eyes.

Now, with shrieks and hoots, the procession approached from the southeast, rerouted to avoid the haunted Wailing Place of Shakespearean quotations. The crowd roared its approval, sending up great swirls and spirals of frightened flies, as the Gateway to the Dey chugged up to the grandstand and dismounted to await the Ineffable Dey. More cheers as the great cloth circle of the Dey's cyclorama now appeared, huge clouds of smoke belching from the Dey's unseen tractor in the center, slaves running with their poles to keep the scene moving at the same speed as the tractor.

Now the cyclorama bulged and wriggled like a cell undergoing mitosis, reshaped itself into a long corridor within which it was known the Dey was walking, then parted slightly to swallow the grandstand and the prow of the battleship. The Dey, everyone knew, was now getting his first look at the His Limitless Majesty's Ship, H.L.M.S. *Ineffability*.

Now the cyclorama of delight could be seen moving at the head of the Dey's retinue along the railing in a tour of inspection of the ship, though whether or not the cyclorama was ever opened a crack so the Dey could actually observe the ship proper or its fittings could not be seen from Cal's vantage point.

Now the procession moved back down the side of the ship and shrouded itself on the grandstand. There was a pause for some kind of fumbling, perhaps, Cal thought, something to do with the champagne bottle, then an expectant hush, and then a huge *kaboom* that echoed back and forth across the prairie under the lowering skies as a great column of smoke shot straight up into the air where the cyclorama had been, and the battleship H.L.M.S. *Ineffability* began to rumbled backward.

"They've blown him up!" Cal gasped. "They've blown up the Dey!"

Through his mind galloped the possibility that Bascomb might have been aboard. Damn the regulations that made him turn away from her, he thought. If he had just one thing he loved . . . But at that instant, a series of blood-curdling whoops went up from all sides, and at the horizon appeared troops of *elik*-mounted nomads bearing down on the celebrating crowd. Terrified royal soldiers raced after the battleship lumbering on its hundreds of tiny wheels, crushing its way through the clattering sawgrass. Some fell and perished among the deadly blades, others found ladders and stairways to haul themselves up into the safety of the ship. Squinting against the sun, Cal could make out the Gateway to the Dey striding grandly across the deck and disappearing into the stairwell that led to the bridge. A moment later a flash of color revealed the Gateway on the bridge itself.

Belching smoke and trembling, the great ship began to wheel, her turrets turning to face the approaching enemy as the crowd dispersed, terrified civilians running for safety in every direction.

"This way," the nomad said, indicating the sheds along the side of the landing field.

Now the crews in the turrets began to crank the eleven-inch guns down to train them on the nomad riders. The gunwales bristled with big cannon and little.

And then the order to fire.

The instant her guns fired, H.L.M.S. *Ineffability* stopped dead. Its huge keel and wheels lifted up off the prairie floor in terrifying slow motion, its guns writhed up and down like fingers drumming out a tattoo on a tabletop, its turrets roofs crashed inward and walls out, disintegrating into spinning, scaling fragments; its superstructure wavered and fell sideways, crashing about the railings and cascading down the undulating side of the ship in a shower of tiny black-and-burning figures that had been crewmen. Every gun on the ship had suffered a fatal malfunction, from jamming to having sawgrass wads stuffed in its barrel. And every one had exploded.

In the next moment, the fire reached the powder magazine. The stern and bow now leaped up into the air, closed together on the cloud of smoke like jaws of a great whale leaping straight up from the prairie, and then slowly subsided into themselves, dissolving into the smoke and dust of their crumbling bases. And for those soldiers left behind, there were the onrushing hoards of Superdeps to hound them all the way to Kabugar.

It was a long time before the noises of the explosions and the thunder of *elik* hooves had died away into the steady crackling of the prairie fire where the battleship had sunk among the grass blades. Twisted ribs of steel stood out against the sky like claws of some murdered beast. To the east rose the dust of the pursued and their pursuers.

"It will be time shortly," said the nomad. "We should go out onto the field to wait."

Cal nodded, followed him out to the fire-blackened landing field. In its panic, the crowd had destroyed most of the neatly stacked supplies, and the field was strewn with debris.

"What will happen now?" the Nuncio asked.

"To the Dey's people?" said the nomad. "Nothing. We are not yet strong enough to take Kabugar. But someday, who knows?" He looked toward the capital. "And then we must begin the long process of rebuilding Depaz, but in a new and better way."

"Built around a strong central authority," Cal said. "Drofsko."

"You are wrong about the shapeless one, you know," the nomad said. "It is we who are strong."

All at once they stopped. Through the twilight of the swirling smoke they could make out a shadowy figure waiting on the other side of the landing field. Cal sensed who it was from the shape and the full Depasian robe, even before he'd seen the face.

"Identify yourself," called the nomad.

Hara turned and faced them, flexing ever so slightly at the knees in readiness. There was no weapon visible, but

Cal was certain she had something cocked somewhere, just in case. Then she seemed to relax.

"So it's you, Cal. And you, Your Excellency. Good to see you."

"What are you doing here?" Cal asked.

"I could probably ask you the same question."

"We're here to take the autoshuttle when it comes in."

Hara's colorless lips bowed in a thin smile. "You get an A for effort, at least."

"You're going to stop us?" Cal asked.

"Stop you? Why in the world would I do that?" She laughed.

Cal shrugged. "Because you tried so hard to kill us the other night?"

"Yes, well, things change."

"And what *are* you doing here?"

"Taking the shuttle with you. Hoping I can hitch a ride with His Excellency here."

"Why?"

"I'm retiring."

"What?"

"You heard me, my boy," Hara said, smiling. In the half-light her gray face had gone dark and indistinct. "My time's up."

"But—"

"What's the matter, my boy? Haven't I earned my pension?"

"I just can't believe it. You caused all this . . ."

"You mean, Project Nimrod?"

"Yes, Project Nimrod. You started it all knowing you were this close to *retirement?*"

"I don't understand you, Cal. If something's right for the Mission and right for Earth, then it's my responsibility to institute it. The fact that I was going short has nothing to do with it—it's my job to do what's best as I see it. What do you think I am, some kind of timeserver sitting out the days till I retire?"

"Don't hand me that. This whole thing was to protect yourself because you were afraid of the consequences of not knowing about the Superdeps in time to protect the Ambassador. You were committing murder to save your pension."

"You're wrong, Cal."

"Am I? Then what about the shipload of dramaturgbots you blew up?"

"I never blew them up."

"Of course you did. You were afraid that First Player would somehow let slip that he was the one you sent to plant a bomb outside the Dey's residence to scare him into going along with your scheme to wipe out the altered Depasians for the Home Office."

"I tell you, you're wrong."

"Sure I am. Well, I've got news for you—you've been wasting your time. Our masters back on Earth could care less about us."

"Masters?" Hara blinked.

"Don't tell me in all your years in the Service you never at least heard rumors about who we really are!"

Hara smiled her grim smile again. "So that's it. The clone business."

"The clone business. And now I know it's true. We're manufactured. We're grown from tissue. Sure, maybe it's human OWS officer tissue, but what's the difference? We're cultured in tanks like bacteria, manufactured, and then we have carefully selected memories implanted. Just enough to make it all seem real, not enough so we care all that much about getting home to Earth. But like most things made up by bureaucrats and government committees, it's superficial. Nothing stands out in all those memories as real—not the decision to enlist, not the decision to go deep-space, nothing. It's just so much varnish painted over raw brain cells."

"And how would you know, Cal? If you're really not quite human, how would you know how memories are supposed to stand out, what they're supposed to feel like? The truth is, it's the years. It's the suppressants and rejuvenators, it's the time in suspension traveling deep-space. It gnaws away at you. The biological clock may be *almost* stopped, but never completely. What you're complaining about is the risk you agreed to when you signed on. And then there's just the fact that you're a lot of years away from your life on Earth. That's what smooths it all out and makes it seem so far away, my boy. Believe me."

"Why the hell would anybody believe you?" Cal spat.

Far off in the darkling sky twinkled two moving pinpricks of light.

"That's the autoshuttle," Hara said matter-of-factly. "You going to let me go with you?"

"Should I?"

Hara shrugged. "In a way it doesn't much matter. All this time waiting to retire, and now I finally realize I don't have anywhere to go. I mean a real place, a home instead of a destination. I'm kind of a woman without a country."

"Because home isn't Earth?"

"No, because I've been away so long. Look, Cal, nobody knows the Service better than I do. If we were counterfeits, I'd know it. What you really know is that you aren't. You want to think you are, because then you wouldn't be quite responsible for what you've been part of. Sorry, my boy. It's not that easy to get out of. You may not want to hear this, but I have no trouble getting to sleep at night with that truth."

"Go ahead, go ahead. What's a few more lies?"

"Why would I lie to you? I'm retired."

"Then tell me—you *were* Intelligence, right?"

Hara shook her head.

"You're just playing Official Secrets Act."

Hara shook her head again. "Cal, believe it or not, I just want what's best for the Depasians. I'm a Development Attaché, pure and simple. That's all I ever was. I was an importer back home; I lost my shirt in a near-solar deal, and I got a lateral appointment into the OWS on a reserve rating because I was coming in by a back door instead of the Academy route, that's all. I love the Service, Cal. It gave me a purpose. It literally saved my life."

"Oh well," Cal said. "I don't suppose Satan identified himself when he slithered into Eden, either."

Hara chuckled mirthlessly.

"This is hardly Eden, Cal."

Cal's eyes skimmed the horizon, from the burning *Inef-*

fability to the dust clouds in the direction of Kabugar, everything bisected by the sharp line of the sawgrass.

"No," he agreed. "It's not Eden." He looked up to the approaching autoshuttle. "And the Ambassador—is it true that he got word from the Home Office to terminate Drofsko's experiments because the Depasians are human?"

"I wouldn't know, Cal."

The air began to thunder with the noise of the autoshuttle engines as it approached overhead.

"Yes or no?" Hara said.

Cal looked into the brown eyes. Again he saw his own reflection, flattened, lifeless on the glassy globes. He did not want to stare out at life through eyes like those, and yet he was not sure there was any way to avoid it. But then there was Bascomb. Could he salvage what might have been? Could he work to save Earth's interests here despite what the Mission would be trying to do? Yet how could he live with himself, flying away in the same ship with Hara, leaving these poor beggars to die?

"All right," Cal said. "Go ahead."

He stepped back to the nomad, leaving Hara next to the Nuncio.

"You are coming, too, yes?" the Nuncio said.

Cal shook his head. "I'm staying," he said.

There was a moment's hesitation, and then the warning sounded. The Nuncio walked up the gangway, followed by Hara. They both stopped at the door to wave, and Cal, next to the nomad, found himself waving back. Then the door shut. In another moment, he watched as the shuttle now rose uncertainly on a tail of flame, faster and faster, the Nuncio and the spy taking wing together, transmogrified, leaping into the heavens, shaking off the tug of gravity.

Maybe someday, Cal thought, he would understand. In the meantime, it was better to do. With fewer questions.

And maybe by then he would have learned to accept the fact that what he'd imagined it was to be an immortal, a true citizen of the universe, was an impossibility for mankind. One could never break the bond of Earth and origin. One could never be more than a displaced human, a timeserver at the edge of the galaxy. But he would do his best, at least, to atone. He would do his penance here for what Hara had done; he would make it up. He would serve his time toward some end.

Explicit.

BIO OF A SPACE TYRANT
Piers Anthony

"Brilliant...a thoroughly original thinker and storyteller with a unique ability to posit really *alien* alien life, humanize it, and make it come out alive on the page."
The Los Angeles Times

Widely celebrated science fiction novelist Piers Anthony has written a colossal new five volume space thriller—**BIO OF A SPACE TYRANT:** *The Epic Adventures and Galactic Conquests of Hope Hubris.*

VOLUME I: REFUGEE   84194-0/$2.95
Hubris and his family embark upon an ill-fated voyage through space, searching for sanctuary, after pirates blast them from their home on Callisto.

VOLUME II: MERCENARY   87221-8/$2.95
Hubris joins the Navy of Jupiter and commands a squadron loyal to the death and sworn to war against the pirate warlords of the Jupiter Ecliptic.

VOLUME III — Coming Soon

ALSO BY PIERS ANTHONY:

BATTLE CIRCLE	67009-5/$3.95
CHAINING THE LADY, CLUSTER II	61614-9/$2.95
CLUSTER, CLUSTER I	81364-5/$2.95
KIRLIAN QUEST, CLUSTER III	79764-X/$2.50
MACROSCOPE	81992-9/$3.95
MUTE	84772-8/$3.95
OMNIVORE, ORN I	82362-4/$2.95
ORN II	85324-8/$2.95
OX, ORN III	82370-5/$2.95
THOUSANDSTAR, CLUSTER IV	80259-7/$2.75
VISCOUS CIRCLE, CLUSTER V	79897-2/$2.95

AVON Paperbacks

Buy these books at your local bookstore or use this coupon for ordering:

Avon Books, Dept BP, Box 767, Rte 2, Dresden, TN 38225
Please send me the book(s) I have checked above. I am enclosing $_____ (please add $1.00 to cover postage and handling for each book ordered to a maximum of three dollars). *Send check or money order*—no cash or C.O.D.'s please. Prices and numbers are subject to change without notice. Please allow six to eight weeks for delivery.

Name _____

Address _____

City _____ State/Zip _____

Anthony 5/84